D1795558

PRELUDE TO WAR

PRELUDE TO WAR

Christopher Nicole

This first world edition published in Great Britain 1999 by
SEVERN HOUSE PUBLISHERS LTD of
9–15 High Street, Sutton, Surrey SM1 1DF.
This title first published in the U.S.A. 1999 by
SEVERN HOUSE PUBLISHERS INC of
595 Madison Avenue, New York, N.Y. 10022.

British Library Cataloguing in Publication Data

Nicole, Christopher, 1930-
    Prelude to war
    1.   Suspense fiction
    I.   Title
    823.9'14 [F]

    ISBN 0 7278 5416 X

B

Typeset by Hewer Text Ltd
Edinburgh, Scotland
Printed and bound in Great Britain by
MPG Books Ltd, Bodmin, Cornwall.

"The end of man in an action and not a thought, though it were the noblest."

Thomas Carlyle

Contents

Prologue

The soldier was shouting and waving his arms. What he was saying was incomprehensible, but he was in uniform and there was a rifle slung on the shoulder of his khaki tunic. "We'd better see what's on his mind," Peter Bentley said.

The four young people brought their bicycles to a halt, stepping down on to the somewhat rough road surface. It was a magnificent early spring day, warm in Albania where there would still be snow on the ground in England. But to their right, where the mountains rose steeply to several thousand feet, they could see snow, however warm and welcoming might look the sea, distantly glimpsed to their left.

The soldier marched towards them, brow furrowed beneath his khaki sidecap, black boots stirring the dust. Catherine Ames reckoned he liked what he saw, and suddenly wished she was wearing slacks instead of shorts. She glanced at Roberta Wilcox. The two had been friends all of their lives, through school, then Teacher Training College, but there could hardly have been a stronger contrast between the tall, strongly built, golden-haired Catherine and the small, generally tightly-framed Roberta, features half-concealed beneath the mass of black curls. Roberta even had tight features, where Catherine's were large and generous, in keeping with her personality. Both were twenty-two and extremely attractive young women, not only because of the length of leg they were exposing.

The soldier was almost up to them. "Do you speak Italian?" Peter asked, in that language.

"Si, I speak Italian," the soldier said.

"Oh, good," Alan Chambers said. "Because we don't speak Albanian."

Both the men, like the girls, were trainee teachers enjoying a

1

last big holiday in this spring of 1939 before taking up their various posts at the end of the summer. They too had gone through college together, and it had been their idea to go cycling through what Alan called the ancient parts of Europe: he was going to teach Greek. He was a short, heavily built young man, like Peter a year older than the girls. And as with the girls, there was some contrast between the pair, Peter being tall and thin and somewhat languid. Catherine wasn't sure about them, sexually. They were fun to be with, but had been nothing more than that throughout the holiday. At least this far. Which was as it should be. She and Roberta had debated for some time before accepting the invitation. It had sounded so romantic, but . . . "There's to be no hanky-panky," Roberta had announced. "We'll have our tent, and you'll have yours—"

"And never the twain shall meet," Alan had grinned.

And there had, in fact, been almost no hanky-panky, not even the occasional holding of hands, as they had prowled through Greece before coming north. Just a lot of ouzo and a lot of fun. Except for one night on a Greek mountainside, after a lot more ouzo, some frantic fumbling and panting, followed by an even more frantic apology from Peter. Apparently Alan had not even got that far with Roberta.

Catherine had felt just a little bit disappointed about that evening; she rather fancied Peter. Although what she would have done had he really started to come on at her . . . it could still happen, as they were not aiming to make Belgrade for another couple of weeks – Albania was such a romantic country: she had a copy of Byron's *Childe Harold* in her knapsack. But she was not yet ready for any permanent commitment. She was even less ready to yield her virginity in passing, as it were.

"You are in the wrong place," the soldier was saying. Both girls spoke Italian, having studied languages in addition to their chosen subjects.

"Isn't this the road from Vallona to Fier?" Peter asked.

"It is a road from Vallona to Fier," the soldier conceded. "But it is not the right road. Not the main road, eh? The main road is by the sea."

"We chose this road for that reason," Alan explained. "To get

2

away from the traffic, and to enjoy the scenery. It is very beautiful up here."

"Very beautiful," the soldier agreed. "But also very dangerous. There are bandits in those mountains. Too close. You do not wish to be captured by bandits," he added, eyeing Catherine and Roberta to suggest they would like it least of all.

"We haven't seen anybody," Peter pointed out. "Save you."

"Ha ha. But they are there, watching. Here you are safe, because there is a military camp just along the road. But after that, you must return to the lower road."

"Anything you say," Peter agreed.

They remounted their bicycles. They had had to push the bikes up the last slope, but there it was reasonably flat for a while, and a few minutes later they saw the Albanian flag and the tents of the encampment. "What are the military doing up here, anyway?" Roberta asked.

"Keeping an eye on those bandits," Peter said.

They were abreast of the camp now, and soldiers were crowding the perimeter, whistling at the girls. "You reckon they're better than the bandits?" Catherine asked.

The camp behind them, they saw the bifurcation. "That's the road that fellow said we should take," Alan said.

"At least it's downhill all the way."

They dismounted to inspect the side road, hardly more than a cart track, that led down to the coast. From their vantage point on the brow of the hill they could see the lower road. There really wasn't all that much traffic down there – Albania was not all that well off for motor vehicles; but the odd very obviously military truck rolled by. "I think they're preparing for trouble," Peter commented.

"I'm not really very well up on the politics out here," Catherine confessed. "I had an idea Albania was an Italian protectorate."

"It was, virtually, down to a couple of years ago," Peter said. "Then people started to get fed up with being told what to do by *Il Duce*. There was a rebellion up in those hills last year. Those so called bandits are merely Muslims who want better treatment from King Zog. So relations with Italy have cooled. And there has been a lot of talk about Musso doing something about it.

3

Won't come to anything, of course. Albania isn't Czechoslovakia. To do a Hitler the Italians would have to cross the Adriatic, and the Albanians aren't about to shout for help – they'll do their own fighting."

"I'd say we should forget the lingering looking at the scenery bit, and get on to Yugoslavia just as quickly as possible," Roberta said.

"Or maybe chuck the whole idea and go back to Greece."

"Hey," Alan said. "What's that you said about having to cross the Adriatic?" He didn't have to point; they could all see, emerging from the heat haze, a vast armada of ships . . . transports as well as warships, steaming north-east.

"Holy shitting cows," Peter remarked. Behind them they could hear the sound of a bugle.

"This is an invasion," Alan said. "How the hell did we manage to ride into a war?"

"That's it," Roberta said. "Back to Greece." Catherine just stared at the ships. She had never seen so many in one place.

"When we can. Get off the road," Peter snapped. Now the bugle calls were being overlaid by the sounds of engines, the neighing of horses. "Quickly." Peter lifted his bicycle and ran up the hillside, panting and staggering amidst the trees and bushes. Catherine followed as best she could before tripping and collapsing in a shallow gully. Alan and Roberta came behind them, joined her. They sat together, gasping for breath, and gazed at the road, and the stream of men; there were a few vehicles, and some of the soldiers were mounted, but most were on foot. There was little evidence of any discipline, but a great deal of excitement. "Look!" Alan said.

There were flashes of red at sea, and a moment later an explosion on the hillside, well below where the four Britons were sheltering; a cloud of dust and stone and shattered trees and leaves rose into the air. "Crikey!" Alan muttered.

Now several more shells fell on the hillside, and these were closer to the road. The soldiers promptly fled into the trees themselves, while the horses stamped and neighed; even the trucks were abandoned. "We have to get out of here," Peter said.

"Where?" Alan asked.

"Up. We'll climb up."

4

"Carrying all this gear?" Roberta asked. Apart from the bicycles, they each had a knapsack.

"Unless you want to abandon it. Come on."

A shell now actually burst on the road, and two of the trucks burst into flames while several of the horses were hit. That was sufficient incentive. Peter lifted his bike on to his shoulder and commenced climbing. Catherine looked at Roberta, then shrugged, lifted her own bike, suddenly terribly aware of the weight of her knapsack, and followed. To fall flat on her face as there was an enormous whoosh and the whole hill seemed to tremble. But the shell had landed a good quarter of a mile away, further scattering the Albanian soldiers. "Come *on*," Peter was shouting from above her.

She scrambled up again, aware of having scraped her knee. She looked back and saw Alan and Roberta behind her. Peter was waiting a few feet further up. "We should be all right here," he said. "Listen."

The barrage had moved further along the coast; through the trees they could see the red flashes of the explosions, and the upsurges of earth where the shells landed. "Wowee," Alan gasped, collapsing beside them. "What an experience!" He un-slung his knapsack, found his canteen, and took a swig. "My mouth is as dry as a desert."

"Nerves," Peter said, but he also drank.

As did Catherine. "I don't have much left. Do you think there's any water around here?"

"Bound to be," Peter said. "A rushing mountain stream. Let's find one."

"And then what?" Roberta asked.

"Like you said, we'll work our way back to Greece," Alan said. "But I think maybe we should stay away from the roads. We don't want to get mixed up in a war."

"Amen," Catherine agreed.

"Right," Peter said. "Here's what we'll do. We'll find some water, have a meal, and then start heading back through the mountains." He was their natural leader.

It took them an hour, slowly picking their way along the hill-sides, and insensibly moving higher all the time, to find a stream

5

rushing down from the higher slopes. They lay on the bank to drink and then filled their canteens. "Cold and clear," Catherine said. "Does that feel good. You know what—" her scraped knee was oozing blood, she was covered in dust, and very sweaty. She looked at Roberta.

"Oh, yes," Roberta said. "A hundred yards, please, gents. Downstream."

Alan made a face, but he and Peter laid down their bicycles and clambered down the slope. A hundred yards away they were out of sight behind the trees. By then the girls had already stripped off, and Catherine sank into the water. She had to crouch to be properly immersed as, standing, it only came to her thighs. Her knee stung, but she was able to wash away the dust and dirt. "It makes me feel almost clean," she said, watching Roberta daintily stepping in beside her.

"Ooh," Roberta squealed at the cold. They splashed water over each other, soaking their hair.

"Incredible," Catherine said, "that we should be skinny-dipping while people are being killed only a few miles away."

They could still hear the crump-crump of the shells, distant now. "Were you scared?" Roberta asked.

"Do you know, I wasn't," Catherine said, seriously. "I felt such a spectator. You know, it couldn't be happening. Not to *me*."

"I know what you mean," Roberta said. "I . . . aaagh!" She stood up, and then hastily knelt again, arms folded across her breasts.

Catherine swung round and gazed at the two men who had suddenly appeared upstream. Both were very roughly dressed, were bearded, and carried rifles. "Heck," she whispered. "Are those the bandits?"

Roberta licked her lips. "Could be. What are we going to do?" Their clothes were several feet away on the bank. And the men were coming closer.

Catherine took a deep breath. "Hello!" she called, as loudly as she could. Surely the boys would hear. "Do you speak Italian?"

One of the men grinned. "You Italian?" He didn't speak it very well.

"No, no," Catherine said. "We are British. Friends." He

6

peered at her, trying to see through the unfortunately clear water. She also cupped her hands over her breasts, for the first time in her life regretting they were so large, and hoped he couldn't see much lower down. Then his companion snapped a remark, and the spokesman raised his head and in the same movement unslung his rifle. "No," Catherine shouted.

"What the hell—?" Peter called.

"They're with us," Catherine said, desperately. Roberta appeared to be struck dumb.

"Your husbands, eh?" suggested the man

"Ah—" Catherine thought rapidly. But probably these men, if they were Muslims, wouldn't go for four people of opposite sexes holidaying together if they weren't married. "Yes," she said. "Husbands."

The man grinned at her. "You come out now, eh?"

"Ah—" she turned round. Peter and Alan were at least wearing pants, hurriedly dragged on. "All right. But you go away, eh?"

"No, no," the man said. "We stay."

Catherine looked at Roberta, and then at Peter and Alan, who were slowly approaching. "Beggars can't be choosers," she said, and stood up, deliberately letting her hands drop to her sides; there was no point in being coy – if they were going to be raped, they were going to be raped. She was amazed at her coolness, even if her heart was pounding. Slowly she waded to the bank and climbed out, terribly aware of the men gazing at her, both Albanian and British. She didn't bother with her towel, dragged her knickers over the wet flesh, added her shirt, and for good measure pulled a pair of slacks from her knapsack in preference to the shorts.

Roberta had remained in the water, but now she also came out and dressed herself. "You come," the Albanian called to Peter and Alan. "You have pretty wives."

"Yes," Peter said as he approached, going very red in the face.

"You come with us," the Albanian said.

"We're trying to get back to Greece," Alan ventured.

"You come now," the Albanian repeated. "You come village."

"That might not be a bad thing, for the time being," Catherine suggested, gaining confidence now it appeared they were not after all going to be robbed or assaulted – merely kidnapped. "There could be someone in authority there."

"Bandits," Alan muttered.

"Our gear," Peter said.

The Albanian nodded, and spoke to his companion. "You go fetch." The boys retreated along the bank, accompanied by the second man, who had also unslung his rifle.

"We really are your friends," Catherine said. "All we want to do is get out of your war."

"Italians," the Albanian said darkly, and came closer. Catherine found that she was breathing very deeply. She seemed paralysed as he stretched out his hand and squeezed her left breast through the thin, wet material. "You are much woman. This husband, he sell you to me?"

Roberta made a stifled sound. "I don't think so," Catherine said. "I am pregnant with his child." Roberta made another stifled sound.

The Albanian studied her for a few seconds, then released her, to her great relief. They heard the other men coming back through the trees. "You come," he said, and started up the slope.

Roberta was gasping. "My God," she said in English. "If—"

"If nothing," Catherine said. "We play this by ear, right?"

"But you're not pregnant."

"He doesn't know that. And we'll be back in Greece long before he finds out."

"I hope so," Roberta said. "Oh, I hope so."

"You two all right?" Peter asked, as he and Alan rejoined them. He could tell they were emotionally excited.

"We're all right," Catherine assured him.

"They didn't—" Alan looked embarrassed.

"They just looked," Roberta said. "As did you."

"Well—" his flush deepened.

The Albanian had advanced several yards. Now he turned to look back. "You come," he called. Neither he nor his companion had offered to help with their loads. Wearily Catherine and Roberta again humped their knapsacks and bicycles and set off up the slope, the stream rushing by on their right. They had covered about half a mile, always upwards, their muscles burning, when their leader stopped and pointed. "You see? Our village."

The village was a cluster of very rough-looking houses set against the hill, and in some places, Catherine reckoned, built into the hillside. She watched people, many of them women in brightly coloured kaftans and headscarves, emerging to oversee their approach. Dogs barked, chickens clucked, and goats bleated. "Here you are safe," the Albanian said.

Safe from what? Catherine wondered. But they weren't safe at all, for suddenly the women above them started screaming and shouting. "Planes!" Peter shouted, and grabbed Catherine's arm to throw her to the ground. The bike and knapsack fell on top of her, and she exclaimed with pain, then he was rolling her away from the stream as the aircraft, a squadron of six biplanes flying quite slowly and very low, came down the side of the hill. Catherine looked up at the village, where the Albanians were clustered, apparently unsure whether to seek shelter or to wave. Then the first bomb plunged downwards into the very centre of the houses, throwing up bricks and stones and pieces of wood, and pieces of people and animals, too, Catherine realised with a sickening roll of her stomach as she rose to her knees. "Get *down*," Peter begged.

For the two Albanians were firing their rifles at the aircraft, and attracting their attention. Now two of them banked steeply and came down the line of the stream, machine-guns spitting red. "Shit!" Alan commented. "Oh, shit."

The lead machine had a bomb left, and Catherine watched this leave the undercarriage and come plunging downwards. It made no sound above the roar of the plane, only a few hundred feet above them. Then the morning was obliterated in searing noise. She found herself lying on her back, her ears ringing. She was looking through the trees, at the second plane, which was firing its machine-guns as it swooped even lower than the bomber. She watched branches snapping and heard high-pitched screams. Then the planes were gone.

Catherine didn't want to move. It wasn't that she felt any pain – would she feel any pain, immediately, had she been hit? She couldn't be sure. But she was afraid of what she might see. The

9

planes were all gone now, and the ringing in her ears had stopped. But the screams persisted, from some distance away. Closer at hand there were only moans. She forced herself to sit up and look down at herself. She looked absolutely normal, save for the mud on her pants and shirt. She hadn't been hit. If her knee was still bleeding it hadn't penetrated her pants. She wanted to scream herself, for joy.

She turned her head to find Peter. He lay on his face, a few yards away. The back of his shirt was soaked with blood. "Oh, God," she muttered. "Oh, God." She crawled to him, stared at the back of his head. She had never seen a dead person before. Her life to that moment had been singularly free of death. Her grandparents had died before she was born, her parents were still in the very best of health and early middle age. But then, up till today her life had been singularly free of anything that could be considered dangerous. To cycle from Athens to Belgrade had been the biggest adventure she had ever undertaken.

Biting her lip, she stretched out her hand to touch Peter's neck. She should turn him over. But she didn't want to do that. She heard a sound from behind her, and turned to look at Roberta. Her face was a mask of pain and fear, and she moved like a snail, dragging herself along the ground, leaving a trail of blood on the leaves. "Is he dead?"

"I think so. Are you hurt?" What inanity!

"My leg," Roberta muttered.

"Alan—" Catherine looked past her.

"Don't go back there," Roberta begged.

Catherine scrambled to her feet and ran towards the stream, checked. Alan lay on his back, his body opened from crotch to breast as if by a huge, jagged knife wielded by an inept surgeon. Amazingly, the bullets had missed his face, and his expression remained one of total surprise. Catherine dropped to her knees, still some distance away. She felt sick, but she couldn't vomit.

"Come, come, you come!" It was their leader. How obscenely absurd, she thought, that this man, who by shooting at them had brought the Italian planes down to destroy her friends, should be quite unhurt. As was his companion. Catherine thought that had she a gun she would have shot them both without compunction.

"My friends," she muttered, her mouth full of saliva.

10

"They are dead," the Albanian said.

"Not that one." She pointed.

The Albanian bent over Roberta, who was now hardly conscious. "She will die too."

"No," Catherine shouted. "Not if she is helped. You must take her to the village."

The Albanian muttered at his companion, and was distracted by shouts from above them. Several men were making their way down the slope by the stream. They carried rifles, wore beards and rough clothes and caps like their compatriots, but one of them had gold braid on his jerkin, and an air of authority. "Please," Catherine cried in Italian. "Are you in charge?"

The man peered at her in astonishment, and their captor spoke rapidly in Albanian, obviously explaining the situation. The headman, as this had to be, peered at Peter and Alan in turn. "They have to be buried," Catherine said. "But my friend here has been hit in the thigh. She must have medical assistance, or she too will die."

The headman gave orders, and two of his men lifted Roberta from the ground to carry her up the slope. Roberta screamed in agony. "Don't you have a sedative?" Catherine shouted.

"No."

"Well . . . a stretcher?"

"No stretchers."

The men carried the moaning Roberta up the slope, greeted now by some of the women coming down from the houses, several of which were burning. As the original two men accompanied Roberta, Catherine was left standing by herself, between the dead bodies of Peter and Alan, suddenly acutely aware of the heat, and that the woods were filled with insects. "You can't just leave them here!" she shouted. The headman, who had been about to follow his people, stopped, turned, and crooked his finger, imperiously. Catherine bit her lip, but went up to him. He pointed at Alan and Peter, then held up his hand, two fingers spread. Then he pointed at the village, opened and shut his hand twice. "Oh, my God," Catherine said. "Look, I'm sorry. But—"

He was walking away from her again. She ran behind him, reached the village. The bombs had landed in the every centre of the houses, and several had been destroyed, apart from those on

11

fire. The stream ran through the centre of the street – to Catherine's consternation as she remembered that a couple of hours ago she had been drinking that water – and the fires were being doused by a bucket brigade. Other men were trying to round up the scattered flock of goats that was the village's wealth. To one side the ten dead bodies had been laid in a row. About double that number of wounded sat or lay close by, groaning and moaning, being tended by the women, and by a man who was definitely not Albanian. But he didn't look Greek or Yugoslav, and she couldn't believe he could be Italian. He was a short man, but very powerfully built. His hair was fair, and thinning. He wore European-style jacket and pants and shoes, somewhat dishevelled and dirty. But he had a bag which obviously contained some medicines. Catherine stood above him, nose wrinkling as she smelt the dead, and the wounded. "Please," she said. "Do you speak Italian?"

He raised his head with a frown, looked her up and down. "Better than you do," he remarked in English.

"Oh, thank God!" She knelt beside him. "My friend needs help."

The man turned his head to look at where Roberta had been laid. She was hardly conscious now, but she still groaned; her pants were a sodden mass of blood. "So do these people."

"She's bleeding to death. My two other friends are already dead. Please," Catherine begged, her eyes filled with tears. "This isn't our war."

The man gazed at her for several seconds. He had quite regular features, although they were remarkably hard. Catherine felt he was no man to cross. But he had to have a spark of humanity, if he was a doctor. "Do you think it is these people's?" he asked, then spoke to the people around him and lifted his bag to where Roberta lay. "Shit," he muttered. "Are you travelling together?"

"Four of us," Catherine said. "The others—"

He nodded. "I have to get these pants off. If you wish, you can go over there."

"I want to help."

He shrugged, produced a hypodermic needle which he carefully filled from a phial, then thrust it into Robert's arm. Roberta groaned, and then subsided. The man selected a pair of scissors and started snipping away at the blood-stained cloth; the flesh he exposed was also a mass of oozing blood. "Is she going to die?" Catherine asked.

"Hopefully not. I wouldn't bet a million dollars on her ever walking again." He was uncovering the wound with deft fingers. "There's still some metal in there."

"Can you take it out?"

"Looks as if I'll have to. It's not something I've ever done before."

"But . . . if you're a doctor—"

"I'm not a doctor. I happen to have a little knowledge of medicine."

"But . . . what are you, then?"

The man's face twisted in a bitter grin. "I'm known as a lot of different things to a lot of different people. My name is Clayton Andrews." He held out his hand. The fingers were bloody. But Catherine clasped them anyway.

The villagers crowded round to watch the operation, not least interested because Roberta was now naked from the waist down save for her bloodstained knickers. Catherine felt she should demand privacy, but she didn't suppose anyone would take much notice of her. She couldn't bring herself to watch any longer, and retreated to sit on the street, against the wall of a relatively undamaged house. It was now mid-afternoon, and she hadn't eaten since breakfast. How long ago breakfast seemed. It had been a different world. A civilised world. But she wasn't hungry, even if her throat was parched. She was too conscious of the heat, and the smells, of what was happening to Roberta, even if she knew nothing about it, of the two bodies lying by the stream . . . she found she was stroking the head of a moth-eaten looking dog. "We're both strays," she said. Clayton Andrews stood above her. "Is it done?" He nodded. "And—?"

He shrugged. "I've sewn it up as best I can, given her another shot. We have to wait and see. Now tell me . . . do you know, I don't even know your name?"

"Catherine Ames."

"And you're English."

13

"Yes, and you're American." She had placed his rather mid-Atlantic accent.

"Right first time. And your friend?"

"Roberta Wilcox."

"And may I ask what you and Miss Wilcox, and your other two friends, are doing in Albania?"

"We're on a cycling holiday. Were on a cycling holiday. My God! Our gear—"

"Will be where you left it. These people aren't thieves."

"We were told—"

"I'm sure you were. But it isn't true. Rebels against Zog and his fascists, yes. Robbers, except when it comes to guns and bullets, no."

Catherine licked her lips. "Do you think I could have something to drink?"

He waved his arm, and a waterskin was brought. "Nothing stronger, I'm afraid. These people are Muslims." He squatted beside her.

"This tastes just fine. May I ask what *you* are doing here, Mr Andrews?"

Another twisted grin. "What I can. Now I am going down to look at your other friends. They *are* dead?"

"Yes."

"Then I'll have them buried. I'm afraid they'll have to be put in the communal grave with these people. There is no way of taking their bodies out."

Catherine sighed. "I understand that."

"I assume you know their parents?"

"Sort of."

"Grim, isn't it."

He made to get up, and she caught his arm. "What happens to me? And Roberta?"

"We'll talk about it," he said.

Time seemed to stand still. Catherine felt it was doing that for the villagers as well as her. Down to this morning theirs had also been a trouble-free existence. No, she reminded herself, that couldn't be true if they had been in arms against their government. But whatever might have happened in the past, they had

14

not been bombed before. Now they were, literally, shell-shocked, wandering about, some of the men firing their rifles into the air. The woman gathered in groups, chattering. Occasionally they, and their children and dogs, would gather round Catherine; hens returned from shelter to peck the ground beside her – several had been blown to bits. She was acutely aware of being scantily dressed, certainly by Albanian standards, due to the haste with which she had dragged on her clothes by the stream. She wore no brassière, her shirt was torn, and somewhere during the day she had lost her sandals. There were clean clothes and another pair of shoes in her knapsack, but she could not face going to find it. Her knee was aching in tune with her head and her feet.

She felt she should at least go and look at Roberta, see if she had regained consciousness, but she could not bring herself to move. She realised that she was in a state of shock, too, constantly shivering despite the heat, which began to fade as the afternoon wore on. She listened to the chanting and the blowing of pipes as the dead were buried. Peter and Alan, laid to rest with ten complete strangers, in an unmarked grave and without a Christian prayer. That was what she had to tell their parents, when she got back to England. If she got back to England.

She wondered how old Clayton Andrews was. Somewhere about forty, she supposed. "Drink this." He held a cup to her lips, and she snorted.

"I thought there was no alcohol?"

"Medicinal brandy. You need it."

She swallowed, and felt her digestive system catch fire. "And now some food," Clayton Andrews said.

"I couldn't."

"You must. You can't just sit there and starve to death."

Lamb stew was brought, and once she had swallowed her first mouthful she realised just how hungry she was. "How is Bobbie?"

"Alive. I'm keeping her under sedation. What she really needs is a blood transfusion, but as that isn't on, we just have to let nature do its work. If it can."

"How soon will she be able to travel?"

"I'm afraid we're talking about weeks, unless we can get hold of some transport, and that isn't too likely at the moment."

"What's happening, really."

"I don't know what's happening, save that we've been invaded. But I wouldn't estimate the Albanians have much chance of resisting the Italian army."

"Surely the League of Nations—"

His mouth gave one of those disconcerting twists. "The League of Nations didn't do a lot to stop *Il Duce* in Abyssinia. Let's talk about you. I'm going to get you out."

"But Roberta—"

"Do you really want to spend the rest of the year here? These people will care for her."

He was asking her to abandon Roberta, one of nature's confirmed virgins, to these mountain savages? "But suppose they're attacked again?"

"If they are, your being here isn't going to help matters."

"You mean, I should just walk away, leaving three of my closest friends behind?"

"The sensible decision isn't always the most acceptable," he pointed out. "What would you like to do most, right this minute?"

"Kill some Italians. I suppose that's not a very ladylike thing to say."

"Wars aren't very ladylike things to begin with. I entirely agree with you. Do you know, I have been fighting Italians for more than ten years now?"

"Why?"

"Oh, I don't have anything against them as people, and I think Italy is a wonderful country. But I don't like their boss and what he stands for."

"Did you know he was going to invade Albania?"

"I knew he had established a protectorate over it, and I also felt pretty damned sure Zog would do as he was told. So I came here to help these people. Well, Zog surprised us all by standing up. But it hasn't done him a damn bit of good."

"And these people have been blown to bits."

"Some of them. There are quite a few in these mountains. And now they really have something to fight against. If only they had something to fight with. I'm trying to arrange that. The guns are there, waiting. But getting them here . . . anyway, that's none of your business. Yes, Catherine Ames, I think you should walk away from here just as rapidly as you can, get down to Athens, and take a ship home. Have you any money?"

"Some. We all had some."

"I would say you're entitled to take whatever you can find in their knapsacks."

"I can't abandon Roberta."

"I've told you, you can't help her. I'll look after her."

"You?" She was immediately suspicious.

He grinned. "She's a little young for me, Miss Ames. Even if she had two good legs. But you go home. Just where is home, anyway?"

"Gloucestershire. Do you know England?"

"I've been there a few times."

"Well, I live in Cheltenham. I'm going to teach in a girl's school there."

"Cheltenham," he said thoughtfully. "Now there's an odd thing. Have you ever heard the name Martingell?"

Despite herself, Catherine smiled; both the food and the alcohol was starting to have an effect. "Sir James? Our most notorious resident. Not Cheltenham. But he used to live in the Chilterns. One of the last great adventurers, my father says."

"I never met him. I suppose you know that his wife was sent to prison for murdering her own son?"

"Oh, yes. She is also a notorious figure. But she was let out because the conviction was eventually considered unsafe. She now lives in the Chilterns herself."

"With a man named Elligan," Clayton Andrews remarked.

"You seem to know a lot about them. I've heard of Mr Elligan. His reputation isn't too good, either."

"They were gun-runners. Still are, when the price is right. I've done business with them."

"And you'd like to do so again," Catherine said thoughtfully. "For these people."

"I've told you. I can get the guns. I need a delivery system. Trouble is, I've fallen out with the Martingell/Elligan set up. Certainly with Elligan's ex-wife, who is the real lynch-pin of their operation. Do you know about her? Name of Sophie, born a German but a naturalised British subject."

17

Catherine shook her head. "They're all just hearsay to me."

"Sophie is quite something. Eats men for breakfast."

"Has she had you for breakfast?"

"More than once," he said ruefully. "I fell madly in love with her. But she was interested only in the money. However, as she *is* interested only in money . . . you could be the answer to a prayer. Would you really like to help these people? Avenge your friends?"

"Yes," Catherine said. "Tell me what you wish me to do."

She sat beside Roberta. Roberta was only half awake, and moaned and groaned. At least Andrews had had the decency to cover her with a blanket. "God!" Roberta muttered. "What happened?"

"You were blown up by a bomb. We all were. I was lucky."

"The boys—"

"Are dead."

Roberta stared at her in disbelief, which changed to horror as memory returned. Then she was overtaken by a spasm of pain. "My leg—"

"You had a bomb splinter in there."

Roberta clutched her arm. "Tell me."

"You still have it. The leg I mean. Mr Andrews took out the splinter. But listen, Roberta . . . you have to stay here for a while. You can't walk, and there's no means of moving you."

"You'll stay with me, Cathy."

Catherine bit her lip. "I'll come back for you. But I've promised to help Mr Andrews get some things he needs. But I'll come back."

"When? When will you come back?"

"Just as soon as I can," Catherine promised.

The Web

"Oh, cease! Must hate and death return? Cease! Must men kill and die?"

Percy Bysshe Shelley

Assassins

"We have prisoners, General," the captain said. Brigadier General Edio Rometti got up from behind his desk and went into the antechamber of the house he had appropriated as his military headquarters. Edio Rometti was a tall, thin man, with a heavily sun-tanned hatchet face and greying black hair, which he wore neatly brushed back from his high forehead. He looked grim most of the time, his expression suggesting the ruthlessness required for command in war, just as his well-pressed uniform and highly polished black boots indicated his attention to detail. He could fight, and often had fought with the best, but he remained, inside, slightly bewildered that he should have risen so far in this army with which he had first seen service at the disastrous Battle of Caporetto in 1917.

Twenty-two years ago he had been a teen-age subaltern, filled with romantic notions of how war should be waged, of the mutual respect that should exist between opposing forces, of the requirements of officers and gentlemen to be chivalrous towards the foe. Then he had served Italy, and been proud of it. More recently he had served *Il Duce*, and he was not so proud of that. But it was his duty. Compared with his previous military experience since the end of the Great War, the long, barbaric brutal struggle with the Senussi in the Sahara, and then the no less bitter campaign against the Abyssans in East Africa, the invasion of Albania had been the simplest thing in the world. Of course, when he had returned from Abyssinia, two years ago, he had discovered that the plans had long been laid for the takeover of the little Balkan country, Italy had already established almost complete financial control of the mountain state across the Adriatic Sea, and her military attachés had covered most of the territory, in the guise of tourists or simply as advisers to the

21

unsuspecting Albanian government, establishing just where was best for offensive manoeuvres and where it might be necessary to stand on the defensive. Nothing had been left to chance.

And in fact the Albanians had put up very little resistance, thus far; the invasion was only a week old. King Zog and his wife and family had fled the country the moment the Italian army had landed, along with the government. Only in these mountains bordering Greece did the remnants of the Albanian army, leaderless and virtually unarmed, still hold out. It was Edio's task to dislodge them and destroy them. That these partisans were in the main composed of Muslims who in any event had been rebelling against the government of King Zog before the Italian invasion only made his orders the more attractive; he had a long memory of campaigns against Muslim guerillas, even if the Abyssinians had in the main been Christians – of a sort. Now he surveyed the two men who had been forced to kneel by their captors. They were very roughly dressed, and stank of fear and lack of hygiene; their beards were as straggly as their hair. They trembled. They were as unattractive as any human beings could be – to Edio Rometti's eyes. "Do you speak Italian?" he asked.

One of the men rolled his eyes. "I speak Italian, Signor General."

"Good. So tell me, how many men are there under arms in the mountains?" Some more rolling of the eyes. Edio drew his revolver. "If you do not answer my questions, I shall blow out your brains. We will still have your friend, eh?" He had long ago discovered that the simple, straightforward approach to these matters was far more productive, and certainly less stomach-churning, than a painful, long drawn-out "interrogation".

Certainly the Albanian did not wish to be shot. "There are many men, Signor General. Hundreds of men. Maybe thousands."

"Men like you?" Edio's contempt was evident, even to the prisoner.

"Better men, Signor General."

"Better armed?" The two men had been captured in possession of somewhat ancient rifles.

"They are not better armed now, Signor General. But soon they will have new rifles, and much ammunition. And machine-guns."

"Is that so? Where are these munitions coming from? Greece?"

22

"I do not think so, Signor General. I think they are coming from a ship."

Edio frowned. "A ship? What nationality? And to which port?"

"I do not know these things, Signor General. I am only saying what I overheard, when Signor Andrews was in conversation with the Englishwoman—"

"What did you say?" Edio's normally quiet voice rose an octave.

"About the ship—"

"The name you said," Edio snapped. "Say it again."

"Andrews, Signor General?"

"Andrews," Edio repeated. "There is a man named Andrews, fighting with you in the mountains. He is an American, about my age?"

"Si, Signor General. He is an American." The prisoner preferred not to suggest an age.

"And this man is going to supply your people with guns?"

"Si, Signor General. That is what he says."

Well, well, Edio thought. How devils do return to haunt one. He had hunted Clay Andrews for some ten years, ever since the American adventurer, whose sole ambition in life seemed to be to oppose Fascism wherever it was to be found, had been identified as fighting with the Senussi. He had been supplying them with arms too, arms which had been manufactured and delivered by the German House of Beinhardt, whose agent was the daughter of Claus von Beinhardt, Sophie, and her husband, Richard Elligan. He had never met Andrews until he had taken him red-handed in Abyssinia, selling guns to the army of Haile Selassie. And then he had foolishly let the scoundrel go, because Andrews had been with Sophie Elligan and Ned Carew, her lover, and that pair had once saved the life of Edio's mistress. It had been the last time he had allowed his belief in chivalry to rule his head.

Well, he had paid that debt. And he had warned them all that if they ever met again he would hang them all. And here was Andrews again. On his doorstep. With the woman? "Tell me about this Englishwoman who is with him. She has red-brown hair, eh? And she is old." That was an insult to Sophie, who could not yet be forty, but he reckoned that to a Muslim man any female age over thirty would be regarded as old.

"No, no, Signor General," the prisoner protested. "This girl has yellow hair. And she is very young. And very pretty," he added, doing some more eye-rolling.

Edio frowned. But the man was obviously telling the truth. "Her name was not Elligan?"

"I do not think so, Signor General. But I have heard that name. Signor Andrews used it to this girl."

"Ah," Edio said. "So this girl is a friend of Signora Elligan's?"

The prisoner looked utterly confused. "I do not think so, Signor General. She was on a bicycling holiday with some friends, when they were blown up with a bomb. She was the only survivor, I think. So Signor Andrews took her over the mountains into Greece, and then returned to us."

"Andrews personally escorted this woman into Greece? Someone you say he had never met before? And you do not know her name? But they definitely talked about Signora Elligan?"

"That is what I heard, Signor General. Signora Elligan is important to them."

"Yes," Edio said. "She is important to them. Now tell me when this happened. When did Signor Andrews take this young woman into Greece?"

"It was three days ago, Signor General. He returned yesterday."

"Very good. Put them in the cage with the other prisoners," he told the captain. He had actually obtained a great deal of valuable information, which he could put to good use, if he acted quickly enough. He returned into the office, where his secretary stood to attention. Edio sat behind his desk. "Get on the radio. I wish the names of everyone who crossed the border from Greece on or about the day of the invasion. I am particularly interested in a group of English tourists, riding bicycles. They will have entered the country legitimately, and thus they will have been checked at the border. I wish their names and the numbers of their passports." The secretary was writing busily. "Then I wish the names of any British tourist who re-entered Greece from Albania within the past four days. This may well have been an illegal entry, but I have an idea it would have been done through a border check point." He knew Clay Andrews would have friends amongst the Greeks, and he also knew Andrews would wish to keep his messenger girl as legitimate as possible. "Get our Greek agents onto it. Immediately, Roberto."

The information was on his desk that afternoon. "Catherine Ames," he said with some satisfaction; hers was the only name that occurred on both lists. "Very good, Roberto. Now get on the phone to our people in Athens, and tell them I wish to know the whereabouts of Catherine Ames, and if she has left the country, by what means and her destination. Immediately, Roberto."

It was the following morning that he got what he wanted. "Freighter for Marseilles," he said thoughtfully. "Arriving tomorrow morning." He picked up his telephone. "Get me our people in Marseilles. This is top priority and the line must be scrambled." The call was through in fifteen minutes. Edio outlined the situation to the agent on the end of the line.

"You wish this woman snatched when she lands?" the agent asked.

"No. That would cause an incident. Besides, she is of no importance. It is the people she is going to meet who matter. I wish her followed until she meets with these people. They will be a man and a woman. The man is very big, rough-looking, English. The woman is tall and red-haired, very handsome. She is German by birth but is a naturalised British subject. Their names are Edward Carew and Sophie Elligan, but I have no doubt they are using an assumed name. I have been looking for these people for several years, and have been unable to find them."

"You say these people are English, but you think they may be living in France?"

"They are living wherever Catherine Ames is going. And at the moment she is going to France."

"And if we find them now?"

Edio sighed. But the days of chivalry were gone; he was fighting a war. "I would not like the meeting to be completed."

"I will have to check this action with the boss."

"Do so. Their names are on file if he wishes any more information. I would like to be informed when the transaction has been completed." He hung up and stared at the wall. Sophie Elligan was *such* an attractive woman.

On a spring day the Mediterranean sea glowed eerily through the heat mist. The holidaymakers were not yet here in force, but they would come in August, regardless of what might be happening in the rest of Europe, as Hitler's Nazis completed the rape of Czechoslovakia. The little man had announced this was to be his last territorial claim, and the people of France were prepared to believe him, because they believed they were too powerful ever to be attacked – did not France have the greatest and most efficient army in the world? So the politicians said. As for strikes and Communist agitation, there had been strikes and at least radical agitation for a hundred years, and the country still prospered.

It was, Sophie Elligan thought, a prosperity that brushed off even on those who were just passing through. She had supposed that she and Ned Carew were just passing through, five years ago. But they had stayed, despite the fact that they were still wanted by the French authorities, at least in North Africa, on charges ranging from gun-running through murder to revolution. But they had never broken the law in France itself, and no one had ever troubled Mr and Mrs Smith, who lived quietly in their villa off their invested income. And now she rather suspected, and hoped, that their stay here might become permanent. She rolled on to her stomach to sun her back. She was a tall, strongly built woman, with long legs, square shoulders, and heavy breasts; even in the modest one-piece bathing costume, with its little skirt to make sure she exposed no hint of cheek or wisp of pubic hair, she attracted glances from the men using the beach. Her auburn hair was bound up on the top of her head and she wore glare glasses to protect her eyes. Her features were surprisingly piquant for the rest of her, but were nonetheless attractive; only her eyes, so carefully concealed, would have revealed to an inquisitive acquaintance that she was a woman who had lived life to the hilt, who had fought and killed and suffered and survived – the dusting of freckles that covered every exposed part of her body indicated that she had spent much of that life in the sun.

Glorious days. She supposed, in the light of conventional morals, that she was a bad woman. Had been a bad woman. Her adventures had not been those of a lady who had been born a German countess, nor had her desertion of her husband in favour of his servant, nor the fact that they lived as man and wife without ever having married; neither she nor Richard had wanted to risk the publicity of a divorce. But all of that was behind her now; for the first time since her return from the desert she had missed a

26

period. The ultimate fulfilment. She often felt that her marriage to Richard had broken down because of her inability to have a child for him – although there had been other reasons. Her relationship with Ned, forged in their battle for life in the Sahara Desert, had never depended on domestic bliss; he had never raised the subject of children. But her lack had remained a great blot on her life, the ultimate non-fulfilment of womanhood. It had been easy to explain away, to herself, during the great adventure, when she had existed on poor food, continual exhaustion, and constant tension for four years. Menstruation had been a rare event. Since her return to civilisation and an ordered existence she had also returned to normal, slowly. But there had been no success. At thirty-seven she had all but despaired.

And suddenly it had happened. She could not imagine what Ned's reaction was going to be when she told him. He would be overjoyed, she was sure. But it would have to wait another month, until she was absolutely certain. Of course she assumed it would be a boy. But the sex didn't matter. The child would be the coping-stone of their middle-aged, retired prosperity.

She heard the hoot of a horn, and pushed herself up, gazing past the grassy knolls that lined the road at the car that had appeared there. She waved, and stood up, folding her towel as she did so, and then walking up the beach with long, positive strides. He stood beside the car, a vast, heavily built man. Her Gargantua, she called him, loving every inch of the massive bone and muscle structure, in perfect condition despite his forty-three years. His face was too craggy to be called handsome, but there could be no doubting his strength of character – without it they would both have died in the desert when escaping the Senussi. His dark hair was thinning, his only concession to advancing age. His clothes, loose shirt and pants, canvas shoes, merely indicated that his was not a nine-to-five existence.

They were, she supposed, the oddest of odd couples, from their background to their appearances. Sophie was the daughter of Claus and Clementine von Beinhardt, of the House of Beinhardt, the arms merchants who had launched James Martingell on his career. She had been an only child, growing up in the Great War and learning the facts of poverty during the great depression of 1923, when a billion marks would not buy a loaf of bread. But the Beinhardts had survived, and even gone back into the arms business, and Sophie had determined to play her part. Thus, as her father's agent, she had joined forces with Martingell and his young sidekick, Richard Elligan. That she and Richard would find each other sufficiently attractive to marry had, she supposed, been inevitable. Besides, she had wanted to be even more a part of the ongoing adventure that had ended so tragically in Martingell's death, along with his daughter and more than one other faithful companion.

By then she had become a naturalised British subject, her back turned on Germany forever – save that it was simpler to buy and export guns from Germany than Britain, where the rules were tightly and more rigorously enforced. The breakdown in her marriage had begun when Richard had decided that a woman should play no part in the increasingly dangerous business of delivering the goods. He had wanted a wife more than a partner. Sophie did not know whether, in time, she would have slipped quietly into domesticity, resenting and regretting the new role being forced upon her, had not Richard broken his leg so badly as to be confined to bed for several months, just before Clayton Andrews had turned up with a quarter of a million pounds to buy guns for his friends the Senussi.

That offer, coming as it had just as the world was being plunged into financial chaos by the crash of 1929, had been too good to resist. But Richard had been unable to move. Sophie could still remember the feeling of triumph she had known when he had accepted that she would have to make the delivery herself. He had unwittingly ended the marriage when he had appointed his servant, Ned Carew, to be her bodyguard. At that time Ned had been nothing more than a servant, large, faithful, reliable . . . but when the delivery had turned into an on-going catastrophe that had left the two of them alone in the desert, every man's hand against them, he had become much more than that. From fighting and killing, shoulder to shoulder, digging for water shoulder to shoulder, sharing everything, it had been a short step to sharing their bodies. They had been sustained by the fortune they had stolen from the Arabs, driven onwards by the knowledge that were they to be captured their fate would have been unthinkable. And they had triumphed, after four unforgettable years.

There had been no question of her going back to Richard.

Besides, he had long given her up for dead, and taken up with his old girlfriend Anne, James Martingell's widow, recently released from prison when the charge of murder against her had been quashed. Sophie had not supposed she would ever see him again, had no desire to, content with Ned. Until Clayton Andrews had re-entered their lives, with another offer they had been unable to refuse, this time on behalf of the Abyssinians. Another catastrophe, compounded by the things she had had to do to get the guns out of Hitler's Germany. But once again, a huge profit, for them, and these three years of total happiness, total commitment to each other. And now, she was determined, total parentage.

"I'm not sure you should spend so much time in the sun," he remarked, holding her robe to wrap it round her.

"I think it's already done me all the damage it can." She sat beside him in the Renault and he engaged gear; to their right the seaport of Sete broiled in the afternoon heat. "All well in town?"

"Depends on your interpretation of the word. The markets are falling while they wait to see what Mr Hitler does next. And of course they're agitated by Mussolini's invasion of Albania."

"How come he's getting away with that?" Sophie asked.

"Who's going to stop him?" Ned asked. "The British and the French could have stopped Hitler, back in 1935. They could have stopped Mussolini then too, when he invaded Abyssinia. But they didn't. They've lost the moral high ground when it comes to stopping dictators."

"This fall in the stock exchange . . . there isn't going to be another crash?"

"I wouldn't bet against it. Depends on what the Germans and the Italians do next, I suppose. With Franco winning in Spain, you have to say it's been a good year for Fascism."

She shuddered. "Is it going to affect us?"

He grinned as he pulled into the forecourt of their little villa, which was set several miles back from the coast and an almost equal distance from the nearest village of Le Pouget, nestling on a shallow hillside well away from any other habitation as well; this area, bordered by the *étangs* or salt lakes that stretched for several miles along the coast, was at the bottom end of the tourist market as opposed to places like Cannes well to the east. Here it was possible to be private. "I may have to get a job."

"I hope you're joking."

"Oh, we've enough tucked away in Switzerland to last us a few years yet. By then . . . who knows?"

The car stopped and Sophie got out, frowned at the bicycle leaning against the front steps. "Are you going in for exercise?" He stood beside her. "That, my sweet, is a lady's bicycle. It doesn't have a crossbar."

"Good thinking. It also has a knapsack, waiting beside it." She looked up as the door opened, and Marie, their cook-housekeeper, emerged. "Do we have a visitor?" Sophie switched to French.

"A young lady, who wishes to speak to you, madame. An English lady," Marie added, dropping her voice. Marie was young, not unattractive, and romantic. To her, everything to do with her somewhat mysterious employers was exciting.

Sophie looked at Ned, who shrugged. They needed their privacy, and prided themselves on maintaining it. There were too many people in the world who had scores to settle with Sophie Elligan and Ned Carew. Sophie pointed at the verandah which ran round the side of the house. Ned nodded, and moved along this, softly on the balls of his feet. "Where is the young lady, Marie?" Sophie asked.

"I put her in the lounge, madame." Marie watched Ned disappearing. "I gave her a cup of coffee while she waited. Have I done the wrong thing?"

"Not at all," Sophie said. "We need to know what she is about."

Sophie entered the hall, drew a deep breath, and went into the lounge. There was always the chance that the young woman was an assassin, who would shoot on sight. But how had she tracked them down? She gazed at Catherine Ames, eyebrows arched. Catherine flushed. "Mrs Elligan?"

She was holding a handbag, in front of her. As she might have been expected to do. She also looked somewhat travel-stained, her blouse darkened with sweat, her slacks crumpled, her low-heeled shoes scuffed; even her yellow hair, gathered behind her head in a pony tail, looked sweaty and untidy. Anyone who looked less like an assassin could hardly be imagined. But then, that was how an assassin would choose to look.

Sophie moved towards her, casually. "I am Sophie Elligan."

"Catherine Ames. We haven't met."

Sophie studied her from a distance of about six feet, while watching Ned enter the room from the back, so softly Catherine did not hear him. The girl was certainly young, and attractive. But her eyes had also looked on the seamy side of life. The legs were long, the blouse well filled. And the hair, untidy and unwashed as it was, was really magnificent. If she *was* an assassin, they were taking them from the top drawer. "I was sent by a friend of yours," Catherine said. "Clayton Andrews."

The name galvanised Ned into action. He had been stealthily approaching. Now he leapt forward, thrust an arm under each of Catherine's, closing his grip across her chest, and jerking her backwards off her feet. She gave a little scream, and her legs flailed. Sophie sidestepped the kicking feet and snatched the handbag. "For God's sake," Catherine protested, as Ned dragged her to the settee and sat her there, sliding his hands up to grip her wrists and hold her hands above her head. She tried to wriggle free, but he was too strong for her.

Sophie emptied the bag on to the table. But there were only women's things, and some money. "She could have something on her," Ned said.

"What are you doing?" Catherine panted. "I came here—"

"From Clay Andrews." Sophie sat beside her. "Please stop fighting. You'll get hurt."

Catherine stopped trying to free herself, mainly because she had run out of breath. "He said he was a friend of yours," she panted.

"He would." Sophie ran her hands over Catherine's blouse, testing under her arms, then her waist, and parted her legs to slide her hands between her thighs.

"You are assaulting me," Catherine shouted. "Indecently."

Sophie leaned away from her. "She's clean." Ned released Catherine's wrists; she brought her arms together to massage herself. Tears trickled down her cheeks. "I think the young lady could do with a drink," Sophie said.

Ned went to the sideboard, while Catherine suddenly swung her right arm as hard as she could. Sophie caught it without difficulty. "You really are asking for a beating," she remarked. The two women stared at each other, the angry colour slowly fading from

31

Catherine's cheeks. "Any friend of Clay Andrews is by definition an enemy of mine," Sophie said. "How good a friend are you?"

Catherine bit her lip. "I think he saved my life." Ned stood before them with a tray and three glasses of Ricard. Catherine gulped at hers. "Gosh!"

"It's quite strong," Sophie said. "You were going to tell me about Clay." Catherine drank some more, and told them about Albania. Ned sat on her other side. "So you're out for vengeance," Sophie said thoughtfully.

"I'm trying to help," Catherine said. "My friend—"

"Where is Clay now?"

"In Albania, so far as I know. He escorted me over the border, then handed me to some friends of his who took me to Athens. I suppose he went back. I was talking about Roberta."

"But he sent you to me."

"I have a message."

"How did you, or he, know where to find us?" Ned asked.

"I don't know. He gave me this address."

"Seems to me we have to consider moving on," Ned said. "Shame, I've become quite fond of this place."

"How well do you know Clay?" Sophie asked.

"Well—" Catherine flushed. "We were together for a few days."

"Did he have you?"

Catherine's head jerked. "Certainly not. He was a perfect gentleman."

"That's our Clay."

"Besides—" Catherine's flush deepened. "I think he is in love with you."

"That's our Clay." This time it was Ned who spoke.

Catherine looked from one to the other. "He needs your help. He said there is a great deal at stake."

"I'm sure there is, Miss Ames. But there is nothing we can do to help him, even if we wanted to. The Martingell Arms Company went out of business years ago. Beinhardt and Company still operate, but they are making arms for the Reich. They went along with us a few years ago, but that was before Hitler and Mussolini became buddies. I don't see them selling arms to us for use by the Albanians against the Italians today."

32

"Clay said there would be no trouble procuring the arms; he has already arranged that. He merely needs you to deliver them. He said you should contact a Mr Walters at the American Embassy in Paris. He gave me the phone number. It's a private line. He said there would be fifty thousand American dollars in it for you."

"That's our Clay," Ned said again.

"Let me get this straight, if I can," Sophie said. "You just happen to run into Clay Andrews, and he just happens to trust you to the extent of sending you off to see us and persuade us to deliver some guns for him. Now you are telling us that he is dealing through the American Embassy in Paris? Miss Ames, we weren't born yesterday. You will have to do better than that."

"Well," Catherine said, sulkily, "as for trusting me, he has my friend Bobbie, in Albania, as a kind of hostage."

"And the American Embassy?"

"I don't know. He gave me a letter to post to them when I reached France."

"To this Mr Walters."

"Yes. I posted it in Marseilles, yesterday."

The whole thing stank, Sophie thought. But . . . "Fifty thousand dollars!" She looked at Ned.

"We're retired."

"With a crashing market," Sophie reminded him. "And if Clay Andrews has discovered our address, and perhaps the American Embassy as well, as you say, it's time to move on. That is going to cost money, and we don't want to start drawing on capital."

"Sophie—"

"Delivery to Albania. That would mean either Greece or Yugoslavia."

"The Adriatic is totally controlled by the Italian Navy."

"So it will have to be Greece. The Italians wouldn't interfere with a ship flying the British flag. Or even better, the German."

"Sophie—"

"Let's sleep on it. I think you had better spend the night with us, Miss Ames."

"Oh! All I was told was to deliver the message and then go home."

"But you're a long way from home," Sophie pointed out. "Where did you intend to spend the night?"

"I was going to find an hotel in the nearest town."

"I don't think that would be a good idea. Not until we've found out how much of what you have told us is the truth. Besides, the nearest town is several miles away. You could wind up sleeping rough. You'll be much more comfortable here."

Catherine's chin came up. "You can't keep me a prisoner."

"We are keeping you as a guest. Perhaps you'd lock Miss Ames' bicycle in the garage, Ned. And bring in her knapsack."

"I am sure we are going to be the best of friends." Sophie showed Catherine into the spare bedroom. "I'm sorry about the bars on the windows, but they're actually to keep burglars out rather than anyone in, although it works very well both ways. Now, I suggest you have a bath, and change into something clean, and join us for an aperitif before dinner." Ned had placed the knapsack on the chair, and the two women were alone.

"Are you going to help Mr Andrews?"

"Does our friendship depend on that?"

"Well – not necessarily. It's just that he desperately needs help."

"He always desperately needs help. It's this habit he has of getting involved in lost causes. But he's always operated on his own, before. I find this American Embassy link intriguing. Have you actually spoken with this man Walters?"

Catherine shook her head. "I was just told to post the letter, and I did that in Marseilles when I landed."

"Yesterday morning. Where did you spend last night?"

"In an hotel."

"And then bicycled all the way down here this morning? How long did that take you?"

"I put the bicycle on a train. I only got off at Montpellier."

"Very sensible." Sophie went to the door. "You have that bath."

"*Are* you going to help him? I think his offer is a very good one."

"I told you, we'll sleep on it." Sophie closed the door.

Ned was waiting in the master bedroom, where Sophie changed her bathing costume for a dress. "What do you reckon?"

34

"That Catherine Ames is either a very dumb blonde or a very deep young woman."

"What are we going to do with her?" Sophie glanced at him. She knew just how ruthless he could be when either she or himself were threatened. Catherine Ames' presence in this house was threatening them both. "She knows where we live," Ned pointed out.

"Because Clay told her. Now that *is* frightening. How the hell did he find out?"

"He could have put the Embassy on to it, if they're in partnership."

"Then how the hell did *they* find out? We've never done anything to upset the Yanks."

"We've done a lot of things to upset Clay Andrews. And if he is now in cahoots with his government, I say we make ourselves scarce. But we'll have to dispose of our little friend along the way. Will that crease you up?"

Sophie led the way into the lounge. "She seems a nice kid. I'd better go see how she's getting on." She glanced out of the window, and frowned. "What the—" A large black car had swung off the road into the forecourt.

"Jesus Christ!" Ned shouted. "Take cover!"

Sophie dived to the floor as the windows shattered to the sound of machine-gun fire. From the kitchen Marie screamed. Sophie rolled over and over to reach the inner door, while the chattering continued and bullets smashed into the walls and pictures, shattered bottles on the sideboard, ripped open the furniture. "Ned!" she screamed, uncertain where he was.

There was no reply. Sophie rose to her hands and knees, crawled into the hall. More bullets shattered the ceiling above her, bringing down a cloud of plaster. "Aaagh!" Catherine screamed. "Mrs Elligan!"

"Here!" Ned had emerged from the study, slid a Browning automatic pistol across the floor. He had another for himself. Sophie grabbed the gun, rolled through the spare bedroom door, saw a man at the barred window holding a tommy-gun. She lay on her stomach and fired twice. She was an expert shot, and both bullets hit. The man disappeared.

"Oh, my God!" Catherine had apparently got out of the bath on hearing the shooting, and had thrown herself down when the

35

man appeared. Now she rose to her hands and knees, water dripping from her naked body.

"Get *down*!" Sophie shouted, and rolled again. At the other end of the hall she saw two men at the front door; they had apparently shot out the lock. Now they were pointing their tommy-guns at her, but before they could fire, Ned stood up from the study doorway, pistol thrust forward as he fired again and again. The men went down, but one of them fired as he did so, and Ned gave a startled exclamation and fell back through the door, hitting the floor beyond with a thump. "Ned!" Sophie screamed, scrambling to her feet.

"Keep down," he shouted. But the two men were both dead. Sophie ran down the hall, pistol thrust forward, held in both hands. She reached the doorway, saw the black car moving as the remaining assassin decided to escape. Sophie stood on the porch, taking deep breaths, and fired again and again. One of her bullets struck the driver in the back of the head and he slumped across the wheel. The car swung sideways and crashed into the bushes by the gate.

"Oh, my *God*!" Catherine stood in the spare room doorway, staring at the carnage.

"For Christ's sake," Sophie snapped. "Put something on!" She ran into the study, knelt beside Ned. Now it was her turn to say, "Oh, my God!" but hers was a whisper rather than a shout, as she stared at the mass of blood covering Ned's chest and dripping on to the carpet. "Listen—"

"You listen," he panted. "Get out of here. Go, go, go! Before the police get to hear of this."

"A doctor. I'll get a doctor."

"Forget it." Now his voice was suddenly faint. "I'm done, Sophie."

"Ned!" she screamed, hugging him against her. "Oh, Ned!"

"It's been such fun," he whispered.

"Oh, Ned." She kissed his head, raised it up, and looked into empty eyes.

"Jesus," Catherine whispered from behind her. Sophie half turned her head; the girl had wrapped herself in a towel. "What *happened*?"

"What happened was that you were tracked here by those thugs." Sophie's words were like drops of vitriol.

36

"But . . . who were they?"

"Let me guess." Slowly Sophie laid Ned's head on the carpet. All gone, she thought. All gone. But already her mind was working at speed. Her parents considered her to be utterly cold-blooded. She knew that wasn't true. Some time very soon she was going to be prostrate with grief about Ned, the only man she had ever loved. But not right now. There was too much to be done. And Ned had given her the priorities. She stood up.

"Are we going to call the police?" Catherine asked.

"Forget that. We'd all wind up in gaol and sitting ducks for the next wave."

"You know these people?"

"Not personally." Sophie went into the hall, knelt beside the two dead men, emptied their pockets, her hands becoming as wet with their blood as her dress was from Ned's. Predictably they carried no identification. But their tommy-guns had been made in Italy.

"Are they dead?" Catherine asked.

"Listen," Sophie told her, "if you utter another inanity, I am going to wring your fucking neck. Don't you realise you caused this to happen, you silly little bitch?"

"I was only doing what Clay asked me to."

"Par for the course. Marie! My God, Marie!" She ran into the kitchen. Marie lay on the floor in a pile of blood, dead. "Shit! You—" Sophie pointed. "Get dressed!" Catherine ran into the spare room. Sophie went into her bedroom, stripped off her blood-wet clothes, showered, then dressed again neatly in a quiet blue suit with a white blouse. She packed a single clothes bag, quickly and economically, and filled her large shoulder bag with all the essentials she knew she might need over the next few days, including her two passports and her first-aid kit. By the time she had finished, Catherine was standing in the doorway, dressed in shirt and pants, her still wet hair bound up in a bandanna. "What are we going to do?" she asked.

"You, are going to do exactly as you are told," Sophie said. "To begin with, pack up your knapsack." She went into the study. Ned had drawn money that day in town, and the notes were in the desk drawer: two thousand francs. She looked at her watch; it was far too late for a bank to be open, but she would need more than this. She went outside, watched by Catherine with wide eyes; the girl was hefting her knapsack and looked ready to run. The house was very secluded. Sophie went on to the road, walked up and down. She could not see the crashed car, only the side of the house. No passer-by could tell there was anything wrong in there, unless he came into the forecourt. And no one had any reason to do that: they did not take deliveries. The only people likely to call for the next day or two would be the back-up assassins – there always was a back-up – and they would hardly go rushing off to the police.

As for Marie's family . . . but Marie often stayed overnight at the villa, and even more often caught the bus into Montpellier or Sete when she had finished work to enjoy some nightlife. They would not get anxious before tomorrow night, at the earliest. She returned to the house. Catherine had come into the yard to escape the smell of death. "I really had no idea this was going to happen," she said. Her face was pale, and she was shivering, but she seemed to have recovered very well. What her reactions were likely to be later . . . "My God, were they after me, or you?"

"Me," Sophie said. "But I imagine they wanted you as well." She went inside, stepping over the dead bodies, stood in the study doorway, looking at Ned. How wonderful it would be if he were not dead after all, if he had moved . . . but he had not moved, and he was quite dead. She desperately wanted to bury him, at the least. But there seemed little point, apart from their relationship; she had no coffin and his body would be eaten by worms long before anyone got around to digging him up. Besides, if he was found by the police, surrounded by the bodies of the men he had killed, it might take some of the heat off her. That was what he would wish her to think, the course he would wish her to follow.

She took the now empty pistol she had used and placed it in his hand, closing the fingers round it. Then she took his pistol, reloaded it from the box of cartridges in the desk, and placed it and the cartridges in her shoulder bag. The ballistics detectives would discover that there had been more than one gun involved, quite apart from the tommy-guns of the assassins, but she reckoned it would take them a day or two to complete their investigations. If it also took them a day or two to find the bodies in the first place, that was more than sufficient time. "Was he your husband?" Catherine watched her with wide eyes.

"He was my lover," Sophie said. "Come."

She carried her bag outside and threw it into the back of the Renault, then added Catherine's knapsack. "Your lover?" Catherine asked. "And you're just going to drive away and leave him?"

"Was any of the people in Albania with you your lover?"

"Well—" Catherine flushed. "No."

"But you were friends. And you walked away and left them, right? We can't do anything for the dead, Catherine. Get in."

"What about my bike?"

"You'll have to leave the bike." Maybe that would confuse the police as well.

They drove some fifty miles in the general direction of Paris, then entered Millau and after two attempts found an hotel for the night. "Two ladies," remarked the concierge. "Wishing to share a room." She sniffed, even more disparagingly. "I must take your passports, for the police, you understand, madame." Sophie still wore a wedding ring.

"Of course." Sophie handed over her Elligan passport, retaining that in the name of Smith, and beckoned Catherine to do the same.

"Dinner is at seven," the concierge said. And added, "It is a double bed."

There was no porter, so they carried their bags up to their room. "There's no toilet," Catherine said. "I need to use the toilet."

"It'll be at the end of the corridor" Sophie said. "Give me your handbag."

"Why?"

"So you don't get any ideas about doing a runner."

Catherine glared at her for a moment, then threw the handbag on the bed and stalked out of the room. Sophie sat in the one chair and looked at a somewhat shabby portrait of the Christ doing something or other; it was difficult to make out what. Just as her future, not to say her present, was difficult to make out. For very nearly nine years she had relied on Ned for very nearly

39

everything, while always managing to convince herself that she was in control. Now . . . she wished she could weep. She wished she could scream and shout and break up the furniture. That wasn't her scene. Which did not mean that she couldn't feel anger, a red-hot fury that would soon enough become white-hot. So then, her future was after all delineated. She got up, opened Catherine's handbag, again emptied its contents. "What are you doing now?" Catherine asked from the doorway.

"Close the door. I am seeing how much money you have."

"Three thousand francs," Catherine said. "It's to get me back to England."

"I told you, you're not going back to England. For a while."

"Because the French police will find me there?"

"Because Mussolini's hit men will find you there."

Catherine sat on the bed, both hands clasped to her neck. "Why me?"

"Because they know you are an emissary for Clayton Andrews, a man they would dearly like to lay hands on. While I am an old partner of his, and by definition, because of you, a new partner as well."

"Then why are we here?" Catherine asked. "Shouldn't we be driving, or running, just as fast as we can?"

"Where to?"

Catherine gulped. "We are actually here," Sophie said, "because in the next big town, which is only half an hour away, there is a branch of my bank. We need more money, and I will draw it out tomorrow morning."

"But—"

"Of course it's a risk. But it has to be taken. And it's less dangerous than you think. I am working on the idea that nobody, except possibly another batch of killers, is going to visit the villa for at least twenty-four hours, maybe longer. When they do, they will start looking for Mrs Smith. Then they will very rapidly find out that Mrs Smith drew a large amount of money from her account in Sete, via a bank in Aurillac. Which will establish that we were there. But by then we'll be a long way away. And they'll be looking for Mrs Smith, not Mrs Elligan."

"Where will we be?"

"I'm working on it."

"You say the police will be looking for you after they go to the house," Catherine said, thoughtfully. "But no one knows I exist. Save you."

"You think too much," Sophie told her. "Let's eat."

"Whatever caused you to go bicycling in Albania?" Sophie asked as she poured the wine. As with even the most shabby of French hotels, the food was excellent, the *vin de table* surprisingly good.

"History, I suppose," Catherine said. "I'm going to teach it." She grimaced. "One day. We had no idea there was a shooting war about to start."

"One never does. You just happened to be in the wrong place at the wrong time. Tell me about Clay. I last saw him standing on the dock in Mombasa. That's in Kenya. And that was . . . three and a half years ago."

"You'd been delivering guns together?"

"In a manner of speaking. We were nabbed by the Italians before we could make the delivery."

"And you weren't sent to prison? Or even shot?"

"I happened to be an old friend of the man who caught us."

"You seem to have got around."

"Some."

"Were you and Clay ever lovers?"

"We came close a few times, but we always seemed to have other things on our minds."

"And now you say you hate him. Tell me why!"

"It really isn't any of your business. But . . . he let me down with a bump, handed me over to an Arab to be executed."

"Good lord! Why did he want you executed?"

"He didn't. The Arab did. I killed his uncle. It's a long story. The point is, Clay is not a man to get too close to. When he is doing a job, only the job matters. If he is helping the Albanian Muslim rebels, then he is helping the Albanian Muslim rebels. Nothing else will matter to him. Even if someone as pretty as you comes along, while he will use you without compunction, if you let him down or get between him and what he's doing, he will kill you." Catherine swallowed. Sophie smiled at her. "So tell me, *did* he get into your sleeping bag?"

"Well—" Catherine flushed. "I was really too cut up about

41

what had happened to Peter and Alan, and Bobbie, of course. I think maybe he had ideas, but he could see I was upset. And like I said, he kept meandering on about you."

"How sweet."

"I'm sure you're wrong about him, you know. About his being heartless when he's on a job. I mean, he was on a job, wasn't he? Yet he took time out to escort me to safety. That wasn't being heartless."

"Darling, he wasn't helping *you*. He was making sure his messenger girl would feel sufficiently grateful to carry out her mission."

"What about Bobbie? I think he saved her life."

"Again, with the main chance in mind. Bobbie was your dearest friend, right? Is your dearest friend. She's another compelling reason for you not to let him down. If those guns don't turn up, I doubt you'll ever see her again."

"Oh, you—" Catherine gulped at her wine. "If you don't help—"

"Don't rush me. What exactly were the plans for Bobbie?"

"Well, Clay was going to nurse her back to health and then get her into Greece. I was going to contact the Foreign Office in England and get them to help, and then go back for her."

"It seems to me," Sophie said, "that you're both in dire need of help."

They finished their meal and went upstairs. Sophie carefully locked the door and put the key on the table beside the bed. "You don't trust me, do you?" Catherine remarked.

"I'm hoping you'll grow on me. But I'm sure you'll agree I'm entitled to have a suspicious nature." She undressed and cleaned her teeth.

"Were you scared?" Catherine asked. "Back at your house?"

"One is always scared when one is being shot at."

"You mean you've been shot at before?"

"Several times."

"The way you reacted . . . you killed all four of them!" She had apparently only just realised that.

"If I hadn't, they would have killed us. Anyway, Ned killed two of them."

"And you've killed people before—" Catherine was equally apparently only just realising she was sharing a bedroom with a mass murderess.

"Always in self-defence," Sophie said. "Well. . . nearly always." Catherine watched her get into bed. "Don't you wear anything?"

"Never have. Don't worry, I'm not in the mood for sex." Catherine cleaned her teeth, put on pyjamas, inserted herself beneath the sheet very carefully. "This isn't a very big bed."

"So don't toss about. Things will look better in the morning." Sophie switched off the light. Would they look brighter? She wondered. How could they? Ned was gone, gone, gone. With every second that passed that realisation was biting deeper and deeper into her subconscious. Quite apart from her feelings for him, she had to come to terms with the fact that she was alone, alone, alone.

She had never been alone in her life before. First there had been Richard, and then there had been Ned. And for the brief period between Richard and Ned, there had been Clay Andrews, even if he had never done more than look, and dream. She had trusted him then. Now . . . he was still in love with her, according to Catherine. After all these years, all those bitter fights, after nearly allowing her to be killed in a most horrible manner. The bastard! But he was *there*. Ned was dead.

She awoke as Catherine left the bed. Perhaps she should have warned the girl that her years of adventure and misadventure had left her the ability to sleep like a cat, apparently deeply but entirely aware of any movement around her. She had been lying with her back to the girl. She remained still, listened to Catherine tip-toeing round the bed. She was coming for the key.

Sophie took a deep breath and opened her eyes, could see almost immediately as there was some light coming in the window. Catherine was standing beside her, her fingers just closing on the key. Sophie grasped her wrist, and Catherine gave a startled exclamation, tugged, and when she couldn't free herself, swung her other hand. But Sophie grasped this wrist as well, at the same time jerking forward. Catherine fell across her, and Sophie rolled over, carrying the girl with her to stretch her on her back while she kicked away the covers. Catherine heaved against her, but she lacked Sophie's strength. "Did I ever tell you that I once spent a week in a harem?" Sophie asked.

Again Catherine heaved against her, without success. "Bitch," she spat.

Sophie rose on her knees above her, straddling her hips. "You and I have just got to come to an understanding," she said. "You have got to accept that I am the boss and you are at very best my assistant, at the worst, my servant."

"You—"

"Cursing me is only going to make me angry." She grasped Catherine's shoulders and turned her over. Catherine made another strangled exclamation and tried to rise, and Sophie put her left hand in the middle of her back and forced her flat again. Then she pulled down the pyjama pants and delivered three crisp slaps on the heaving backside beneath her.

"Ow!" Catherine screamed. "Ow!"

"Now there," Sophie panted.

There was a banging on the door. "Madame? Madame?" It was the landlady. "What is happening in there? Are you all right?"

Sophie released Catherine. "Quite all right, madame. I just fell out of bed. I am sorry to have disturbed you."

Madame muttered something indistinguishable, and went off. Sophie switched on the light. Catherine was kneeling on the bed. She had pulled up her pyjama pants but was massaging her bottom. "I would really like us to be friends," Sophie said. "But we have to be friends my way."

"Your way." Catherine snorted.

"My way," Sophie repeated. "You see, my dear little girl, I have decided to help Clay."

Conspirators

"Mr Walters? My name is Sophie Elligan. I think you have heard of me."

"Mrs Elligan," agreed the nasal voice at the other end of the phone. "Where are you?"

"In Paris."

"It's a big city."

"I'm glad of that," Sophie said. "We need to meet."

"Can't you come to the Embassy?"

"No. You come to the Bois de Boulogne at six o'clock this afternoon. Take the Allée de Longchamp. Just before you reach the Hippodrome there is a path to the left. Turn down that and sit on the third bench. What do you look like?"

"I'm five foot eight inches tall, fair haired. I wear glasses."

"There's an honest man."

"So what do *you* look like?"

"I'll surprise you. Six o'clock." Sophie looked at her watch. "Two hours. And please be alone." She hung up, stepped out of the phone booth.

"Contact?" Catherine asked.

"Contact. Let's have a cup of coffee."

"When can I go home?" Catherine asked. They had left Millau at dawn, and driven all day apart from the short, nerve-wracking but trouble-free stop in Aurillac, where Sophie had cashed a large cheque drawn on Mr and Mrs Smith's account in Sete. The Aurillac branch had naturally telephoned for clearance, and this had been given without hesitation on presentation of Sophie's passport – as she had assumed, the bodies had not yet been found. They had reached Paris at three, parked the car, taken their bags, and walked away from it.

There was so much to be considered, so much that needed to

45

be done. Sophie had determined that her highest priority had to be Walters, because he was the future. But she also had to bear in mind what would soon be happening down at Le Pouget. She had calculated it would be tomorrow before anyone would visit the villa – except the back-up assassins. So what would they be doing now? "You can't go home." She studied a newspaper with her coffee. There was still nothing about any massacre in Le Pouget.

"But every minute I spend with you puts me in danger," Catherine said.

"Not so much danger as if you were on your own. You're an innocent in a rough world, Catherine. The Italians know who you are, and that you are Clay's messenger girl. They'll want you as much as they want me, maybe more."

"I feel sick."

Sophie signalled the waiter and ordered two cognacs. "It'll settle your stomach," she told Catherine. "And you don't want to forget you're helping Bobbie."

"But my parents—"

"Still think you're bicycling in the Balkans."

"They know we were going into Albania. They'll know about the Italian invasion."

"So they're probably raising all kinds of hell with the Foreign Office. But as the Foreign Office won't know what has happened to you—"

"They'll be worried sick."

"Yes, it's tough. I once went missing for four years."

"Suppose I just got up and walked away from you?" Catherine asked. "I know you have a gun in your bag. Would you just shoot me down?"

"I don't think so. That would be messy and public. I might telephone the Italian Embassy and tell them where you are and where you live."

"You are a—".

"Please don't say it." Sophie closed her hand on Catherine's. "Or I might just break all of these fingers." The two women glared at each other. "I will tell you what I'll do," Sophie said. "Behave yourself, and come with me to this meeting, when we'll hear what Mr Walters has to say. After that we'll be moving on from France, one way or the other. And before we do, I'll let you send your parents a telegram, to let them know you're all right."

"Why can't I do that now?"

"Because the telegram will have to be sent from a Paris post office. And will be traced back there in a matter of hours. It can't be sent until just before we leave." She released Catherine's hand.

"You're so . . . I don't understand you. That man was your lover. You watched him shot to death, and you've never shed a tear."

"They're there," Sophie said. "Did you cry when your friends were blown up?"

"I . . . I can't remember. There was so much going on—"

"Snap. And the gallant Clay came to your rescue. My trouble is, I don't have anyone to ride to *my* rescue. Let's move; it's a long walk."

"Why don't we drive?"

"That's why we brought our bags. Once the French police go to the villa, that car is going to be very hot. It's registered in the name of Mr Smith."

"But then . . . they'll know we're in Paris."

"As I told the man, it's a big city. And if it's not till tomorrow, we'll no longer be in Paris. Right?"

It was just before six, and the sun was well down when they reached the Bois de Boulogne, sauntering down the Allée until they reached the chosen corner. "We'll stand over there," Sophie decided, pointing at a clump of trees which overlooked the bench she had recommended.

"Suppose he doesn't come?" Catherine asked.

"He'll come. He needs us more than we need him. There. He's even punctual." The short, dapper, somewhat stout man was hurrying along the path, carrying a briefcase. He reached the bench, looked left and right, laid the briefcase on the seat, and took off his glasses to polish them. Sophie studied the path along which he had walked, the trees to either side. "Looks all right," she said. "Go talk to him."

"Me?" Catherine asked in dismay.

"You're our lead," Sophie told her. "Leave your bag."

Catherine placed the knapsack on the ground beside Sophie's

suitcase, drew a deep breath, stepped out from the trees. And walked towards the bench. She wore a dress today – her only dress; they were running out of clean clothes – and her hair was as usual tied with a ribbon. Walters, his back to her, did not hear her approach until she was nearly up to him, then he turned, sharply. "Mrs Elligan?" He appeared totally surprised.

"A friend," Catherine explained.

"I'm afraid I need to speak with Mrs Elligan, personally."

"She's around," Catherine said. "Shall we sit down?"

Walters hesitated, then picked up his briefcase, and sat. Catherine sat beside him. He was effectively distracted by Catherine's legs, which were very good, and her hair, and her general ambience. And there was no sign that he had provided himself with any back-up. Sophie left the trees and advanced, carrying both bags. "Are you in Mrs Elligan's confidence?" Walters was asking. "Part of her team?"

"I work for Mr Andrews."

This seemed to confuse him even more. "Well, Mr Andrews, of course—"

"I am Sophie Elligan," Sophie said. Walters leapt to his feet and turned to face her, jaw sagging. Sophie placed the bags on the ground and held out her hand. "I'm sorry we had to handle it this way, Mr Walters, but I'm conditioned to suspicion."

Walters squeezed her hand. "Well . . . I must say, you are more of what I expected, Mrs Elligan. Mr Carew—" he looked past her, as if expecting Ned in turn to materialise from thin air.

"Let's talk," Sophie said, and sat down, indicating that Walters should sit between her and Catherine. Which he did, after a moment's hesitation.

He licked his lips, and looked from one to the other. "What I have to say is in the strictest confidence."

"Of course," Sophie agreed.

"What I mean is, should you ever attempt to repeat it, I should deny that this meeting ever took place. This is because the United States Government cannot in any circumstances be involved."

"Absolutely."

"Well . . . you know Clay Andrews, of course."

"For years."

"For some time he operated on his own, aiding various anti-

48

Fascist organisations in the world. In recent years, however, he has found it increasingly difficult to find adequate supplies of guns for the people he has elected to help."

"He's had some bad luck." Sophie decided against confiding that the bad luck had been principally herself.

"Absolutely, thus, after the defeat of Abyssinia, and his determination to assist the Muslim people of Albania against King Zog's Italian-oriented regime, he conceived the idea of approaching the United States Government for help. This approach was of course rejected."

"Of course."

"That was, officially. Privately, he obtained a hearing. The Administration has long been opposed to Mussolini's expansionist ideas, but of course we could only express such disapproval through proper diplomatic channels. Andrews worked away, however, seeing all the right people – his family is fairly prominent in New England—"

"I know that."

"Well, at last it was agreed, in the strictest secrecy, that a supply of surplus *matériel* could be made available for his friends, provided he could arrange the delivery, which must in no way involve the United States, or any United States carrier. This was several months ago and we heard nothing further. Presumably Andrews was already in the Balkans, seeing what could be arranged. Then, as you know, he was overtaken by events two weeks ago when the Italians suddenly invaded. Still we heard nothing from him, until yesterday, when I received a letter, mailed in Marseilles."

"I mailed that letter," Catherine said with some pride.

"It was given to you by Andrews? Where and when?"

"A week ago I was in the Albanian mountains with him, Mr Walters." Catherine spoke with even more pride.

"Ah—" Walters looked as if he would like to have asked some more, but changed his mind. "Did you know the contents of this letter?"

"I knew it had to do with Mrs Elligan."

"What did he have to say?" Sophie asked.

"He said in the letter that I would be contacted by a Mrs Sophie Elligan, with whom he had worked in the past, and who is a member of a gun-running consortium, and who, in return for a fee, would be able to deliver the *matériel*, in conjunction with her partner, Mr Edward Carew."

"He says the nicest things." Sophie looked past Walters at Catherine, willing her to keep her mouth shut.

"Well," Walters said. "Of course the Administration utterly condemns the Italian action. That has been said publicly. However, as I have said, it is not part of official American policy to become involved in any European dispute. Thus the need for secrecy in any transaction we may undertake is increased."

"I can deliver the goods," Sophie said. "In secrecy. Italians or no Italians. For a fee."

"He did mention that you were a—" again Walters changed his mind about what he might have said. "That you would require payment. He suggested fifty thousand dollars."

"He meant, a hundred thousand . . . pounds," Sophie said.

Walters goggled at her. So did Catherine.

"It is a highly risky business," Sophie pointed out. "The Italian Government has a price on my head, and is prepared to shoot me on sight. And I have to find and charter a ship."

"A hundred thousand pounds," Walters muttered. "My dear lady, that is an enormous sum of money."

"It'll deliver your guns."

"Yes. Well—"

"Twenty-five thousand down," Sophie said. "That will cover the charter of the ship and various immediate expenses. Twenty-five thousand when the goods are loaded. And fifty thousand on completion of the delivery. I'll take the first payment in cash. The remainder, as it becomes due, will be placed in a deposit account in Switzerland in my name, and only to be accessed by me, but such access will be dependent on a clearance from you. However, just so we're not cheated, you will give me written confirmation of the financial transaction now. What is involved need not be mentioned. When we return from Albania, the delivery successfully completed, and you hand over the authority for me to use the account, I will destroy the confirmation. Should the authority not be handed over, or the final payment be in any way interfered with, I shall sell the story, and the confirmation, to the highest bidder."

Walters was looking slightly dazed. "How do we know you would not do that anyway, Mrs Elligan?"

"I'd be throwing away both fifty thousand pounds and my own anonymity."

"Hm," Walters commented. "The handing over of our authority regarding the money and the confirmation of the delivery would have to be done simultaneously."

"That suits me."

"Then tell me your time schedule."

"I'll need a week or two to organise the ship. Where are the goods?"

"You will be told that when you have your vessel. However, they can be collected by ship."

"Right. So all I need is the first payment, and I'll go find our ship."

"You do realise, Mrs Elligan, that should we pay you twenty-five thousand pounds, and you do *not* secure a ship, the United States Government would take a very serious view of the situation."

"I'm sure you would. I don't break arrangements, Mr Walters."

"I should also like to meet Mr Carew, before the transaction is finalised."

"Why?"

"I hate to be indelicate, Mrs Elligan, and I am sure you are a most experienced, ah, person, but frankly, in a transaction of this nature we would like to feel we are dealing with a man."

"You, sir, are a male chauvinist pig," Sophie said. "I'm afraid Ned is not available right now, but he will be with the ship when we pick up the goods."

"I would prefer to meet him before the transaction is finalised," Walters repeated, politely.

"Well . . . he is currently on a business trip, but he will be back in a day or so. Shall I bring him here, say in two days' time?" She smiled. "Same place, same station? You'll have all your paperwork completed by then, I hope."

He gave a cold smile. "I shall be here, Mrs Elligan."

The two women watched Walters walk away. "Whew!" Catherine said. "I didn't know things like this really happened."

51

"They're happening all the time, if you know where to look."

"But what are you going to do? When he finds out about what happened in Le Pouget—"

"How is he going to do that? Or at least, relate it to us? So someone named Smith gets killed in what the police will assume is a gangland feud, and his wife disappears. What has that got to do with Sophie Elligan. Oh, they'll work it out eventually, but by then the transaction will have been started, and Walters won't be able to stop it."

"But . . . how can Mr Carew meet Mr Walters in two days' time, if he's dead?"

"We'll have to bring him back to life, won't we?"

Sophie's car remained where she had parked it, and was as yet apparently attracting no attention. They observed this from the other side of the street. "What happens now?" Catherine asked.

"We need to change. Just about everything."

They went to a clothes store, bought two headscarves, and then to a chemists', where Sophie bought some bottles of dye as well as a pair of scissors. "You're not going to cut off my hair," Catherine protested.

"Mine too. It'll grow." They checked in at another cheap hotel. As before they had to hand over their passports for the night, but Sophie was again gambling that the name Elligan would mean nothing to anyone for at least another twenty-four hours. "We need to leave early in the morning," she told the concierge, "to catch the train for Strasbourg."

"They will be here, madame." She had hardly looked at them.

"Why are we going to Strasbourg?" Catherine asked.

"We're not. But it will help if, when the police finally trace us, she tells them that."

"Will they trace us? You said they'd be looking for a Mrs Smith."

"Never underestimate the police. They always get there in the end."

Once in the bedroom Sophie got to work, cutting Catherine's hair short, then Catherine did the same for her. Neither cut was in the least stylish, but they served their purpose. then Sophie dyed Catherine's hair black, and Catherine dyed hers yellow. Then they looked at each other and had to laugh. "Won't the concierge notice the difference?" Catherine asked.

"I doubt it. But for the time being we'll use these headscarves." They found a sidewalk café, ate snails and shared a bottle of *vin de table.* "Do you know," Catherine said. "In the oddest fashion I feel I've known you all my life."

"It could turn out that way."

"Do you really eat men for breakfast?"

Sophie raised her eyebrows. "I seldom breakfast. Is that what Clay said?" Catherine flushed. "I think he means I don't suffer fools gladly, especially when they wear pants," Sophie suggested.

"About Ned—"

"No," Sophie said. "Nothing about Ned. Not ever again. Nothing about Ned."

Catherine stared at the tears in her eyes. "I am so sorry. Right. I was going to ask, those men you shot . . . had you ever shot anyone before?"

"A considerable number."

Catherine swallowed some wine. "And were you really in a harem?"

"Briefly."

"Was it . . . well—?" Catherine toyed with a piece of bread.

"There were about twenty women, mostly young and pretty, who were required to service one rather old man whenever he could get it up. What do you think?"

"It's unthinkable."

"Have you never?"

"Well . . ." another flush. "The odd fumble at school. You know—"

"What about boys?"

"Not really."

"Not even when bicycling with them in Albania? You'll be telling me next that you're a virgin."

"I am."

Sophie refilled their glasses. They had been travelling so far and so fast she hadn't really had the time to consider the situation regarding Catherine. But now she was back to her last conversation with Ned. God, how it hurt to remember that. But

53

what was she to do with this girl? She had brought total calamity in her wake. And now, by confirming to Walters the reality of Clay's position and requirements, she had served every useful purpose. The most sensible thing to do would be to depart the hotel at dawn tomorrow, by herself, leaving Catherine in bed by herself, dead. She would be in England before any proper hue and cry could be raised. But that hue and cry would be looking for Sophie Elligan, the name on the passport she had used, rather than Eloise Smith, the missing woman from Le Pouget. So that simply was not on. Here.

Besides, although Sophie liked to consider herself an utterly ruthless woman, and had proved it sufficiently often in the past, she had never killed anyone in cold blood. She wasn't sure she could. And certainly no one as attractive as this girl. "Did you enjoy being in the harem?" Catherine asked.

"I wasn't there long enough to come to a decision."

"But you had to . . . service the sheikh, or whatever?"

"I was supposed to. But instead I hit him over the head with a washbasin, and fractured his skull."

Catherine stared at her. So, Sophie thought, if I can't kill her, at least right now, equally I can't turn her loose. Not only was she as vulnerable as she had pointed out, but she might also get an attack of nerves and go to the police, regardless of the consequences. But keeping her virtually a prisoner while they were travelling would be an impossible task. She had to be sucked right into Sophie's world, and want to stay there. "But you like sex with men," Catherine was saying. She had definitely had a little too much to drink. Another danger sign if she was ever on her own. "I mean, you were living with . . . oops, I'm so sorry."

"I like sex with the right man, at the right time. I think we had better be getting back to the hotel. Put on your scarf."

"When can I send my parents that telegram?"

"Tomorrow," Sophie promised.

It was a different concierge, who again hardly looked at them as she handed over the key. "I wish you'd tell me just what your plans are," Catherine said, when they were in the bedroom. "I mean, where are you going to find a man to pretend to be Mr Carew?"

54

"We," Sophie said, cleaning her teeth. "The word is we. We're a team, now."

Catherine sat on the bed. "I don't know anything about gun-running, or killing people. The whole idea gives me the heebee-jeebees."

"It'll grow on you." Sophie undressed and got into bed, while Catherine used the basin.

"Yes, but . . ." Catherine spat and dried her face. "What about my job?"

"What job?"

"I have a post at a school in Cheltenham, starting in September."

"September is five months away. I should think you'll be able to make that. Drop that and come here." Catherine had been balancing on one leg while she inserted the other into her pyjama bottoms. Now she hesitated, then let the garment fall and went to the bedside. "Sit." Catherine obeyed, their naked thighs touching. "Now listen to me, very carefully," Sophie said. "Like I told you, we are now a team. You joined the team, whether you were aware of it or not, when you agreed to carry Clay's message for him. From here on I cannot afford to let you out of my sight, because if I do you will almost certainly be nabbed, sooner than later. Do you know what they will do to you if they nab you?"

Catherine's eyes were enormous. "Shoot me?"

"Not right away. The Italians will want you to tell them all about me, about what I am doing, about Clay, and what he is doing. And just to encourage you to deliver, they will do certain things to you. Savvy?"

Catherine licked her lips. "What things?"

"This particular breed believe in the efficacy of castor oil. They will fill your gut full of castor oil, and you won't care whether you are alive or dead."

"Has that ever happened to you?"

"Yes. And when they have reduced you to a wreck with castor oil, if they reckon you still haven't told them everything they want to know, they will probably start beating you. Of course there may well be the odd rape thrown in on the way." Sophie touched Catherine's cheek. "You are a very pretty girl. You also want to remember that should you try to go it alone, you will

55

certainly wish to return to your home, and when they find you, they will also find your parents and any other relatives you may have, and put them through the same routine. We are dealing with utterly ruthless people here. On the other hand the French, if *they* nab you, or if you are foolish enough to go to them for help, will be utterly and scrupulously polite, but they will soon link you to the killings in Le Pouget, and then, with the same scrupulous politeness, they will cut off your head with a bloody big knife dropped from a height. Do remember all of this."

Catherine's face seemed to have closed. "And they won't do these things if I am with you?"

"The Italians certainly won't find it quite so easy, firstly because as I am the person they are actually looking for they'll be more interested in me than in you, and secondly because, as you my have noticed, I am prepared to kill any and all of the bastards who get too close. Then there's your friend Bobbie. We are going back to Albania, or close to it, and then leaving again. Stick with me, and we'll bring Bobbie back out. That's a much better bet than relying on Foreign Office representations."

"And when we get back, you'll let me go?"

"If that's what you want, yes."

"And the Italians won't still be looking for me?"

"Their business is to stop the delivery of any guns to the Albanian partisans. Once the guns have been delivered, you are no longer important. Sadly, there are quite a few Italians who would still like to get their hands on me."

"Doesn't that frighten you?"

"I found it necessary to stop being frightened long ago," Sophie lied. "So, partners? Till death do us part? Or until the guns are delivered?"

"Well . . . all right."

"You are growing on me," Sophie said, and kissed her on the lips.

When Sophie awoke, just before dawn, Catherine was still lying in her arms, breathing slowly and evenly. The things I do to survive, she thought. But it actually was what she had needed. The previous night she had been exhausted, mentally as well as physically. Too exhausted for grief. Last night she had been more relaxed, and thus less able to exclude thoughts, memories, despair. Ned was dead, dead, dead. After nine of the most stimulating, productive, *happy* years of her life. And he had never known he was going to be a father. That thought haunted her as much as any. She had wanted, needed, to hold someone in her arms, as tightly as possible, to scale a peak of physical stimulation, to share, body and mind, with someone, to lose herself in a cocoon of intimacy.

She supposed, had Catherine not been available, she might even, in her desperation, have gone out and picked up a man off the street. Thank God Catherine had been there, as bewildered as ever, but beautifully and adorably compliant. She was clearly entirely overawed by the dominant woman into whose orbit she had so carelessly drifted. Sophie had never considered herself a dominant personality, but she supposed she had lived an unusual life, quite out of the ken of a would-be schoolmistress in a country as civilised as England. Presumably Catherine would never be the same again. But would she ever have been the same again in any event, after her experience in Albania? She slipped out of bed, put on her dressing-gown to go to the bathroom. When she came back, Catherine was sitting up. "Gosh," she said. "I reckon a lot of wine must have flowed last night. Did we really—"

"Put it down as a dream," Sophie recommended. "Let's move." The concierge of the previous day was on duty, putting out coffee and croissants. She made no comment at her two early guests wearing headscarves to breakfast. Sophie paid the bill and collected their passports, and they caught a taxi for the station. While waiting for the train, Sophie bought a newspaper, but there was still nothing concerning her from the south of France. "We've another ten minutes," she said. "There's a post office over there. Why don't you send that telegram?"

"Oh, may I? What should I say?"

"Say, Alive and well, on my way home. Love."

"What about Bobbie? Her parents will be worried too."

"They'll have to worry for the time being. Do they know your parents?"

"Sort of."

"Well, if they contact them, they'll probably believe Bobbie is with you and just hasn't bothered to get in touch. Now send that telegram, or leave it for good."

Catherine obeyed, and copied out the words while Sophie looked over her shoulder. Ten minutes later they were in the train, in a compartment to themselves, and able to remove their headscarves, stare at each other, and again burst out laughing.

"It feels so odd, not to have hair," Catherine said.

"It won't take long to grow."

"Have you ever had to cut yours before?"

"There's a first time for everything," Sophie said.

"About this man who's going to be Mr Carew—"

"I'm working on it," Sophie told her.

At Dover, they caught a train for London, then one for Bristiol, getting off at Swindon to hire a taxi. "You certainly know your way around," Catherine said.

"I used to live here, remember," Sophie said.

"Andoversford?" asked the driver. "That's a good way, missus."

"I know," Sophie said. "The cost is not relevant."

He shrugged, and they got into the back. What memories, Sophie thought, as she watched the familiar countryside drifting by. She had lived in the Chilterns for four years, as Richard Elligan's wife, walking the dogs, riding, the perfect consort of an apparent country squire. If from time to time they had disappeared from view for a few months, it had been accepted that they were great travellers. Only the Foreign Office and the Special Branch knew differently, and they had never been able to accumulate sufficient evidence to do anything about it. "I'm so close to home, here," Catherine said, wistfully. "Don't you think—"

"You're still on your way back from Greece," Sophie reminded her. They left the main road outside the village and bumped down a cart track. She half expected to see a woman walking the dogs along the ridge to their right. But the woman who had owned the dogs was now seated in this taxi, and the dogs were long gone. The car pulled into the yard. Again, Sophie half expected to see a man emerge from the woodshed, questioningly. But that man was now lying dead in his study in the house outside Le Pouget.

She paid the driver. "How do we get another one?" Catherine asked, as they took their bags.

"Hopefully, we won't need to." Sophie went up the short flight of steps. Catherine looked around her. The property had once been a farm, but there had been no animals here for several years. Yet the old smells persisted, mingling with the aroma of neglect; the house badly needed painting. "See what I mean?" Sophie asked, as she rang the bell.

It was some moments before the door was opened, and she gazed at the tall middle-aged woman standing before her. Anne Martingell's hair was now quite white, and she moved stiffly, but her splendid bone structure left her still a most handsome woman. She wore a dress, stockings, high-heeled shoes, and might have been about to entertain, deliberately. Her hair was in a bun. She in turn stared at Sophie in total disbelief. "Well, hello," Sophie said. "Won't you ask us in?"

"What do you want?" asked Lady Martingell.

"To see Richard." There was no point in beating about the bush.

"He's not here."

"But he still lives here, doesn't he?"

Anne Martingell's mouth twisted. "Yes."

"Then we'll wait for him to come back. Do we get to come in, or do we sit on the step?"

"Oh—" Anne stepped back, leaving the door open.

"Thank you." Sophie picked up her bag. "Come along, Cathy."

Catherine, who had been looking from one to the other in uncertain embarrassment, hastily gathered up her knapsack and followed her into the house. "You're not planning on staying?" Anne inquired, anxiously.

"As a matter of fact, yes. We have so much to talk about."

"Do we?"

"I meant, Richard and I. This is Catherine Ames, by the way. She is a schoolmistress. And this is Lady Anne Martingell," Sophie said. "I know you've heard of her."

"Pleased to meet you, my lady," Catherine said.

Anne did not offer to shake hands. Instead she sat down, carelessly throwing one leg over the other. "No doubt you are going to explain why you are here?"

59

"When Richard comes." Sophie went to the icebox, opened it.
"No champagne?"
"Times have changed."
"I thought they might have. Do you suppose we could use your laundry facilities? We have quite a load."
"Well—" Anne Martingell listened to the sound of a car engine in the yard. "Here's Richard," she said with some relief.
Both Sophie and Catherine faced the door as it opened.
"Passed a taxi on my way in," Richard Elligan said. "Who . . . my God!"
"Well, hello," Sophie said again. "You're looking well."
As a matter of fact he was. He was a tall, well-built, good-looking man in his early forties. His black hair was streaked with grey, and his handsome features were lined with strain, but he moved well and his colour was good. His clothes, as always, were immaculate: brown three-piece suit, highly polished brown shoes, matching tie. "So are you," he said. "But . . . what have you done to your hair?"
"Cut it and dyed it. It's all the rage. This is Catherine Ames. My husband."
"Your—" Catherine swallowed.
"Richard and I never got around to divorcing."
"They just came bursting in here," Anne said.
"Business," Sophie said. "Aren't you going to invite us to dinner? But first, laundry."

"I think we could all do with a drink," Richard said, when the women had returned from washing and hanging out various garments, watched by Anne Martingell as if they might run off with the kitchen sink.
"There isn't any champagne," Sophie pointed out. "I looked."
"I'm afraid champagne every day is a little out of our price range, nowadays. Scotch will have to do."
"Do you drink Scotch?" Sophie asked Catherine.
Who sat down, uninvited. "I think I might."
"It's been one of those days," Sophie said, sitting beside her. "One of those weeks, in fact. So times are hard."
"Times are always hard," Anne said, "when one has been cheated of a large sum of money."

"I cheated you of nothing. You tried to rob us, and we responded in kind."

Catherine looked from face to face. "Do you know anything of what they are talking about?" Richard asked, handing her a glass, and inspecting her as he did so.

Sophie recalled that he had always had an eye for pretty young women. But in that respect, Catherine was one of her trumps. "I suppose it's to do with running guns," Catherine said.

"Ah, then you do know something of what is going on." He handed a glass to Sophie.

"Catherine has just come into the business," Sophie explained. "She knows you and I were partners for a while. However, now I have a proposition for you," She looked around her; the inside of the house needed decoration as badly as the outside. "I'm sure you'll find it interesting."

Richard had reached Anne in handing out glasses. "If you ever do business with this bitch again," Anne said, "you will need your head examined."

"Twenty-five thousand pounds," Sophie said, quietly.

Richard turned so sharply he nearly spilled his own drink. "Doing what?"

"Helping me make a delivery."

"You have got to be joking," Anne said.

"Take it or leave it," Sophie said. "I can do it without you. It just happens that I need a man, and I know you have the know-how and experience to do the job. But if you're not interested, I can find someone else."

"Hold on there." Richard sat on the settee beside Anne. "What about Ned?"

"Ned and I have split," Sophie said, staring at Catherine.

"Well, well," Richard said. "It had to happen. So you found out he was not, after all, a knight in shining armour."

"Something like that," Sophie said.

"And now you need a new partner," Richard said thoughtfully. "Someone to take care of the heavy stuff."

"Quite. Are you interested?"

"Fill me in."

"Richard!" Anne protested.

"Can't do any harm to listen."

"It's very simple," Sophie said. "I am being funded to make an arms delivery to the Albanians who are fighting Mussolini. The deal has been set up by Clay Andrews—"

"Now you need *your* head examined," Richard said.

"I think we can keep things under control," Sophie said. "We are dealing with certain people high up in the US Administration. They have the goods, they have the money. But they don't want any involvement. All I have to do is find a ship and make the delivery. Unfortunately, you know what governments are. The American official who is handling the transaction was informed by Clay that Mrs Elligan and Mr Carew, experienced gun-runners, would be the delivery merchants. This man is, I am afraid, somewhat old-fashioned as well as being a pedant. Ergo, he wants to meet Mr Carew before he will hand over the down payment, which I need before I can charter the ship. He does not feel a woman can handle this, you see, and he assumes Mr Carew will be in command."

"I see," Richard said thoughtfully. "So you wish me to appear instead of Ned."

"I don't think that will take us very much further, Richard. My friend, as I say, is a pedant, and he wants to be sure that Ned is running the show. So . . . I wish you to appear *as* Ned."

Policemen

"Well, really," Anne commented. "You are asking me to act the part of my own servant?" Richard asked.

"Don't make me angry," Sophie said. "It is damn near ten years since Ned was your servant. In that time—"

"He has cheated me of a fortune and been your lover."

"You cheated yourself of that fortune. And yes, he became my lover. Because we adventured together, and learned to live together and love together. And I discovered that he was more of a man, and a gentleman, than any man I have ever known."

"*Touché*," Richard said quietly. "Until he walked out on you. Or did you walk out on him?"

"What happened is my business."

"And am I expected to act as your lover too?" But he glanced at Catherine.

"You may take your pick," Sophie said.

Catherine gave a little gasp, and pink spots flared in her cheeks. "I might just do that," Richard said. "Give me a schedule."

"Richard!" Anne snapped.

"Immediately, you will come to Paris with us," Sophie said. "We will have another meeting with our principal, at which time the formalities will be completed. Our exact schedule after that depends on the Americans, and their contacts with Clay, but my first business after the receipt of the down payment will be to procure the delivery vessel."

"And the payment schedule?"

"I am receiving twenty-five thousand pounds down. I will pay you six and a quarter thousand of that money. When I pick up the goods, I will receive another twenty-five thousand. Again, I will pay six and a quarter thousand to you. When the delivery is completed, I will receive the balance of fifty thousand, at which time you will receive your remaining half of twelve and a half thousand."

He stroked his chin. "You are receiving seventy-five thousand to my twenty-five thousand. That isn't very equitable."

"It is entirely equitable. I am hiring the ship, and the entire operation is being carried out in the name of myself and Ned Carew. Once it is completed, you will just disappear, and resume your life here, considerably better off than you are now. But I will have to make a new life for myself somewhere the Italians can't get at me."

"And Miss Ames?"

. "She's in the vengeance business. Some of her friends were killed when the Italians invaded Albania. Besides, she's a friend of Clay's."

Richard got up and refilled their glasses, then he went to the bookcase against the wall and took out a large atlas. This he spread on the table. "News reports claim that the Italians have completed the conquest of Albania."

"News reports," Sophie said. "Put out by Italians."

"Good point. Still, it would be a shame to go all that way and find there is no one to receive the goods."

"That isn't our responsibility. We will be given a time and a place and it is our business to be there with the goods."

"I hope the Yanks understand that. News reports also claim that the Adriatic is an Italian lake."

"Again, news reports. Yugoslav shipping is still moving, as is German shipping. The Italians aren't going to interfere with a German ship."

"And you intend to use a German ship? Tricky."

"As I am sure you remember, I have contacts in Germany."

"I remember very well. All right, Sophie, I'll come with you to Paris, and act the part of your lover. For six and a quarter thousand pounds."

"I'm afraid you will have to come the whole way."

He shrugged. "Sounds like fun."

"You can't!" Anne shouted. "You're stark, raving mad! Don't you remember the last time we tried to do business with her? And Carew?"

"We didn't cheat you," Sophie said. "All the attempted cheating came from your side."

Richard grinned. "I suppose there is some truth in that."

Anne threw up her hands in despair. "You'll be killed. The Italians are fighting a war. If you are captured running guns they will put you against a wall and shoot you."

"Hasn't happened yet," Sophie pointed out.

"That's true," Richard said. "Well, won't you stay to dinner?"

"And the night?" Sophie suggested.

"I'm afraid we only have the one spare room," Richard said, carrying Sophie's and Catherine's bags upstairs after the meal. "And it has a double bed."

"We're used to sharing," Sophie said.

"Is it an early start in the morning?"

"Very early. I want to be in and out of France just as rapidly as possible."

Richard raised his eyebrows. "Is there something you should be telling me?"

"Not a thing," Sophie lied. "It's just that Ned and I lived there for a while, and I have unpleasant memories."

"Oh, quite. Well—" He hesitated, then came into the room, closing the door behind himself. "God, it's good to see you again, Sophie. You look so . . . so huggable." Sophie allowed herself to be hugged, and kissed. Once she would have given all she possessed to be in this man's arms – and indeed, *had* given all she possessed. He kissed her mouth, then pulled his head back. "I shall enjoy being your lover, and taking a sea voyage with you. It will be quite like old times."

"Quite."

He released her, looked at an embarrassed Catherine. "Oh, go ahead," Sophie said. "She won't mind."

Catherine gave her a startled glance, then also submitted to a hug and a kiss on the mouth, while Richard massaged her bottom through the summer frock. "I look forward to getting to know you better," he said, and left the room.

He whistled as he went downstairs, where Anne was still drinking her after dinner port as she cleared away the plates. "You are a bastard," she remarked.

"That's a well-known fact. I've an early start tomorrow. Coming up?"

"What have you been doing? Fucking them both at the same time?"

"Not possible," he said easily. "Even for me."

"Richard!" She caught his hand. "Why? Do you still have a yen for her? Or is it that long-legged sidekick? I'd bet my last penny they're lessies."

"Sophie is, and never has, been anything you could label. Just Sophie. She makes up her own rules as she goes along. As I imagine the Ames girl is finding out."

"But you want to get between both their legs. Is this why you're risking your life?"

"I am prepared to risk my life, my darling, partly because we desperately need that money, and partly because . . . Christ, I need to adventure. For the past three years I have sat here, quietly going mad."

"Thanks very much."

"Oh, it has nothing to do with you. It's just that—"

"I'm a fifty-nine-year-old hag and you're looking forward to adventuring with a twenty-two years-old pair of legs."

"Think of the money."

"And what am I supposed to do while you are gallivanting around the Mediterranean with your two beauties? I assume you don't wish me to come with you?"

"Ah . . . no. I think that would be unwise."

"Because you think I'm past it."

"Not in the least. We need you here, protecting home base. Remember that Foreign Office fellow Pemberton? He threatened us with gaol if we ever got involved in gun-running again. I wouldn't be surprised if he's not still keeping an eye on us. So you stay here, and if anyone inquires after me, tell them I've gone up to Scotland for a day or two." He pulled her to her feet. "And the moment I get hold of that money, I'll send it to you. Won't that be nice? Now come to bed."

Anne followed him up the stairs, undressed, and got into bed beside him. Predictably he did not want sex. His mind was already drifting into the future. She knew he loved adventure; he hadn't been lying about that. But she also knew he loved the adventure of woman, to be pursued and hopefully conquered. As twenty years ago he had pursued and conquered her, when she had still been married to James Martingell, and when he had been officially been trying to become engaged to James' daughter. The bastard! Pemberton, she thought, as she drifted off to sleep. Walter Pemberton. She remembered Walter Pemberton very well.

"Sophie," Catherine said, as they got into bed. "Why did you tell Mr Elligan that you and Mr Carew had split up, instead of telling him that Mr Carew had been killed? Would he have been frightened off?"

"No," Sophie said. "Richard Elligan doesn't get frightened off very easily. But it pays to keep certain things to yourself. What might upset him would be to discover that the French police are probably looking for us by now."

"Gosh. But we're going back?"

"In and out. I reckon they'll still be looking for Eloise Smith. The landlady down in Millau didn't look a very avid newspaper reader; it'll take her a day or two to link up the descriptions of Mrs Elligan and her companion with Mrs Smith and *her* companion. By which time we'll be long gone."

Catherine lay in silence for a few minutes, then she asked, "You're not really going to let that man, your husband, have me, are you?"

"Forget the husband bit. That's dead water under the bridge."

Catherine rose on her elbow. "But I don't want to have sex with him. He's—"

"Richard Elligan," Sophie said, "has modelled himself on the only man he ever respected, James Martingell. Thus he is an adventurer, brave, a crack shot, a man who loves challenges, and a born philanderer. He is also selfish, ruthless, occasionally savage, and always ready to cheat and steal and lie to obtain his objectives."

"I think you admire him."

Sophie smiled. "Once I thought I loved him."

"Then why did you split?"

"Because, if you take everything I have just said about him, and substitute the word woman for man, you have a picture of myself."

"You can say such things of yourself?"

67

"It's not a bad principle to be honest, at least with oneself. Two people with such personalities and such outlooks on life can never get on for very long."

Catherine lay down again. "And are you lying, and cheating, and getting ready to steal, as regards me?"

Sophie switched off the light. "Not so long as you're my partner. Remember that."

"But you'll let him have me."

Sophie kissed her. "You have got to get it into your head that we are engaged in the second most immoral business in the world. Only war is more immoral, and we provide the means for men to go to war. Once you accept that, you have also got to accept that if we are going to be successful, we need to be as immoral, and indeed amoral, as the people we are dealing with. It is the only way to survive. So we use our brains, money, and when we have to, our bodies, our sex, to their best advantage, regardless of personal feelings. Okay?"

Catherine sighed. "And your gun."

"At the end of the day," Sophie agreed. "It usually comes to that."

Anne Martingell drove them into Cheltenham to catch their train. No one spoke much; they were all bound up in their own thoughts of the immediate future. When she had dropped them, Anne drove home, and went into the study. In one of the desk drawers there was a collection of cards left by various visitors over the years. She riffled through these until she found the one she wanted, picked up the phone, and gave the number; as it was in London it counted as a long distance call, and she had to wait some time before a voice said, "Yes?"

"Mr Pemberton? Anne Martingell. I hope you remember me."

"Lady Martingell!" Suddenly the voice was interested. "Indeed I remember you. Is there something I can do for you?"

The bastard had once threatened to arrest her, Anne recalled. "I'd like you to come down and visit me, Mr Pemberton. There may be something I can do for you."

When they landed in Calais, just after lunch, Sophie bought a newspaper, which she read as the train sped towards Paris;

Richard was happy to engage Catherine in conversation, in which she confined herself to monosyllables. Poor child, Sophie thought; she still hadn't really a clue as to what she had got herself into. But she was more interested in the newspaper, and on an inside page she found what she was looking for. *Strange case of English couple in Le Pouget*, said the small item under "Provincial News". *Mr James Smith was found shot dead in his villa outside Le Pouget yesterday morning. With him, also dead, were his cook/housekeeper, Marie Etienne, and four men who have not yet been identified. A crashed car was also found in the grounds of the villa; the driver is one of the dead. The bodies, it appears, had lain undiscovered for two days and several policemen were affected. A search is now being made for James Smith's wife, Eloise, who has disappeared. Police are assuming she was also killed and her body disposed of elsewhere. Also disappeared is the Smith's blue Renault car, and the police are also mounting a search for this. Although Mr and Mrs Smith, who have lived in the villa outside Le Pouget for four years, are regarded locally as prosperous, law-abiding retirees, police regard the killings as gangland connected, although the actual motive has not yet been discovered,*

Sophie folded the newspaper and placed it in her shoulderbag; she had no desire for Catherine to know she was still totally unconnected with the murders, or for Richard to discover the true reason she had come looking for him. And things were working out exactly as she had planned. She had the highest regard for the French police, but she did not think even they would locate the car for a few hours, and even if they did, it still could not immediately be related to Sophie Elligan, until they got around to interviewing the landlady in Millau, and then the landlady in Paris. There were a lot of landladies in Paris. Nothing would devolve before tomorrow, and by then she would be out of the country. But when she thought of the true meaning of what the report had said, that the disintegrating bodies had affected even the French police . . . oh, Ned!

It was mid-afternoon by the time they reached Paris. They deposited their bags at the Left Luggage counter, and Sophie led them first of all to where they had abandoned the car; sure enough, there was a policeman standing beside it. He could merely be docking it for overparking, but she suspected he was on guard duty over it, from the way he was not moving, "Oh, lord," Catherine said. "They've—" Sophie squeezed her hand to shut her up.

Richard was frowning. "I have a notion something is going on of which I know nothing. I don't like that. Is that gendarme anything to do with you?"

"Never saw him before in my life," Sophie said, truthfully enough. "Let's get ourselves placed." They went to the Bois, and Sophie made her arrangements; being a Sunday, the park was much more crowded than usual. "You sit on the bench, Catherine. Richard – from here on you're Ned – come with me into that clump of trees."

Catherine duly sat down and crossed her legs, apparently waiting for a date. "Seems to me you don't trust this Yank," Richard remarked.

"I don't trust anybody," Sophie said.

"As I recall, you never did. So tell me, why did you and Ned split?"

"People do. Like you and me."

"Oh, quite. Would you like to come back?"

She glanced at him. "Just like that? What about Lady Martingell?"

"She's past her sell-by date, wouldn't you say?"

"You really are a bastard, Richard Elligan. And she might be a little difficult to get rid of. She knows a great deal about the business."

"Because it's her business too," Richard pointed out. "She's not really in a position to sell her story to the newspapers. In any event, she's a lonely, frightened widow. She needs me."

"Which is why she's quite happy for you to go off into the blue with Catherine and me?"

He grinned. "She isn't happy; she's spitting mad. But she's used to accepting the facts of life. Besides, twenty-five thousand pounds is worth a lot of sacrifices. Is that your man?"

Walters was approaching Catherine with his usual precise steps, his briefcase at his side. "That's him," Sophie said. "Just let's make sure he's alone." As before, she studied the trees to either side, but there did not seem to be any people hovering, although there were quite a few people about. In any event, she had to believe that Walters was now committed. "Let's go."

She led Richard to the bench, and Walters stood up. "Mrs Elligan! I'm glad you made it back."

"Was there ever any doubt? This is Mr Carew. Ned, Mr Walters of the US Embassy."

"My pleasure," Richard said, shaking hands.

Walters frowned at him for a moment; obviously Richard was not quite what he had expected. Then his face cleared. "You know the situation, Mr Carew?"

"Sophie has outlined it."

"So, can you do it?"

"I don't see any reason why not. Once we get the details right."

Walters sat down, laid his briefcase on his lap, and opened it. Sophie sat beside him with Catherine on his other side. Richard stood in front of them. "I have here the documentation you required, Mrs Elligan," Walters said, taking it out. "Together with a certified cheque for twenty-thousand pounds. I trust that is satisfactory."

Sophie studied the cheque, and then the letter of confirmation, placed them both in her shoulderbag. Richard's nose wrinkled; obviously he was intrigued by the letter, which she hadn't mentioned. But he kept his mouth shut. "You realise," Walters said, "that should that letter fall into the wrong hands, all deals will be off, and we will denounce it as a forgery."

"Absolutely," Sophie agreed.

"So tell me what you are going to do now."

"I am going to secure a ship. As I said last time, this should take about a week, but allow two for us to get into position. Where will the goods be loaded?"

"The goods are in Ireland. Eire, not Ulster. You will pick them up in Clew Bay. Can you do that, at night?"

"I would think so."

"We'll need an exact date and hour."

"I will enter the bay on Sunday 29 April, at midnight."

Walters made a note. "When you call me, to confirm that you have the ship, I will give you precise instructions."

"These goods are being supplied by the Irish?" Richard asked in surprise.

"They will be handled by Irishmen working for us," Walters said. "They are experts at this sort of thing, although . . ." he actually smiled. "In the past to be sure they have more often landed goods than shipped them. I should tell you that the goods are mainly explosives and ammunition, together with a few machine-guns and tommy-guns and a quantity of rifles. When will you be in a position to confirm this date?"

He was addressing Richard, but Sophie answered. "A soon as I get the ship."

"Very well. Here is a phone number. Call me there. You have merely to say, as instructed, and you will receive your further directions."

"And the second payment will be made when the goods are on board?" Richard asked.

"That is what Mrs Elligan and I agreed, Mr Carew. Is there anything else?"

"Yes," Sophie said. "I assume you have means of contacting Mr Andrews?"

Walters nodded. "Through our people in Greece, yes. It's a slow business, but messages do get through."

"We will need a designated landing place. That can be given to us when we load. When we have loaded, I will be able to give a date and time of delivery." Sophie held out her hand. "Will you be in Ireland?"

"No, you will be met by a Mr Gannon. But he will have the necessary credentials."

"Then it's been a pleasure."

Walters squeezed her hand, and peered at her. "I hope you have no illusions as to the danger of this enterprise, Mrs Elligan?"

"None, Mr Walters. That's why the price is so high."

"And you, young lady?" Walters squeezed Catherine's hand in turn.

"I'm with her," Catherine said.

Walter Pemberton stood up as Harold Eisener entered the club smoking-room. "My dear fellow," he said. "Good of you to come." Pemberton was the epitome of a successful middle-class Englishman, from his somewhat heavy moustache, through the gold watch-chain decorating the front of his prosperously bulging waistcoat, to his brown brogues. His height was medium, his black hair receding and streaked with grey. Eisener was entirely different, tall, thin, precisely dressed and precise in manner. He had a hatchet-face and his dark hair was still thick. As they were both policemen, after a fashion, they had known each other for years, had become almost friends through a dozen international investigations. Pemberton couldn't blame his German associate for having thrown in his lot with the Nazis; he knew all too well that if in some mysterious fashion Mosley's blackshirts had managed to become the government a few years ago, he would have worked for them with as much loyalty as he worked for Neville Chamberlain; in his heart he didn't have much time for either, but he was a professional.

But the friendship had withered on account of some of the things German policemen were reported to be doing in Germany. Pemberton couldn't envisage that sort of thing ever happening in England. Equally no Englishman could approve of Hitler's takeover of the rump of Czechoslovakia, in direct contravention of the Munich agreement. On the other hand, they still needed each other from time to time. He escorted Eisener to a couple of deep leather armchairs in a discreet corner. Whiskies and soda were brought. "Mud in your eye," Pemberton said. Eisener smiled politely, sipped, and waited. "What do you think of *Il Duce*'s latest adventure?" Pemberton asked.

"He has his own way to make. I hope you did not invite me here to talk politics, Walter."

"Only after a fashion. I had lunch today with a most charming if somewhat tawdry lady. Anne Martingell."

Eisener raised his eyebrows. He was not a policeman for nothing. "Don't tell me she is back in business?"

"*She* is not. But her partner is. With his wife."

"Sophie von Beinhardt. She was in Germany, buying guns, in 1935."

"I've never quite understood how she obtained a licence from your people."

Eisener tapped his nose. "When Sophie von Beinhardt waggles her arse, Walter, men fall about trying to get hold of it."

"Ah. Yes. I only ever met her once, but I do remember that she had that effect on men."

"But not on you," Eisener suggested slyly.

73

"Not that I recall. But she has caused us some problems, from time to time, and in the present state of the world we can do without any more. She is now engaged in shipping guns to the Albanian partisans."

Eisener frowned. "You are certain of this?"

"I have been told this, by Lady Martingell, who sat in on the meeting that set it up. Lady Martingell is not happy at the idea of her lover, Richard Elligan, gallivanting off into the Mediterranean with his once-estranged wife, who, I gather, is still in the arse waggling business. Hell hath no fury, eh? However, neither are we happy at the idea. You may not wish to discuss politics, Kurt, but I'm sure you'll agree that fanning the flames of war is a bad business. Albania has accepted Italian sovereignty."

"And you think she may be obtaining the guns in Germany? That is not practical any longer, Walter, no matter how much she waggles her behind. The last deal was done when we were not getting on too well with the Italians. Now they are our allies. Between you and me, I won't pretend we are entirely happy about this Italian adventure, but there is no way the House of Beinhardt is going to get a licence to ship arms to their enemies."

"I don't think she is intending to buy the arms in Germany," Pemberton said. Anne Martingell had told him the entire set-up, but it was not his business to let the Germans know that the Americans were involved, even clandestinely. "I think she has another source of supply."

"Where?"

"Lady Martingell didn't know that," Pemberton said smoothly. "We are working on it. What we do know is that Sophie Elligan needs a ship, and I suspect that is what she is hoping to obtain in Germany."

"Ah," Eisener said.

"In fact, I would say she is on her way there now, with her husband and a third person, a young woman who is the go-between for the Albanians. They left Dover on the ferry to Calais this morning."

"My God!" Eisener said. "They could be in Germany already."

"Lady Martingell's understanding was that they would spend the night in Paris. Apparently they have some business to complete there."

"With the Albanians," Eisener said thoughtfully.

"Probably. So they'll not be crossing to Germany before tomorrow at the earliest. When they do, they will almost certainly be going to the House of Beinhardt in Hamburg. Not only is Mrs Elligan's family there, but all her shipping contacts are there too."

"I will get through right away," Eisener said. "We will have the house watched, and the moment this Sophie and her companions turn up, we will arrest them."

"My dear fellow, you can't do that. They haven't committed a crime, yet. Merely seeking to charter a vessel isn't against the law, even in Germany, is it?"

Eisener smiled. "In the new Germany we have developed the concept of protective custody. This saves a great deal of trouble. Don't you want this woman taken out?"

Pemberton stroked his moustache. "All we want is for her to be stopped from making the delivery. If she can't obtain a ship, she can't deliver. If you just have her met, and told it's not on, we will be perfectly happy."

Eisener chuckled. "You British. Very well, Walter, she will be prevented from obtaining a ship. But the easiest way to do that is to arrest her."

"On what charge?" He really didn't like the idea of Sophie Elligan being arrested by the Gestapo.

"She is of recent Jewish ancestry. We are locking up all people of recent Jewish ancestry. For their own protection."

"You are saying the Beinhardts are Jews? I find that difficult to accept."

"I am saying that we will produce information to prove that their grandparents were Jews. That will be sufficient."

Pemberton swallowed. "What will happen to them?"

"They will be sent to a camp."

"For how long?"

"That I cannot say. But it will be amply long enough for this Albanian business to be finished. Leave it with me, Walter. Surely it is far better to put Sophie Elligan where she can never ship guns again than just to put her off in Germany? She will then merely go elsewhere for her ship."

"I feel like another whisky," Pemberton said.

*   *   *

"I feel like a night on the town," Richard said. "Gay Paree, what?"

"It'll have to do without you," Sophie told him. "We are catching the train to Geneva."

"Am I allowed to ask why? You are surely not hoping to charter a ship in Switzerland?"

"No. But we need to be out of France just as quickly as we can."

"Tell me why. We aren't breaking any French laws."

"I have an account in Geneva. I need to unload this cheque."

"You said I'd receive my first payment, now."

"As soon as I have unloaded this cheque, and got the ship, yes."

"And just where are you hoping to obtain this ship?"

"Hamburg," Sophie said.

They reached the border just after midnight. Both Sophie and Catherine were tense as their passports were inspected, but there was no trouble. Sophie and Richard were clearly married, and Catherine's name was still not involved. Sophie had telephoned ahead, to an hotel where she had stayed before with Ned, and they had two rooms waiting for them. "Mr and Mrs Elligan and Miss Ames," said the sleepy reception clerk. Sophie signed his book. "I'm afraid the kitchens are closed."

"We ate on the train," Sophie said.

"Three nights?" Richard asked, as they rode up in the lift; he spoke English, and the bellhop merely looked bored.

Sophie looked around the bedroom. "Where's Catherine?"

"Across the hall," Catherine replied.

"Well, come in here a moment." Sophie closed the door on the three of them. "Tomorrow I am going up to Germany."

"Hamburg," Richard said.

"That's right. I have to organise the ship. You two will stay here until my return, or until I send for you to join me, which hopefully will not be in more than two days' time."

"What a delightful prospect, eh, Cathy?" Richard said. "There's so much I look forward to showing you." Catherine gulped. "But you'll arrange the money before you go," Richard added.

"I will deposit the cheque before I go," Sophie said. "But there will be no payouts until after I come back, or get in touch. I'm sure you have enough pocket money to last you two days. If you wish champagne, have it in the hotel and put it on the bill. I'm arranging for that to be paid."

"I'm beginning to get a distinct feeling that you don't trust me," Richard remarked.

"I just want you to be here when I get back. Or when I send for you."

"May I have a word?" Catherine asked. Sophie followed her across the corridor into her room. "Why can't I come with you to Germany?"

"Because what I have to do is best done alone, and I need you here to act as watchdog."

"If I stay here with him, I am going to have to act as more than a watchdog."

"That's your job, my dear girl. You're the honeypot to keep him stuck in."

"And suppose he, well . . . wants to get stuck in? I don't want that."

"Close your eyes and think of all that lovely lolly."

"That's another thing," Catherine said. "All this talk about who gets what. My name hasn't been mentioned at all."

"You seem to forget that I am doing you a favour, firstly in helping your friend Clay—"

"I'm beginning to wish I'd never met the fellow."

"He does have that effect on people, when they get to know him. But secondly, I am helping you to rescue your friend Bobbie. Right?"

Catherine sighed. "Right."

"However, if you stick close and prove yourself a faithful second-in-command, I will pay you ten per cent of everything I earn for myself. That should come to seven and a half thousand pounds."

"Gosh. Well, I suppose . . . but what about Richard? I'm—"

"A virgin. That is a nuisance. I'll have a word with him. But you must agree to go along with anything he has in mind, save actual fucking. As I remember, that's not the top of his list, anyway. If you handle him right, you'll have no problem. The essential word is handle."

"I wouldn't know where to begin."

"You'll pick it up as you go along. You may find it fun."

Catherine licked her lips. "I suppose so."

Sophie kissed her. "He can be quite good company."

Richard was already in bed, naked. Sophie undressed. "I'm not in the mood for sex," she said.

"But I'm your lover."

"That's our secret. I'm sorry, Richard, I'm still suffering from a Ned hangover. And—" she changed her mind about telling him she was pregnant. That was *her* secret. In any event, it would only annoy him, as he had never succeeded.

"I've a notion that bastard is going to haunt me for the rest of my life." He gazed at her as she raised the sheets and got into bed. "Do you know you still have the most superb body?"

"Thanks for the word still." She looked under the sheet. "And you're raring to go."

"Sophie . . ." he reached for her. "Can't you at least, well—"

"Oh, all right." She supposed she had to keep him happy. He kissed her mouth, savagely, fondled her breasts and her pubes and buttocks while she relieved his anxiety, then lay back, gasping, while she got up and washed her hands. "About Catherine."

"Is she as good as you?" he muttered.

"Listen. I love that girl as if she were my sister. If anything happens to her all deals are off. She's prepared to be nice to you, but she's a virgin and intends to remain that way until she meets the right man. And you're not it."

"But you say she'll be nice to me."

"You may have to teach her," Sophie said, and went to sleep.

She made an early start, kissed Richard tenderly, and gave Catherine a hug. Catherine was in a highly nervous state. "Pull yourself together," Sophie told her. "Here is a list of things you will have to do, should I send for you instead of coming back. There is no need to show Richard this." Catherine swallowed, and put the list in her handbag.

Sophie went first to her bank, where she deposited the cheque in the account of Elligan and Carew, open to the signature of either. She then drew out sufficient cash to last her for two days – she knew Swiss francs would be most acceptable in hard-currency starved Germany – and waited while four bank drafts were issued, one in the amount of one thousand English pounds, one in two thousand, one in two-and-a-half thousand, and one in five thousand. "I am going to need some guaranteed money to complete a business transaction," she told the curious clerk. "But I do not know how much. The drafts I do not use I will redeposit when I return to Switzerland, Now, I wish to open an account in the name of Mr Richard Elligan and . . ." why not, she wondered? There was no guarantee Richard was going to survive, "Lady Anne Martingell. You will transfer six thousand, two hundred and fifty pounds from my account to this new account, and you will give me a number that will allow either of the principals to access the account. I would also like a cheque book for that account. You may obtain specimen signatures from whoever uses the access number, with proper identification."

The clerk worked busily, while Sophie did some writing herself, on the bank notepaper. "Lastly," she said. "I will give you this letter of instruction to be acted upon should a Miss Catherine Ames present herself to you, and identify herself by means of her passport." He nodded wisely, and Sophie went off to place the letter of confirmation in her safe deposit box.

It was four years since Sophie had been in Germany. She had come here, on behalf of Clay Andrews, to buy arms for the Abyssinians in their struggle against Italy, in 1935. Before then, she had revisited her homeland once, in 1934, for the first time in several years. On both occasions she had been shocked and disturbed by what she had seen. The Germany she had remembered from her girlhood and as a young woman might have been in a permanent state of economic disaster, but the people had laughed, and lived their lives in their own chaotic but enjoyable fashion. Hitler had changed all that. Germany was now a place of disciplined order. She knew the finances had not improved, but Hitler had a knack of doing without real money – how long he could keep that up was anyone's guess. The people and the countryside and the towns all looked far more prosperous than she remembered . . . but no one smiled any more. "Mrs Elligan," said the very smartly uniformed border guard, opening her passprt. "Born in the Reich."

"A long time ago. I have been a British citizen for fifteen years."

"And the purpose of your visit?"

He looked her up and down. Sophie could look extraordinarily elegant when she chose, and today she wore a cream linen summer dress under a red and black striped bolero jacket with a matching sash. She wore no stockings, carried a white linen handbag to match her white canvas sandals, and topped the ensemble off with a broad-brimmed red and black hat. Her short yellow hair made her the more striking. No wonder heads were turning to look at her. She also carried her heavy shoulderbag as well as a small overnight valise. "I am on my way to Hamburg to visit my parents."

"Their name?"

"My father is the Count von Beinhardt."

"Ah," he commented, stamped the passport and handed it back. "Have a nice visit."

Sophie lunched on the train as it went north, and had a glass of wine. She was bracing herself. She and her parents did not see eye to eye. They never had, but their estrangement had been completed first of all by her four-year disappearance into the desert with that mad Englishman, as they regarded Ned, and then by her discovery, on her return, that they had embraced Nazism, fervently. Of course they had explained that they had had very little choice; in the new Germany one was either a Nazi, and prospered, or one was not, when life could be very grim. What rankled with Sophie was that everyone seemed to have accepted that Nazism had been an inevitable political process; those who had attempted to oppose it had simply disappeared.

It was late afternoon when she arrived in Hamburg. The city was as bustling as ever and, as she remembered, there were more uniforms to be seen on the streets than was usual in other western cities. She took a taxi to the family house. Time was when the Beinhardts, as dominated by her grandfather and her Aunt Cecile – neither of whom she could remember – had lived in a large house on a huge estate outside Bonn. Sophie could just remember the house, and the woods, and the horses, and the servants, from her childhood. That was after both Grandfather and Aunt Cecile – James Martingell's mistress and partner in those far-off, romantic, pre-war days – were dead, and the last surviving Beinhardt, Cecile's younger sister Clementine, had married; Sophie was the only child of that marriage.

Claus Schmitt had been required to change his name to Beinhardt to carry on the family name, and that he had done happily enough, especially as his new title carried a "von". Sophie did not suppose her father had ever been as successful a businessman as her grandfather, but they had prospered enough, until the war. They had prospered even more during the first days of that conflict, but it had all ended with the crash of the German defeat, when the country had been wracked by civil war, and arms manufacture and sale had been forbidden by the victorious Allies. They had recovered, of course. Laws in Weimar Germany had been there to be broken, and besides, the military had always been prepared to encourage and if necessary protect those who manufactured arms for their future use.

But the early twenties had been a difficult period. It had been during this time that she had met both James Martingell and his beautiful wife, and their partner the dashing young ex-Guards officer, Richard Elligan. They were engaged in the business she, even as a girl, had known so well. She had wanted to be a part of it again. Thus marriage to Richard. It might not have been love, but it had certainly been romantic, as they had adventured in Central Asia together, until the death of James Martingell had brought their joint dream-world to an end. They had both continued to dream, but in different directions, while using the same product. Which was why they were so strangely back together.

So again, what was she going to do? She needed a man representing Ned to satisfy the Americans. Once the guns were loaded and in transit she would have no more use for him. But she could not turn him loose until after the delivery had been made; he knew too much of her plans and she could not bring herself to trust him. But if he made himself a nuisance . . . she realised she was still on a killing high, the adrenalin still flowing, even several days after Ned's death. But Richard?

*   *   *

81

The doorbell on the house just off the Budapesterstrasse – conveniently close to the dock area – took some time to be answered. Sophie, waiting on the steps, glanced left and right, and was surprised to catch a glimpse of a familiar face. It was no more than a glimpse, because the face immediately disappeared as she looked at it, its owner stepping into a doorway some fifty yards along the street. But it had been familiar. Why? Then she remembered that she had seen the man, or his double, on the train coming up from Munich. She was being followed! But how on earth, and why on earth, should anyone in Germany be interested in an itinerant Englishwoman, even if her passport had revealed her German birth and parentage? Although, because of her last transactions here, she was almost certainly on several police files, even if she had broken no laws. The Gestapo! She felt quite cold. Another country to be in and out of as rapidly as possible.

The door opened. "Yes?"

The woman wore the uniform of a servant, white pinafore and cap over a black dress. She was not the same servant as the last time Sophie had been here. "Is the Countess at home?"

"Who shall I say is calling?"

"Just tell her Sophie. And may I come in? It is tiresome standing out here on the street."

The maid stood back, reluctantly, and Sophie entered the hall. "The Countess is upstairs. I will give her your name. Heil Hitler!"

"Absolutely. And thank you." Sophie went into the drawing room, which overlooked the street. She stood at the window, to one side, watching, and sure enough, the man from the train, the moment he had ascertained she was safely inside, crossed the street to the far side – where he was joined by another man. Sophie suddenly felt very hot, and then ice-cold again. Shooting her way out of a similar problem in France had been relatively simple: it had not, directly, involved the police. But the Gestapo . . .

"Sophie?!" Clementine von Beinhardt's voice was incredulous. As usual. Both mother and daughter always assumed that when they parted, they would never see each other again. Some time soon that had to be true. Sophie arranged her features into a smile, and went forward, arms outstretched. Clementine von

82

Beinhardt had always been a large woman; now she was positively mountainous, not as tall as Sophie but covered in rolls of jellylike flesh. Her dress strained and her stockings might have contained table legs. She wept easily, and was doing so now, the tears obliterating the very last remnants of the once attractive face and expression. Sophie, who kept her figure strictly under control, had often wondered how she came to be the daughter of such a creature – but then, it had always been accepted in the family that she took after her aunt Cecile. "Oh, Sophie!" Clementine held her daughter close. "You have come back."

"Briefly," Sophie said, deciding against inducing hysterics by informing her mother she might be about to be arrested. "I must leave again this evening."

"But—" Clementine peered at her, then released her. "What have you done to your hair?"

"Cut it. It's all the rage."

"And dyed it?"

"That too."

Clementine snorted. "You are not back in the arms business?"

"I have never left the arms business, Mama."

"Well, you are wasting your time coming here. Your father has nothing for you. His work is now exclusively for the Reich. I doubt he will even want to see you, after the last time. Would you like a cup of tea?"

"Thank you." Sophie sat down. Clementine rang the bell, and when the maid appeared, gave the necessary instructions, before sitting down herself, looking very hot and bothered. "I did not come here to buy arms from Papa," Sophie said. "And if he does not wish to see me, well, I do not wish to see him. All I wish is the whereabouts of Captain Pfuhl and the *Bremerhaven*."

"Ha!" Clementine said. "You *are* shipping guns. At your age?"

"I do not see what my age has to do with it," Sophie said. "And it would be best if you did not inquire into what I wish the ship for. I merely wish to charter it for a month."

Clementine sniffed. "The *Bremerhaven* went to the breakers yard a year ago. She had become quite unseaworthy."

Damnation, Sophie thought. She had used Captain Pfuhl's tramp steamer on several previous occasions, had always found him utterly reliable and entirely professional. They had both understood and respected each other. She managed not to let her disappointment show. "Well, then, I shall have to look elsewhere. But I would like to see the captain, as I am in Hamburg. Have you his address?"

Clementine waited until the maid had served the tea, then went to the desk in the corner of the room, opened a large diary, and wrote rapidly on the back of a visiting card. Sophie glanced at it, put it in her handbag; the address was quite close. "Thank you. I'll go along there now."

"You have come all this way . . . where have you come from, anyway?"

"Somewhere."

"And you are spending only five minutes in my company?"

"I had thought you would be glad to see the back of me. Would you like me to come back, after I have visited the captain?"

"Of course I would like you to come back. Perhaps it might be possible—"

"For me to be reconciled with Papa? Who knows. They say that miracles do happen. I will return this evening." Sophie stood up. "Oh, by the way, may I leave by the back door?"

"The back door? Whatever for?"

"I met this masher on the train from Munich. I am sure he has followed me here, and I can do without hasslement like that."

"Oh, help yourself," Clementine said.

"Thank you, Mama." Sophie kissed her on the cheek. "I'll see you later."

She went into the hall, and thence into the kitchen, where the maid was seated at the table reading a novel. She sprang up as Sophie entered. "MeinFrau?"

"I am just leaving," Sophie said. "Through the back."

The woman opened her mouth and then closed it again. Sophie smiled at her, opened the door, and found herself looking at a large man in a trench coat and a slouch hat. "Good afternoon, Frau Elligan," the man said. "You are under arrest."

The Trap

"Thou shalt not kill; but need'st not strive
Officiously to keep alive."

Arthur Hugh Clough

Yachting

S ophie was taken utterly by surprise. But she retained all the speed of thought and action she had accumulated over the years. The man was alone, but he had his partners out front, and of course the maid would undoubtedly be on his side. "You will have to explain," she said, stepping back into the kitchen.

The man came in, and as she had supposed he would, closed the door behind him. Then he took his hands from his pockets, empty. Sophie did not doubt he was armed, but he presumed he was dealing only with a surprised and frightened woman. The maid gave a little scream at his entry, and backed against the wall beyond the table. "You are wanted for questioning," the man said. "Raise your arms."

Sophie obeyed, her shoulder bag dangling from her left hand; she allowed her handbag and valise to fall to the floor. The man stepped up to her, ran his fingers over her blouse, squeezing her breasts, then slipped his hands down to her thighs, and lower, to raise her skirt. Now his head was on a level with her waist. As his fingers moved up her legs, beneath the skirt, Sophie struck downwards with her right hand, with all her considerable strength. The blow thudded into the nape of the man's neck, and he went down on to his hands and knees with a grunt.

Sophie stepped away from him, bringing down her shoulder-bag and opening it to take out her pistol in the same movement. The man recovered, reared back onto his knees, saw her gun yet did not stop himself reaching inside his jacket for his own weapon. Sophie shot him through the head. Blood scattered in every direction, and the maid screamed. She had been starting forward from the far side of the table, now she retreated against the wall as Sophie turned, gun levelled. "Don't shoot me," she begged.

The inner door burst open, and Clementine came in. "That noise . . . it sounded like a—" she gaped at the dead man, mouth opened wide.

"Don't scream, please, Mama," Sophie said.

Clementine closed her mouth again, and slumped onto one of the straight chairs at the table. "They will cut off your head. That is what they do to murderers in the Reich. They will cut off your head with a sword."

"Then I'd better hang on to it for as long as I can," Sophie said. "You . . ." she pointed at the maid. "Open that cupboard." The maid hastily opened the linen cupboard. "Take out those sheets." The maid dumped the sheets on the table. "Now, both of you, stand over there against the wall."

"I am your mother," Clementine protested.

"And I am your daughter. Who I am sure you do not wish to see rolling about the floor, headless. Besides, I am saving you from at least imprisonment. Hurry now. I have little time."

Clementine lumbered to her feet and stood beside the maid. "Imprisonment?"

"I am going to lay this gun on the table," Sophie said. "Please understand that if either of you moves before I tell you to, I will pick it up and shoot you." Clementine gulped; the maid looked about to faint. Sophie laid down the gun and began tearing the sheets into strips. "You see," she explained, "if I leave here, with both of you active, you will either immediately summon the police who are at the front of the house, which will give me very little chance of escaping, or you will not, in which case you will be arrested as my accomplices. But when the police get tired of waiting for me to come out, or of hearing nothing from their friend here, and break their way in, if they find you both bound and gagged they will have to accept that you were as much my victims as this poor fellow. You first, young woman."

Sophie made the servant lie on the floor and bound her wrists and ankles together. Then she bent her legs backwards at the knees and bound all four together in the small of her back. Then she gagged her. "Mama."

"Sophie, you cannot do this to me."

"Please, Mama, do not make me use force." Clementine lay down beside the maid and submitted to being bound and gagged.

"When next we meet," Sophie suggested, "we will have a good laugh about this." She stooped beside the detective, put his Luger pistol in her shoulderbag together with her Browning, and stepped out of the back door.

Sophie reckoned she had about two hours. By the end of that time either her father would have come home or the men in the front would became alarmed and force their way in to see what had happened to their comrade. But Captain Pfuhl's lodging was only half-a-mile away, a garret situated at the top of a four-floor walk-up. "Frau Elligan?" He peered at her in consternation. Sophie was no less taken aback. The big, bluff sea captain she remembered had dwindled in an obviously penurious retirement, his shoulders bowed, his hair white, his cheeks and neck emaciated. "Captain." She rembraced him, and he ushered her into his tiny bedsitter. The air was rancid, the bedclothes clearly not washed for some time.

"You are looking splendid, as always." Pfuhl gazed at her short, dyed hair, but did not comment.

"Thank you. I have very little time. I need a ship."

Pfuhl poured coffee. "I do not have one, any more."

"And no job?"

He shrugged. "It became known that I had engaged in gun-running. No job."

"Will you help me?" Sophie drank the unsweetened coffee and gave a little shudder. "I can put you back on your feet."

"I would like to help you, Frau Elligan. Oh, how I would like to help you. But—"

"You have no ship. But you must know where I, we, can obtain one."

"In this Germany?" He rubbed the back of his head. "How big?"

"Big enough to carry a load of guns and ammunition."

"Then it must be ocean-going."

"Sea-going, certainly. I am not going to cross the Atlantic."

"A big yacht," he said thoughtfully.

"It would have to be a very big yacht."

"A *boier*."

"What is that? It sounds Dutch."

"Yes, it is Dutch. They are designed as bulk carriers on the Dutch canals. They are large and roomy, and they can keep the sea, in reasonable weather. Some of them have been converted to very comfortable yachts."

"And you know where I can get hold of one of these ships, for immediate use?"

"There is one in Cuxhaven at this moment."

"What is it doing there?"

"It is impounded."

"Then what use is it to us?"

"It is impounded for non-payment of harbour dues and a fine. It is a Dutch ship, which has been chartering in the North Sea, and was forced to put into Cuxhaven by bad weather. Once there, because of certain . . . irregularities, it was fined, and as the skipper lacked the funds to pay, it has lain there for the past month, while he has tried to arrange to obtain the money. But so far he has had no success."

"So if someone paid his fine he might be willing to do business."

"I am sure of it. If the fine is not paid he will lose his ship."

"Then we leave for Cuxhaven immediately."

"We?"

"You cannot remain here, Captain. The Gestapo will track me soon enough, and they will undoubtedly require you to tell them where I have gone. I cannot allow that, or the ill-treatment you will receive if you deny them. Besides, do you not wish to adventure one last time, with me? I will pay you well."

"But . . . why should the Gestapo wish to track you here?"

"Because half an hour ago I shot and killed one of their people."

"You—" Pfuhl's mouth opened and shut like a dying fish.

"He tried to arrest me," Sophie explained. "I could not permit that."

"They will track you to the ends of the earth."

"Then let us remove ourselves to the ends of the earth, as rapidly as possible."

The captain was very shaken. Sophie helped him pack a small bag, then tied up her hair in her headscarf and put on her glare glasses. They went to the station and caught the next train to Cuxhaven. Again, they would easily be traced, but she still reckoned she had some time in hand, although they would have to find concealment for the night. But if this yacht skipper would help them . . .

It was dusk when they reached the seaport at the mouth of the Elbe, and they hurried to the docks. "There." Pfuhl pointed to the odd-shaped vessel lying alongside, rising and falling as the river rushed by outside the harbour walls. The *boier* certainly looked big enough to accommodate a few tons of weaponry. She was about sixty feet long, Sophie estimated, and something like twenty broad, a very generous ratio. She was single-masted, but the exhaust sticking out of her stern indicated that she had an auxiliary engine. She was also shallow-drafted, Sophie suspected, but her stability was ensured by the two huge leeboards which were presently secured clear of the water, one on each side under the fenders. She lay some feet below the dock level, as the tide was not yet full; there was a ladder leading down to her deck. "Do you know the skipper?" Sophie asked.

"I have met him," Pfuhl said cautiously. "There is something you should know about him. He is a black man." Sophie turned her head, sharply. "That is why he has been fined, for entering German waters without permission. Black people are not popular with the regime. Does this bother you?"

Sophie thought of the years of faithful friendship given to James Martingell by Mbote, the East African erstwhile slave who had become his closest associate, and who had died at his side. "It does not bother me in the least," she said.

They made their way along the dock, and looked down onto the deck of the *boier*. "Ahoy, *Christina*," Pfuhl called. There had been no one on deck, but now a forward hatch opened and a white man emerged, dressed in a jersey and canvas trousers, barefooted. He was very fair and wore a short yellow beard. "We wish to speak with your captain."

The seaman hesitated, and the after hatch opened to allow the skipper on deck. He made an impressive sight, being over six feet tall and built to match. His face was handsome, with dark eyes and a strong chin. His skin was ebony. He looked a man to respect, and even to fear, if crossed. "Captain Pfuhl." German was obviously not his native tongue. "Come aboard. Bring your friend." Sophie climbed down the ladder, acutely aware of her skirt flaring in the breeze. The captain waited at the foot to hand her over the rail. "You'll forgive me, Fräulein, but I was in need of a sight like you."

"And I am in need of someone like you," Sophie riposted, and held out her hand. "Sophie Elligan."

She had taken off her gloves, and he looked at the rings. "I apologise, Frau Elligan. Dennis Overcamp."

"And you are Dutch?"

"That's what my passport says. Captain." He shook hands with Pfuhl in turn. "Come below."

He escorted them down a short ladder into a very comfortable saloon, lit by electricity from a gently rumbling generator in the bowels of the ship. There was a table and chairs in the centre, and three doors leading off, one right aft and one to either side, indicating staterooms. There was even ample headroom. "Nice," Sophie said.

Dennis Overcamp went to a fitted sideboard. "What do you drink?"

"Whatever you do." Sophie sat down.

Overcamp poured three glasses of schnapps, seated himself. "It's not every day I get visited by a beautiful woman. There has to be a reason."

"I wish to charter your ship."

"That I like. Trouble is, I'm in hock."

"How much?"

"These characters say I owe them four thousand guilders. Which I ain't got. And I ain't got too much chance of raising that kind of money, save I sell the ship."

Sophie opened her shoulderbag and took out the bank draft for two thousand pounds. "Will that do it?"

Overcamp picked up the draft and scanned it. "It surely would."

"How soon can you get clearance?"

"Not before the harbour office opens tomorrow morning."

"Not too good. There'll be people here looking for me in a couple of hours."

"Why?"

Sophie drew a deep breath. But if she was going to sea with this man, she had to trust him from the start. "Two hours ago I shot and killed a Gestapo agent."

Overcamp looked at her for several seconds, and she opened her shoulderbag again, took out the Luger she had taken from the German, and laid it on the table. She kept the Browning concealed. "Am I allowed to ask why?" Overcamp inquired.

"He was going to arrest me."

"Why?"

"I didn't give him time actually to state a reason, but I think it was because the Gestapo are interested in my activities as a gun-runner."

Overcamp had laid the draft on the table. Now he picked it up again, as if to reassure himself that he wasn't dreaming. "You, are a gun-runner?"

"Mrs Elligan is one of the most famous gun-runners in the world," Pfuhl said. "To those in the know."

"And you want to charter my ship," Overcamp said.

"For one month, for five thousand pounds," Sophie said.

"To carry guns. From where to where?"

"I will tell you that after you have accepted the charter, and we are at sea."

"But if we're caught, I'm liable to lose my ship."

"If we are caught, Captain Overcamp, you're liable to lose your life. But you'll see, I'm still here."

She decided against telling him that she had twice been caught, and each time escaped by the skin of her teeth – and various other parts of her skin as well. She glanced at Pfuhl, who knew her history, willing him to be quiet. "And the Gestapo?" Overcamp asked.

"If we cannot obtain clearance until tomorrow, you will have to hide us."

Overcamp looked at Pfuhl. "You in on this?"

"Yes," Pfuhl said. "Are your crew trustworthy?"

"I have only two crew. The rest went home when they realised we were stuck here. The two who stayed are trustworthy. But if the Gestapo are really looking for you, Frau Elligan, they are going to take this port and everything in it apart. Hiding you is going to involve a certain amount of discomfort."

"I can stand a certain amount of discomfort. Does this mean you'll take the charter?"

Overcamp grinned. "For five thousand pounds? Sure. How do you mean to pay me?"

"Half down, and half on completion. In English pounds."

"You have two-and-a-half-thousand English pounds on you?"

Sophie picked up the pistol and restored it to her shoulderbag. "Yes, Captain Overcamp, in the form of another draft, which I will retain until we are at sea. Should you change your mind about our arrangement, I will destroy the draft and then shoot my way into hell, taking you with me. And perhaps a few policemen as well."

Overcamp grinned. "You're quite a lady. I'm not going to betray you. I just hope you don't suffer from claustrophobia."

He put them in the engine-room bilges, situated beneath the saloon, the deepest part of the ship, where he kept spare bottles of beer and various cheeses. The space was both confined and noisome, and half full of water. The engine itself was a large MAN diesel. Beyond it, the generator rumbled. "Won't they look down here?" Sophie asked.

"Sure they will. Once you're lying down, I'm going to put some more stuff on top of you."

"And if we drown?"

"I'm hoping you won't do that. But I'll have to close you in."

Sophie had been in worse situations. She took off her bolero jacket and dress, watched with interest by the two men. "All your gear has to be down there with you," Overcamp pointed out.

"I understand that. But there's no point in ruining it. My shoulderbag is waterproof." She packed away her outer clothing, and her handbag, took out the Luger. She didn't mean to be taken alive. Then she inserted herself beneath the floorboards, the valise, which was fortunately also waterproof, between her legs, the shoulderbag under her arm. "Do you come in with me?" she asked Pfuhl.

"If you've no objection, Frau Elligan."

"I guess we've known each other a long time, Captain."

Pfuhl did not bother to take anything off; he probably reckoned his clothes were already too decrepit to be ruined by

94

prolonged immersion in dirty water. They lay on their backs, shoulder to shoulder and thigh to thigh; they were resting on the ballast bricks, but the water remained about a foot deep, gurgling to and fro as the ship moved to the tide; their heads were floating. By now Overcamp had been joined by his crew, and they began placing additional stores on top of the two bodies; Sophie finished with a cured ham on her groin, and several more cheeses on her breasts and stomach. Then a net was placed over her and the captain's face. They could see, and breathe, but it was impossible for anyone standing above them to tell they were beneath the green gauze, unless the searchers were to empty the entire bilge. "You don't reckon we'll suffocate when you put those boards in?" Sophie asked.

"No," Overcamp said. "They all have air holes bored in them; I like to keep my bilges clear of rot. I'll see you later."

The boards were put in place; Sophie reckoned there was about an inch left between her nose and the wood. But as Overcamp had promised, the air remained clear, apart from the stench of diesel oil. "We are buried alive," Pfuhl whispered.

"Then let's look forward to the resurrection," Sophie suggested.

Half suspended as they were in the water, they were not too uncomfortable. But the claustrophobic element, as Overcamp had warned, was strong, compounded as it was by not knowing when the Gestapo would arrive. Or if they would come at all. Sophie found herself thinking about Overcamp. She didn't think he was really Dutch. His voice had a slightly sing-song intonation, and he rolled his "r"s. She did not doubt he was a strong character, or that he would prove an asset, once they got underway. The trouble was, he made Richard even more redundant, once the goods were loaded.

As it was not possible to move sufficiently to look at her watch, so she had no idea how long they lay there before the *boier* trembled to the arrival of several booted feet on deck. The voices were still some distance away, but the tramp of feet came steadily closer as ladders were descended. They were certainly making a thorough search of the ship. Sophie found her brain ranging wildly over possibilities, that she might have forgotten something in the cabin, that they might be betrayed . . . she wrapped her fingers round the butt of the gun resting on her stomach. The boards immediately above their faces trembled. "What is down there?" asked a voice.

"The bilges," Overcamp said. "And some stores, to be sure."

"And rats, eh?" The policeman guffawed.

"I do not have rats on my ship."

"Show me." Sophie held her breath, but only one of the floorboards was lifted, not over them, and a torch shone briefly inside. "Lots of beer, eh?" The Gestapo agent seemed a good-humoured chap.

"There is some more in the saloon." Overcamp replaced the board.

"A nice ship," the German commented. "But you will lose it, if you do not pay the fine."

"The money arrived today. I will pay the fine first thing in the morning."

"Then you are to be congratulated, Captain. Now remember what I have told you. These dangerous criminals are known to have left Hamburg for Cuxhaven earlier this afternoon. The stationmaster in Hamburg distinctly remembers them. If they are in Cuxhaven, they will wish to escape Germany, perhaps by stowing away, perhaps by buying a passage. You will keep a lookout for them at all times, and should they approach you for a berth, report immediately to the police. And, my friend, do not be taken in by the woman. She is very handsome, very attractive. But she is a murderess."

"I shall look out for her," Overcamp promised. The voices faded. Sophie had hoped the agent might reveal something of what had happened at the Beinhardt house, but he did not, at least when within earshot. Ten minutes later the boards were lifted again. "Are you all right?" Overcamp said.

"Surviving."

"I will leave the boards up for the time being to give you more air, but I think you should stay down there for the night, just in case those people come back." He grinned at her. "Like I said, you are quite a woman, Mrs Elligan."

Sophie reckoned that was the longest night of her life, and she had spent quite a few very long nights in her time. She began to worry about Pfuhl, who was overtaken by an attack of coughing. Suppose he had done that while the Gestapo has been standing above him? Overcamp came down at dawn with some breakfast, which they were allowed to sit up to eat, together with mugs of steaming, sweet black coffee. "When can we get out of here?" Sophie asked.

"When we are at sea. I am going ashore in the next hour to pay off my dues and the fine. I will be in a hurry, because the tide is right at ten o'clock. They will understand this. So we leave just before ten. You look like a drowned rat."

"I feel like a drowned rat. Can I have a hot bath, as soon as we're away?"

"You can have a hot shower. I do not have a tub."

Another long wait, but at last the heavy diesel engine began to throb, and the *boier* pulled away from the dockside. This was actually the most uncomfortable part of their confinement, for the engine was only feet away, and the noise was sickening. But once they were in the mainstream of the river, they were allowed out. "Just remember not to go on deck," Overcamp said. "You wanted a bath, Frau Elligan." Dripping stagnant water, with which was now mixed a solution of diesel oil, Sophie followed the captain into the saloon and thence his own cabin. "The heads are here." He opened another door into a tiny bathroom with a grating for a floor, laid over the deck in which there was a drain, and containing a toilet, basin, and shower. "Soap." He showed her the cake attached to a string. "Hang it round your neck."

He closed the door. Sophie was beginning to feel she had known him all her life. She stripped off her underwear, trampled it under her feet as she stood beneath the shower, which was delightfully warm . . . but salt! So what, she wondered, standing there for several minutes before even beginning to soap, allowing the heat to penetrate. Then she washed her hair as well, for the first time appreciating having so little of it. "I have put your bag here," Overcamp called through the door.

"Thank you." She dried herself, stepped into the cabin, half-expecting to find him waiting for her. But he was not. She pulled on the most suitable clothes she had, which consisted of a pair of slacks and a blouse, then peered at herself in the mirror above the dressing table. "Shit," she muttered. The long immersion, followed by the thorough soaking she had given her head, had caused the dye to run in places, and auburn streaks were coming through. But did it matter? She was on her way.

When she went on deck they were at the mouth of the river, and Germany was fading into a cloudbank astern. Sophie wondered if she would ever see it again. "Let's talk business," Overcamp suggested. Once they were clear of the sandbanks, the engine was stopped and the sails set, a huge main and a smaller jib; *Christina* heeled slightly in the fresh breeze as they headed south, but the leeboards, now lowered and secured in place, kept her from rolling. Sophie and Overcamp sat at the saloon table, and Sophie took the draft for two-and-a-half thousand pounds from her shoulderbag and gave it to him. "Just how many of these things do you have in there?" he asked.

"That's the last," she lied. "The remainder is paid on completion of the delivery, remember?"

He placed the draft in his Log Book. "I guess I am now in your employ, Frau Elligan. What are your orders?"

"There are people I need to contact. I don't suppose you have a radio?"

"Nope. We can put into port, though, as soon as we get down to the Dutch Frisians."

"Which will be?"

"Tomorrow morning, if the breeze holds. I'll need to top up on diesel and water, anyway. You still haven't told me where we're going."

"I will. You tell me, Captain, where exactly are you from?"

"South America, Frau Elligan. A place called Surinam. It's a Dutch colony. They call it Dutch Guiana."

"That explains your accent. How did you come to be owner of this yacht?"

"I went to sea as a lad, worked my way up. I got my master's ticket, and found myself in Holland with a few guilders to spare. I have a house in north Holland. But then I found this ship going cheap. So I invested everything I had left. Went out for charter, fishing parties, a few longer trips. I was doing pretty well till I got blown into Cuxhaven a couple of weeks ago, and was promptly arrested. They sure don't like black people in your country, ma'am."

"It's not my country. I just happened to be born there. Do you speak English?"

"Sure I do."

"Then let's use it."

"You going to tell me what this is all about?" He listened in silence, then gave a low whistle. "Like you said, some risk."

"Some profit. Where do we stop first?"

"Terschelling is our best bet."

"Show me." He spread the chart, identified the offshore island on the outer side of the Waddenzee. "The people who will be joining us are in Switzerland."

"You need to give them two days, if they leave immediately you contact them."

"And from Terschelling to Clew Bay?"

He changed charts to a small scale one of the whole British Isles and North Sea, did some work with his dividers. "Depends on the weather, but that looks pretty good at the moment. Five to six days."

"We actually have more than that to play with. Now, once we pick up the cargo, we need to disappear. Will we have to stop between Clew Bay and our delivery point?"

"In the Adriatic. Say three weeks under sail with a full cargo. If we top up in Terschelling and don't have to do much motoring, no. But we may need another top-up to get back out."

"Will that keep until after the delivery?"

"I reckon so."

"Well, Captain, I feel like a celebratory glass of schnapps."

He poured. "You really shot a lot of people?"

"Hasn't everyone?"

He scratched his head. "I've never shot anybody."

"You remind me of a young friend of mine. She's joining us in Terschelling. Keep your fingers crossed, Captain, and maybe you won't have to. Shoot anyone, I mean."

She wondered what he really made of her. But then, she wasn't sure what she made of him. All of her previous adventures, deliveries, mishaps, had been in the company of men she had known for years, men she had evaluated before the delivery was undertaken at all, and in most cases had known she could rely on, whether they had been James Martingell himself, Mbote, Richard, or Ned. Even Clay Andrews, if they had fallen out time and again over his peculiar ethics, had been a man to be relied on when it came to facing danger and possible death. Dennis Overcamp, although he might be an excellent seaman and navigator, was by his own admission a tyro in the art of risking his life, and employing the ruthlessness necessary for success in the business of gun-running. But as she had said, perhaps he wouldn't have to, if everything went according to plan. The trouble was, in her considerable experience, nothing ever went quite according to plan.

She reminded herself that she also had Pfuhl, almost as experienced as herself, at least in the seagoing side of the business, and soon she would have Richard. She wondered how he and Catherine were getting on? But she was feeling more relaxed than at any moment since Ned had been killed. She always enjoyed being at sea, and now she was not only away from the grasp of the police, whether French or German, but she was working. She always enjoyed that as well. Even when she was in someone else's hands? "What do you reckon?" she asked Pfuhl.

She had been in his hands often enough, in sticky situations at sea. "He's a good man," Pfuhl said. "And he knows the sea. He'll not let you down."

They entered the harbour at West Terschelling the next morning, as Overcamp had promised. A berth was found alongside for the big yacht, whose captain was apparently well known in the port, and he and his two crew got to work immediately topping up the water and fuel tanks. Sophie didn't know whether the two Dutchmen had been told what was going on, but they seemed happy enough. She was able to go ashore and change some money and make her telephone calls. She began with the number Walters had given her. "We shall be in the bay as arranged," she said. "Sunday week, as arranged."

"Thank you. Enter the bay south of Clare Island, then turn north towards the Corraun Peninsular. Steer towards this until you see two red lights, then reduce speed. Three lights means anchor. You will be met. Once the cargo is loaded, you will receive both your next payment and further instructions. Have you written that down?"

"Yes." The phone went dead, and Sophie called the hotel in Geneva.

"Sophie?" Catherine asked. "Oh, thank God!"

"Have you been having a hard time?" Sophie asked.

"That is exactly right," Catherine said.

"Well, now you have to move. Quickly. I am in Terschelling."

"Where?"

"It's an island off the Dutch coast. Take a train for Amsterdam, then another to Leeuwarden. From Leeuwarden you will have either to hire a car or take a taxi to Harlingen."

"Wait while I write those down," Catherine said.

"Harlingen is where the boy stuck his finger in the hole in the dyke. There is a monument to him."

"Will I have time to look at it?"

"No. In Harlingen you will catch the ferry for Terschelling. The ferry will bring you into the harbour of West Terschelling. I will meet you there."

"Right. How do we pay for all this? I'm afraid we're just about broke."

"Go to the bank I listed, identify yourself, and they will allow you to draw sufficient money to pay the hotel bill and get you here. I will expect you on the evening ferry the day after tomorrow. Please do not be late."

"Marseilles is on the line, General," the secretary said.

Edio Rometti picked up the phone. "Is it done?"

"No," the voice said.

"What do you mean?"

"The affair was botched, Signor General. Our people, as instructed, picked up the girl when she landed in Marseilles. From Marseilles she took the train to Montpellier, where she got out and used her bicycle. Our people had her in their sights the whole way. She went to a villa outside the village called Le Pouget. This villa is, was, owned by an English couple named Smith."

"They would be the people we want," Edio said.

"I think you are right. Our people then sent in a hit squad to finish the job."

"And?" The man's tone had Edio frowning at the phone.

"They got shot up, Signor General. Four men."

"Holy Jesus Christ! Four men? Four experienced men?"

"The best we have, Signor General."

"How many were opposing them?"

"We don't know. Apparently there were two other dead people in the villa when the French police got there. But that was not for two days; the villa is very isolated."

"Who were the other dead people?"

"One was a man, and the other a woman."

"Ah," Edio said, relieved. "Then it is done, after all. I am sorry about your people, Colonel, but—"

"The man was big, early forties. The French police have identified him as Mr Smith."

"Yes. That's the one."

"The other was the maid."

"Repeat that."

"The maid, Signor General. A Frenchwoman, who lived locally."

"Not Mrs Smith?"

"No, Signor General. Mrs Smith has disappeared. The police are looking for her. They feel she probably had something to do with the deaths, or is dead herself. I do not think she is dead. My information is that two automatic pistols were used to kill my people. One of these guns was found with Mr Smith. The other has disappeared, along with Mrs Smith and the Smiths' car. The police have traced her as far as Aurillac, where she cashed a cheque the day after the killings. Since then they have traced the car to Paris, where it was abandoned. After that, nothing. She has simply disappeared. It seems obvious she has left the country."

"Shit," Edio said. "Shit, shit, shit!" That woman, so beautiful, so sexy, so utterly delightful . . . so utterly ruthless. And so utterly deadly! "But wait a moment," he said. "You say the French police are looking for Mrs Smith. What about the girl?"

102

"There is no mention of anyone else."

"There is no mention of another body? The girl your people traced to the villa?"

"*Si*, Signor General. The French police are not looking for her for the simple reason that they do not know she exists. My guess is that she left the villa with Mrs Smith. Whether of her own will or not I cannot say." He waited. "Are you there, Signor General?"

"Yes," Edio said. "I am here."

"Are there any further orders?"

Edio sighed. Sophie Elligan had disappeared, having killed, or helped to kill, four top-quality Italian secret agents. And with her had gone Clay Andrews' messenger. So the gun-running deal was still on. And he did not know how, or where, or when. "No," Colonel," he said. "There are no further orders. But just in case the French police do pick up Mrs Smith, I wish to be informed immediately." He hung up and surveyed his secretary, who was hovering anxiously in the doorway. "Summon Colonel Barthes and Colonel Malingi," he said. "It is time we found out what is in those mountains."

"You're not serious," Walter Pemberton said.

"I am very serious, Walter," Eisener said. "Your woman shot and killed one of our people, in Hamburg."

"And then disappeared? I thought you were efficient."

"Oh, we will catch her. We cannot have women shooting Gestapo officers and getting away with it. As I began the operation, I have been placed in charge. I am returning to Germany this evening."

"Is she still in Germany?"

"We do not think so. We questioned her mother, who of course pretended to know nothing of her daughter's activities. But as we do not believe that, we persuaded her to tell us where Frau Elligan had gone."

"Persuaded her?" Pemberton asked, uneasily.

"Ah, she was not difficult. Once we stripped her and tied her to a board and showed her the whip she was stammering in her anxiety to co-operate."

Pemberton swallowed.

"So we know that Frau Elligan went from her mother's house to the lodgings of a man called Pfuhl. He is a sea-captain who has worked for the Elligan-Beinhardt set-up before, but is presently unemployed. Frau Elligan and Captain Pfuhl left Hamburg immediately and travelled to Cuxhaven. We were on their trail within a couple of hours. But in Cuxhaven they vanished."

"Obviously they left the country."

"That seems probable. But in Cuxhaven they could only have done this by ship. Our people mounted a very complete search of the town, and of all the ships in the harbour. Neither Frau Elligan nor Captain Pfuhl were found. And a watch was maintained on the harbour all night; they certainly did not board any ship *after* our search."

"Yet they got out." Pemberton shook his head. "I assume you have a list of all the ships leaving Cuxhaven the next day?" Eisener gave him a sheet of paper. "Hm. German, German, German, Dutch . . . that's the one."

"That is hardly possible. Not only was that ship searched more thoroughly than any of the others, because she was foreign, but she was impounded for non-payment of dues."

"Yet she sailed the next day."

"As it happened, the money had apparently arrived the previous day. The account was settled first thing Tuesday morning, and she was released. Elligan and Pfuhl could hardly have known this was going to happen." Pemberton looked at him, and he flushed. "You are suggesting that Frau Elligan travels with several thousand guilders in her handbag?"

"At the very least. And I would say, if you check, that the payment was actually made in pounds sterling." Pemberton studied the list. "The *Christina*, a Dutch *boier*, in the charter business. Actually, old man, you've done very well. We have the name and the nationality of the ship. We'll find her."

"We would hope to pick her up first."

Pemberton shook his head again. "Best to leave it with us, now. This will require finesse. We can't very well arrest a Dutch ship on suspicion."

"I do not think you understand, Walter. This woman is wanted for the murder of a Gestapo officer. We intend to have her."

"And 'persuade' her to answer questions, as you did her mother?"

Eisener grinned. "Of course. I understand she is a very handsome woman. Our people will enjoy having her in custody."

"I'm sure they will. I will wish you the best of luck. Have a safe journey." He watched Eisener leave the room, then unfolded the newspaper that had lain on the side of his chair throughout their talk. He had been intending to show it to the German, but now was glad he had not. He found the small item, read it again.

French police investigating the shootings at the villa outside of Le Pouget in the Riviera, are now seeking a Mrs Sophie Elligan, who, it is suggested, may well be the same person as the Mrs Eloise Smith who disappeared from the villa at the time of the shootout. Mrs Elligan, with a female companion, checked in for the night at an hotel in Millau, and she answers the description being circulated of Mrs Smith. In addition, a Mrs Elligan, travelling with a female companion, checked in at an hotel in Paris the following night, that of Friday 14. As Mrs Smith's car has been found abandoned in Paris, it seems almost certain that Mrs Smith and Mrs Elligan are the same person. The police are anxious to hear from anyone who may have encountered these two women. Mrs Elligan is described as tall and well-built, handsome of appearance, with auburn hair worn long. Her companion, named as Catherine Ames, is also tall, of slim build, very good-looking, and has yellow hair, which she also wears long. The public are warned that these two women are armed and very dangerous, and should not be approached under any circumstances.

Pemberton let the paper droop from his fingers as he drank whisky. He remembered Sophie Elligan from nine years before, a very beautiful, very elegant, but slightly disturbed young woman – she had just had her first brush with the Italian secret police, and had come off definitely second best. Now . . . four men dead outside Le Pouget. A Gestapo officer dead in Hamburg. And he had no idea how many itinerant Arabs, Italians and Abyssinians left scattered across North Africa.

Armed and dangerous! Sophie had grown up. Now she had to be considered the most deadly woman who had ever walked the face of the earth. And now he might be able to nab her at last. Although, sadly, he reflected, he would not be allowed to

"question" her in quite the Gestapo manner. But then, she had
never actually committed a crime in England.

But she would have to be stopped. He returned to his office,
picked up the phone. "Put me though to the Admiralty, please,"
he said.

Friends

"We have to hurry." Catherine brushed her hair, peering at herself in the dressing mirror. "You pack up here, and I'll settle up."

Richard reclined on the bed to watch her. He enjoyed watching her.

Every movement was as smooth as silk. She fascinated him, because she was so utterly Sophie's creature – and Clay Andrews' to be sure. How he loathed that man! But this girl . . . when she submitted to his caresses, he knew it was because Sophie had told her to do so. When he complained that she was not responding, not indeed showing the slightest interest in what he was doing to her, or even what she was doing to him, she immediately became a bundle of sexual activity – because those were Sophie's instructions. And that she would not let him enter her was again undoubtedly Sophie's instruction.

Of course he could have taken her by force. She wore pyjama bottoms in bed, but those were no protection. But however much he enjoyed putting his hands inside to play with her bottom and pubes, he had never attempted rape. Was he then, still too much of a gentleman? Or was he, like her, Sophie's creature, at least for the duration of this deal? Or did he hope, by patience, to possess this bundle of delight, utterly, in the course of time? "What are you going to settle up with?" he asked.

Catherine picked up her jacket. "I have my instructions."

"Which involves going to a bank, I'll bet." He sat up. "I'll come with you,"

She shook her head. "I'm to go alone. But when I come back you must be ready to move. We have a long way to go by tomorrow."

107

He caught her wrist. "Will you answer me one question? Just what is Sophie to you? Are you lovers?"

Catherine looked down at him, and he released her. "Sophie is my boss. Yours too. As for being lovers, how could anyone not love Sophie?"

Catherine studied the bill. It seemed awfully large, but then it was in Swiss francs. "I will have to go to the bank to draw this," she told the manager. "Mr Elligan will remain here until my return."

"Of course, mademoiselle."

Catherine wondered what he, and his staff, made of it all, as she went out into the bright spring sunshine. She did not suppose any member of the staff was unaware that she and Richard had been sleeping together, even if she made sure to rumple the bedclothes in her room every morning before getting dressed. Why was she doing this? Is Sophie your lover? Richard had asked. Catherine actually could think of no one in the world she would rather have as a lover. It had far less to do with sex than with Sophie's ability to dominate; to make one feel that one was actually a part of herself; the knowledge that if you were on her side she would kill without hesitation to protect you; the cold, almost casual way in which, indeed, she could kill; and then, the passion with which she could feel, and love, and demand. And above all, the utter control she seemed able to have over her life, even when in the gravest danger. Catherine had never dreamed people like that actually existed.

Was Sophie a monster? Or just a supreme example of the sort of woman likely to develop out of the Stalin-Hitler-Mussolini syndrome, where moral values no longer had any meaning, and one dealt in profit and survival. In which case she was to be envied, as long as she kept shooting first. But how did *she*, who did not even enjoy violent movies, get involved in this? She supposed the answer to that was simple enough: Italian bombs on an Albanian hillside, and an overwhelming desire to *do* something to retaliate. In that sense, she supposed, she was really no different to how Sophie herself might have been ten or fifteen years ago. She had accepted Clay Andrews' mission in that mood. But the mood had faded long before she had reached France. She would deliver his message, and then continue to

England. She would go and see the Wilcoxes, and explain what had happened, and then do everything she could to help them get Roberta out of Albania. She had meant what she had promised, that she would return for her friend, even if only as far as Greece. Instead of which she had found herself in the middle of a gun battle, and then been swept off her feet by the most marvellous woman she had ever met. And been kept off her feet ever since. Every step Sophie had taken had been logical and calculated, given she intended to deliver the guns Clay wanted, whatever the difficulties. And every step *she* had taken, at Sophie's behest, had also seemed perfectly logical. But the fact was that at Sophie's behest she had lied to her parents, that the Wilcoxes still did not know what had happened to their daughter, and that went for the parents of the boys, too, that she was rushing along like a blind woman, responding only to the stimuli afforded by Sophie . . . and loving every moment of it. Here was a freedom she had never expected to exist for any well brought-up young woman. To go to bed with a man she had only just met and didn't really like, but whose body she enjoyed. To travel all over Europe, feeling protected by the umbrella of Sophie's personality. And now to begin a great adventure . . . with death and destruction at the end of it?

"We need to add to that total the cost of two persons travelling from here to Holland," Catherine explained to the clerk in the bank. "That may involve at least one overnight stay."

"Of course. May I ask where in Holland is your destination?"

"I don't think Mrs Elligan would wish me to reveal that. Just allow enough for any eventualities."

"Quite so," he agreed, unruffled. "I will just make a calculation . . ." he did things with his calculator, winding the handle to and fro with great vigour. "Swiss francs for the hotel and the train fare, Dutch guilders once you reach Holland . . . and Mrs Elligan maintains her account in pounds sterling. All very complicated. Do you wish cash, or drafts?"

"I'd prefer cash."

"It will be quite a lot of money to carry around with you."

Catherine gave him a sweet smile. "I have a bodyguard."

Clay Andrews lay amidst the rocks high up on the hillside, and surveyed the slopes below him through his binoculars. After their initial bombardment, the Italians had concentrated for the first week or so on consolidating their hold on the towns and cities, on the communications systems and the harbours, while they poured more and more men into the country. They could now be said to be in total control of all of Albania that mattered – only the mountains of the south-east were left, and the invaders had hitherto shown no sign of wishing to probe into those treacherous fastnesses. Until today. Assembling on the road several hundred feet below Clay's position was a sizeable force. They even had guns, howitzers able to throw shells upwards for more than five miles, and as soon as they were ready, the planes would arrive, to harry the partisans from village to village, from position to position.

It was obvious that a pre-emptive strike was called for. Clay wanted to fight the bastards, but he could not do so on any scale until new guns and more ammunition and explosives arrived. Far better to lure patrols into the mountain recesses and cut them off. Very carefully he wriggled back into the shelter of the trees; he had no doubt the enemy were inspecting the hillsides through their glasses, and all morning reconnaissance planes had been soaring overhead. Once sure he was out of sight, he got up and resumed his climb to regain the encampment, passing on the way the communal herd of goats, with their attentive goatherd. They would have to go too. "Well?" Dino demanded, sitting on the slope and cleaning his rifle. The gold braid on his jerkin glinted in the sun.

"I think they are coming," Clay said.

"Good. Then we will kill a few."

"Not a good idea, if they kill more of us. They will have air support. We must withdraw to the higher ground, and hope they will attempt to follow."

"Withdraw," Dino growled. "Always withdraw. When do we fight?"

"When the guns and bullets arrive. We certainly don't have enough ammunition to sustain a battle right now."

"And when do these guns and bullets come, eh?"

"Soon, I hope." If he only knew. Catherine Ames had disappeared into the sunset and he had heard nothing further. It had been nearly a fortnight. If something had happened to her, or if

110

Sophie Elligan had turned her down flat . . . but in that case surely Walters would have been in touch? He went into the tent he had appropriated as his own, knelt beside the young woman. Roberta Wilcox was no longer sedated, simply because he had run out of the morphine he had been using. He knew she was in pain all the time, but she was being very brave.

As he was her only nurse, in every possible sense, and as she could do very little for herself, he felt he knew her better than any woman previously in his life – he had never really had the opportunity to *know* Sophie, even when they had crossed the Sahara together. But this girl, so small and so shattered . . . he had begun by feeling for her as a father might for his daughter. Now . . . he couldn't be sure. Her future remained too clouded for mental intimacy. His great fear had been the appearance of gangrene, and to fight against this he had bathed her thigh again and again in every antiseptic he could think of, including the last of his medicinal brandy. And so far the wound had remained clean. He moved the blanket and carefully unwrapped the bandage. She had not spoken when he came in. But the question was always there. "Getting better," he said cheerfully, changing the dressing. "One of these days we'll have the stitches out."

"When will I walk?" Her voice was quiet, and faint; she was still very weak from loss of blood.

"A few weeks. Not so long, really."

"Have you heard from Catherine?"

"No. But it's early days. Now listen, Roberta, you are going to have to be moved."

"Moved? I am going to Greece?" Her face lit up.

Clay sighed. "I'm afraid that's not on. It's a long way and you wouldn't stand it. No, the Italians are about to attack, and we are going to have to retreat." She was biting her lip to keep back the tears. "Who's a brave girl, then? I'll be with you all the time."

She caught his hand. "Am I going to make it, Mr Andrews?"

"Sure you are. Never lost a patient yet."

"If only I could tell my parents—"

"Catherine will be doing that, probably has done so. Who knows, they might even be able to interest the British Government in what is happening here. Now—" he turned his head as he heard a commotion outside, went out himself.

111

"A messenger," Dino said.

"From Greece," said someone else.

"Tell me." Clay surveyed the very travel-worn man who had crossed the mountains.

"It is from your embassy in Athens, Mr Andrews. Sent from France by a Mr Walters. It says, simply: Five, and then: Number. This is a question." He peered at Clay. "You understand this?"

"Yes. How soon can you return?"

"As soon as I have eaten and rested, Signor."

"Good man. Excuse me." He went back into the tent.

"Is it good news?" Roberta asked.

"The best." Clay knelt to open his satchel and take out his map. This was divided into small but neat squares, each numbered. He studied these for a few seconds, then returned to the people gathered outside. "My reply is seventeen."

"Seventeen," the man said. "Just seventeen?"

"Just seventeen. But I shall need local support. I also badly need a radio. Tell them this is urgent. Do not forget this."

"I shall not, Signor."

The shepherd was running up the hillside, his goats braying behind him. "Planes! Planes!"

They could see the biplanes soaring towards them. "You must get out now," Clay told the messenger. "Take some food and go. Deliver that message."

The Greek looked left and right, uncertainly. A woman threw a loaf of bread into his arms, another handed him a skin of water. Then they grabbed their children and began fleeing for the hoped-for safety of the rocky slopes.

"I am going to have to carry you," Clay told Roberta. "I had hoped to arrange some sort of litter, but there isn't time." He hastily repacked his maps and medicines, slung his knapsack, added hers, and bent over her. "It may be painful." He wrapped her in the blanket and she put her arms round his neck. He hefted her from the ground – she really was very light in her weakened condition – and smiled at her. "If you feel like screaming, go right ahead. Everyone else is."

Which was true enough as the Albanians shrieked their fear. But they had more knowledge now than to risk staying with their encampment as the planes came sweeping in, machine-guns chattering. Clay checked in the tent doorway as the aircraft made their first pass. Bombs drifted down and stone and rock flew in every direction. But the tent had not been hit. Then the planes were gone again, soaring upwards to turn and come back for a second run. Clay drew a deep breath and dashed across the open ground, past the next couple of tents, seeking the shelter of the trees and the hills beyond. He stumbled over rubble, and Roberta gasped in pain, then he regained his balance and ran a few steps before falling to the ground as the planes swooped low once again.

This time Roberta did cry out in agony as she struck the stony earth. Her arms were tight on Clay's shoulders, her fingers biting into his flesh. He kept his head down, his body shielding hers while the machine-guns chattered, until the noise slowly faded, as did the aircraft engines. Then he raised his head to grin at her.

"Okay?"

"Okay." But her face was twisted with pain.

It was Clay's turn to bite his lip. He did not know for how long she could stand this, and a quick look under the blanket told him her stitches had burst and her wound had opened again. And now he could hear whistles, and shouted words of command. The Italians were close behind their aircraft. He looked left and right. But the Albanians had all fled. Roberta had sized up the situation as well. "You must leave me."

"My dear girl—"

"Leave me, or you will be captured. You are these people's leader. You know where and when the guns are coming. You cannot afford to be taken."

"But you—"

"So the Italians will find me. I'm a non-combatant."

"They may not so regard you."

"I'll insist upon being taken to our consulate."

"You still have your passport?"

She opened her knapsack, which he had laid on the ground beside her, riffled through the contents. "Yes. I'll be all right, Mr Andrews. And I want you to know how grateful I am to you, for saving my life."

"Shit," he said. "Shit, shit, shit!!"

113

"Go," she commanded.

He hesitated a last time, then bent his head and kissed her on the forehead. "I'll be seeing you, Roberta Wilcox. When this is over."

"The very minute," she assured him.

He rose, looked back down the slope. Someone saw him and fired, then he was off, bending double, his bag and his rifle banging on his back. The Italians continued to blow their whistles, and several men came running up the slope, bayonets thrust forward. They almost stumbled over Roberta before they saw her, and for a moment, as she rolled onto her back, she thought she was going to be bayonetted. Or worse, because they now realised she was a woman, young and pretty. The blanket was torn away and they stared at her. They were young too, they were conscripts, and presumably none of them knew exactly why they were engaged in this war. But here perhaps were the first fruits of victory. Roberta closed her eyes and wondered what it would feel like. And heard a barked command.

She opened her eyes again and gazed at the sergeant, who was not a great deal older than his men, but a regular soldier, with a hard-bitten but not unkind face. "I'm English," she said, in Italian. "English. And I am dying."

He knelt beside her to look at the bandaged thigh; the bandage was soaked with blood. "No, no," he said. "You will not die, Signorina. We will not let you die."

Being carried down the hillside on a stretcher was excruciatingly painful, but they had not got very far before they encountered a medical unit, and an injection had Roberta drifting away into blessed unconsciousness. When she awoke it was to a feeling of incredulity, as she lay on a camp cot, beneath a clean white sheet, with a white-clad nurse standing by her head, checking the flow of blood into her arm from the bag hanging above her head. Roberta licked her lips. Never had she been so thirsty.

The nurse saw the movement and shut down the transfusion. A glass of water was brought for Roberta to drink, and she discovered she was wearing a blue hospital gown. "Please," she said. "Is there someone in authority?"

114

"He will come, soon enough." The nurse resumed the transfusion. "You have lost a lot of blood."

Once again, pain, but thanks to the sedatives she had been given, sufficiently dull to be bearable. She lay still, trying to work out where she was. In a room, certainly, and therefore in some sort of civilisation. She could hear the sound of car engines outside her opened window. She was also quite close to the sea, she thought, because the breeze coming in the window smelt of the sea. And there was no firing, no explosions, no screams, no clatter of collapsing hillsides. That was the greatest relief of all. Some broth was brought for her to drink, and with it a glass of wine. "Where am I?" she asked.

"Fier," the nurse replied.

They had cycled through Fier on that fateful Thursday, 7 April, before taking the high road into the mountains. How long ago that seemed. Had they stayed on the coast road they might all still be alive. "Are you Italian?" she asked.

"Albania is Italian," the nurse said with a smile.

Touché, Roberta thought. A doctor arrived. The sheets were turned back, her gown was turned up. Roberta closed her eyes, but opened them again as the doctor spoke. "This is a bad wound. How did you get it?"

"It was caused by a bomb splinter. From an Italian bomb."

His mouth twisted. "Bombs are terrible things. Who attended you?"

"One of the partisans."

"I do not think he had seen a wound like this before. You are lucky you have not lost the leg. Now——"

"You are not going to take my leg," Roberta shouted.

"Be calm. I do not think I will have to amputate. But you will have a scar." As if that was important, she thought. "You have also lost a lot of blood. But we are doing something about that."

"Listen," she said. "I am a British citizen. My passport is in my knapsack. I wish to contact the British Consulate in Tirana."

"That is not my concern." The doctor applied antiseptic to the wound, which made her jerk with the sharp pain. "You are a prisoner-of-war, Signorina Wilcox."

So he had looked at her passport. "I demand to see the British Consul."

He was bandaging her, quickly and expertly. "Regardless of the fact that you are a British citizen, Signorina, you were taken in battle with the insurgents. You were fighting with them."

"Fighting?" she cried. "We were running away. And how could I have been fighting? That wound is more than a week old. You can see that."

"It is a military matter. What is to be done with you. I will inform the commanding general of what you have said."

"Thank you." Roberta subsided. "May I see this general?"

"I am sure you will," the doctor said, replacing the sheet.

The Italians were clearly not using morphine as a sedative, Roberta realised, for where over the past fortnight she had hardly known reality, her drugged semi-consciousness a mass of frightening images, today her brain felt quite clear. Had she really lain in an Albanian village for a fortnight? For the most part naked from the waist down, surrounded by men as well as women and children and goats and dogs and chickens? Her only coherent memory was of their kindness.

But that could also be said of the people who had blown her up in the first place. Now the nurses were clustering round her bed – hers was the only bed in the small ward, whether because she was a woman in a man's war or because she was a prisoner she couldn't be sure – to give her a bedbath. How good it felt actually to be clean again. Then she was dressed in a fresh gown, and tenderly laid back on her pillows, and it was time for more blood. They were pumping strength back into her body, for what purpose? Clay had said they were inclined to shoot prisoners out of hand. Were they so determined she would be able to stand against the wall, or the post, or whatever method they used?

Clarity of thought brought the enormity of her situation back to her in the fullest force. Quite apart from the possibility of being shot. The boys were already dead. All they had been doing was enjoying themselves. And Catherine . . . Catherine had gone off. Roberta could understand that, which did not stop her resenting it. Catherine had promised to come back, with help. That would not do her much good now. And Mummy and Daddy would not even know what had happened to her. Supposing Catherine had got out, and visited them, all they would ever know was that their daughter was probably lying in an unmarked grave on an Albanian hillside. Which could well be true. Tears trickled out from her eyes, and the nurse seated beside her bed started up in alarm. "It is not so bad." She wiped away the moisture. "We are kind people, Signorina."

"I know. Thank you. But you will still shoot me."

"Shoot you?" The nurse's attractive little face screwed itself up into a ball. "Those people you fight with, the partisans, are very wicked."

Roberta almost smiled. "That's what they think of you."

"When they capture our people, they torture them," the nurse pointed out. Roberta didn't believe that. Such things were caught up in her morphine-induced nightmares. "You cannot blame our people for being angry," the nurse explained.

"Then you cannot blame me for being angry too."

The nurse looked puzzled, then stood to attention as the door opened. "The General has come," she said.

Edio took the chair by the bed, handing his cap and swagger stick to the waiting woman. He was carrying a clipboard, and this he laid on his lap. Only when he was settled did he look at the woman on the bed, who had been staring at him since his entry. He saw a very young, extremely pretty woman. Her cheeks were pale from loss of blood, and her face was gaunt from privation, but she would fill back out. She was the last person he had wanted to see. Although a professional soldier all of this life, he did not care for the underside of warfare, the taking and inter- rogation of prisoners. As with leading his men into battle, it was a duty, which he carried out professionally. He had even devised his own method of getting it over as quickly as possible, as with the two Albanian prisoners who had first told him Andrews was in the mountains. But he had not anticipated ever having as a prisoner an extremely attractive girl who also happened to be British.

But he had never shirked his duty, however unpleasant. "I understand you speak Italian," he glanced down at his clipboard, "Signorina Wilcox."

"Yes," Roberta said, breathlessly. Her instincts told her that this man had the power of life and death over her.

117

"You understand the seriousness of your position?"

She was not going to give up without a fight. "No. I was on holiday with my friends when the invasion started. Two of my friends were killed in the first bombing raid and I was badly wounded. The people in the mountains cared for me. Their intention was to evacuate me to Greece as soon as I could walk. But we were overrun by your people . . . yesterday?"

He nodded. "Yesterday. Why did the partisans care for you?"

"I suppose because they are kind people."

Edio looked sceptical. "Do you know a man named Clayton Andrews?" Roberta gazed at him. "You must answer my questions, truthfully. Was it not Andrews who persuaded the partisans to care for you? There is no use in your attempting to lie about this, Signorina Wilcox. We know Andrews is fighting with those people."

"Mr Andrews took out the shrapnel and bound up the wound," Roberta said.

"Because he is a kind person? Or because your other friend, the one you have not yet mentioned, Catherine Ames, was undertaking a mission for him?" Roberta took a sharp breath. "Quite," Edio said. "Now, we do not know whether Signorina Ames succeeded in her mission, but I can tell you that she has become involved in some very dramatic circumstances, including several deaths."

"Is she all right?"

"She may well be. But if she is, she has become associated with some very dangerous people. Now, you know what her mission was, I think."

"No," Roberta said.

"It is very unwise of you to lie to me, Signorina. *We* know what her mission was. It was to contact a certain arms dealer in France, with a view to supplying the partisans here in Albania with munitions. And we are fairly certain that she did complete her mission, and that the purchase and delivery of these arms is in progress. You will understand that we do not wish this to happen. Indeed, we cannot allow it to happen."

"I can see that."

"So, for the past fortnight you have been in the care of Signor

118

Andrews. You must know all of the comings and goings in and out of the partisan encampment—" he paused, expectantly.

"I'm sorry. He kept me drugged most of the time, to relieve the pain."

"But you could still see, and hear. Tell me about yesterday."

"Yesterday? You attacked us."

"We did. However, before we attacked you, our reconnaissance aircraft flew over the area, several times, as far as the Greek border. One of them reported seeing a man using one of the mountain trails from Greece towards the partisan headquarters. It is my opinion that this man was a messenger, from someone in Greece, to Andrews. Am I right?"

"I wouldn't know," Roberta said.

"Tell me of this man, who came to your village yesterday morning."

"I know of no man. I only know of your attack. Mr Andrews tried to move me with the others, but I was in too much pain, so he was forced to leave me. Now, please, I would like to see the British Consul."

Edio regarded her for several seconds. "What was the first thing I said to you, when I came in?"

"You asked me if I understood the seriousness of my position."

"I will ask you that again. Do you understand the seriousness of your position?"

"I understand that you have no legal right to hold me, Signor General."

"There you are mistaken. Let me give you one or two facts. The Government of Albania has fled the country. The rump government that remains has surrendered unconditionally to Italian arms. That is to say, Albania is now a province of Italy. That means that anyone, be he a soldier or a civilian, who does not adhere to the surrender of his government is an outlaw, and may be treated as an outlaw. This applies equally to those who give such outlaws food or shelter, or who elect to share their lives with them."

"I did not elect to do anything," Roberta snapped. "I was wounded. I had no choice but to stay with them."

"That is your story, and obviously it is the story you would

119

tell. But the fact is that you were with the partisans when you were wounded, is that not correct? And now you have been captured still in the company of armed rebels who have been killing my men. The British Consul cannot interfere. Indeed, he need not even be informed of your existence, until and unless we are ready to do so."

Roberta was panting. "So you mean to shoot me."

"I would like to help you. I can help you. I can hand you over to the British Consul. But first, you must help me, to extirpate these vicious outlaws. We know that a messenger came to your camp yesterday, shortly before we began our attack. He came to see Andrews, and you were there, in Andrews' care. I wish you to tell me what the messenger said."

"I do not know what he said."

"You are lying, Signorina Wilcox."

"I do not *know*." Once again her weakness and her frustrated anger at her situation made her weep.

Edio leaned forward so that his face was close to hers. "I think that messenger brought information about the arms' shipment. That information would have been times, and places, and dates. This information I must have, Signorina."

"I don't know," Roberta shouted.

Edio sighed. "There are men downstairs now who wish to speak with you. These men are not soldiers. They are intelligence officers. They have no sense of . . . shall I say, honour, when dealing with a prisoner. If you will not give me the information I need when I have asked for it in a civilised manner, I will have to allow those men to ask the same questions. They do not have a civilised manner. Please, Signorina, tell me what the messenger said, and I swear to you that you will be on a ship home to England in a week."

"I do not know!" Roberta screamed.

Sophie and Dennis Overcamp strolled along the beach on Terschelling's outer shore. Here they looked at the North Sea, over which clouds were gathering and a fresh breeze was whipping the waves into white caps. Sophie was hatless and her still short hair was rippling like the sea itself; she had washed out the last of the dye and was now again entirely auburn. Dennis had his captain's cap pulled well down over his eyes to stop it blowing off. They had spent the morning shopping, stocking up the *boier* with sufficient food to last them more than a month. Then they had lunched well. Walking on the beach was pleasantly relaxing. But only briefly. "What time is the ferry?" Sophie asked.

"It gets here about five. Think they'll have made it?"

"I can't see any reason why not," Sophie said, thrusting her hands into the pockets of her windcheater.

"I hope they do. The sooner we're out of here the better."

"Are you bothered about the weather?"

"No, no. *Christina* can take anything the North Sea can throw at her, and I'm not expecting a blow, anyway. But I wouldn't like any German agents to find us."

"Would they be looking here?"

"They know I'd have to put in somewhere along this coast to fuel up, and it's not very likely I'd risk Den Helder."

"Why not?"

"It's a Dutch naval base. Full of people liable to ask questions."

"You're assuming they have a reason to look for you in the first place."

"Well, by now they'll have figured out that you and Captain Pfuhl are no longer in Germany. And neither am I. Those guys don't believe in coincidences." He glanced at her. "That bother you?"

"That is one of the least things I have to bother about."

"Like I said before, you're some woman." He was the perfect gentleman, had made no attempt to get too close to her. He could turn out to be an absolute treasure – if he could stand up to the real pressure, when it began. But he was also human, and curious. "How'd you get into this business, anyway?"

"I was born into it."

"Come again?"

"My family have been arms' manufacturers for three generations. When you manufacture arms, it follows that you also need to sell them. Sometimes you can do so legitimately, other times you have to do it clandestinely. Once you get into the delivery side of the clandestine business, you become a gun-runner. My husband and I operated quite successfully for a few years."

"And he's on his way to join you now."

"That's right. With my assistant." She stopped walking, turned to face him. "I should tell you, Captain Overcamp, that my husband and I are separated, and have been for some years."

"But you still do business together."

"When necessary, yes."

They resumed walking while he considered what she had just said. "So I guess you want separate cabins. I have only three cabins, aft."

"My husband will share with Captain Pfuhl. Miss Ames will share with me. Tell me, is there a Mrs Overcamp?"

He gave one of his easy grins, and led her up the ramp onto the wall, from where they could overlook the Waddenzee, and the distant shoreline of the mainland. "There was. But one day she up and left me."

"I'm sorry. Did you ill-treat her?"

"I don't reckon so. I just wasn't making it fast enough, and she found someone who was." He pointed. "There's the ferry."

Sophie and Catherine embraced. "Am I glad to see you," Catherine said.

"Problems?"

"None we hadn't anticipated. But I've brought him here."

"Don't I get a hug and a kiss too?" Richard asked.

"No," Sophie said. "This is Captain Overcamp."

Both Catherine and Richard did a double take, but for different reasons; Sophie reckoned Catherine liked what she saw, Richard didn't. "Welcome aboard," Dennis said. "My ship's over here."

Another double take. "That's a canal craft," Richard objected.

"She can keep the sea," Dennis said easily. "Especially when she's well loaded."

Richard looked at Sophie. "He know what it's about?"

"Of course. And he'll get us there. You remember Captain Pfuhl?"

Richard shook hands. "There's a relief. For a moment I thought we were in the hands of this nigger."

"You are," Pfuhl told him. "I'm strictly a supernumerary."

"This is something." Catherine was inspecting the saloon. "All mod cons."

"Nearly." Dennis carried her bag into the third cabin. "You have to share the heads."

"That's not a problem." Catherine held out her hand. "I'm Catherine."

He squeezed her fingers. "Dennis."

"Neat," Richard remarked, placing his bag in the second cabin. "It's a long time since you and I shared a cabin."

"A very long time," Sophie agreed. "And we are not going to share one now. You'll have Captain Pfuhl in here with you."

"What the shit—"

"You'd not expect Catherine to share with Pfuhl, would you? Even if I suspect the old dear is past it. And certainly not with you. I gather you've been making a nuisance of yourself."

"While you have been shacking up with a darkie."

"Your racism is showing."

"Just how did you get involved with something like that, anyway?"

"Something like that saved my life, and is prepared to go the distance with us. And if you are rude to him, Richard Elligan, I will let him duff you up."

Richard grinned. "But you need me, darling."

"Not after we pick up the cargo, darling." She suspected it might be a stormy cruise.

They put out that afternoon, into a lumpy sea. But they were all good sailors, and *Christina* proved a sturdy seaboat, even if she had a tendency to wallow. "We have about nine days to play with," Sophie said after dinner, wrapped up in her windcheater and wearing a headscarf, standing beside Dennis as he took the helm. "But I'd like to get there in eight."

"Point taken. That shouldn't be a problem."

"What is your watch rota?"

"I've a crew of three, including me. So it's four hours on and eight off, round the clock."

Sophie watched the afterglow of the sunset, varying light and dark as the clouds scudded across the horizon. "Can't Captain Pfuhl help?"

"I reckon he's a bit old for a four-hour watch. Anyway, you're the passengers. I'm on charter, right?" The bows dipped, and water came over the bows; some spray rattled aft. "It's gonna be a wet night. You'd better go down, Mrs Elligan."

"I'm happy where I am, Captain, for the time being."

He glanced at her. "Where'd you pick up the young lady?"

"She's an agent for the man to whom we're delivering."

"Is that a fact. Doesn't quite look the part."

"Do I?"

They gazed at each other, and he grinned. "No, I guess you don't, Mrs Elligan. You belong in a first-class lounge, wearing a dinner dress. You always wear your hair that short?"

"This is the first time."

"The Nazis get to you?"

"I got to myself. It was necessary. I think you should know that I am wanted by the French police. So is Miss Ames."

"As well as the Gestapo? Like they said, you're a dangerous woman." But he spoke admiringly. And at least he hadn't asked her for what she was wanted, by the French.

Catherine was already in the upper bunk, rolling to and fro with the ship. Sophie observed that she had so far followed fashion as to be naked. "Why don't you wedge yourself?"

"I like the movement. It's sort of . . . you know."

"I would have thought you'd had enough of that," Sophie said, getting into the lower bunk and drawing the covers to her throat; it wasn't cold, but the movement and whine of the wind in the rigging and the slapping of the waves against the hull increased the need for security.

"I think I'm growing into it," Catherine said. "Where on earth did you find that gorgeous hunk of man?"

"He's married. Sort of. And whatever would your parents say if you brought him home to dinner?"

Catherine giggled. "You know what? I can't sleep. Excited, I suppose. I think I'll take a turn on deck."

Sophie watched those very long and shapely legs sliding past her nose as they reached for the deck. "At least put on a pair of knickers."

*   *   *

124

"Hi." Catherine emerged from the hatchway.

"Hi." Dennis did not appear either surprised or concerned to see her. She had in fact fully dressed herself and put on her coat; with the daylight gone it was quite chilly on deck. But utterly romantic, with the white foam hissing away from the bows and steaming aft, and the clouds scudding across a starlit sky, low above the masthead.

She moved to stand beside him. "Oh, for a something and a something to steer her by," she said.

"You mean, *I must go down to the seas again, to the lonely sea and the sky, And all I ask is a tall ship and a star to steer her by, And the wheel's kick and the wind's song and the white sail's shaking, And a grey mist on the sea's face and a grey dawn breaking.* Masefield."

"Gosh," Catherine said.

"It goes on for a long time."

"And you know it all by heart?"

"Just about."

"Gosh," she said again.

"Why does that surprise you so much?"

"Well—" she was grateful to the darkness for hiding her blush.

"Black men don't study poetry where you come from, right?"

"I never said that."

"Keep your shirt on. I said that. Now you answer one: what's a nice girl like you doing on a trip like this?"

"Hasn't Sophie told you? Or maybe you didn't ask."

He turned his head to look at her for the first time. "I asked, Miss Ames. She said you're the agent for the guy we're delivering for. Doesn't quite fit."

"I was with some friends in Albania when the Italians invaded. Two of them were killed in the bombing, and the other one was badly wounded. She's still there, with the partisans. So . . . I suppose I wanted to *do* something. Can you understand that?"

"Sure."

"So when this man asked me to carry a message to Mrs Elligan, to arrange a cargo of arms and ammunition for the partisans, I said I'd do it. I didn't really mean to get involved, personally. But . . . Sophie's a difficult woman from whom to get uninvolved, if you follow me."

125

"I do. You lovers?"

He had been staring ahead, at the compass and beyond. Catherine turned her head sharply. "Whatever makes you think that?"

"Observations." He grinned. "Seamen are trained to observe. Sometimes it's a matter of life and death."

"Would you be disappointed if I said we were lovers?"

"Sure. It's an evocative thought, but kind of wasteful. I'd like it better if you were into men."

"Maybe I haven't met the right man."

He glanced at her. "Not even one of those friends in Albania?"

"They were friends. So I was very angry and upset when they were killed."

"I can imagine." He watched the seaman coming aft along the deck. "My watch is up, and I am going to bed." Another grin. "Alone. I suggest you do the same thing, Miss Ames."

"You could at least call me Catherine."

"Catherine. I like that. Catherine."

"May we talk again, tomorrow?"

"Sure. When you've slept on it. And thought about it." He drew his finger down the side of her cheek. "And maybe even asked permission from the boss."

Guns

The man on the telephone said, "The *boier Christina* spent two days in West Terschelling harbour, and sailed yesterday afternoon, Herr Eisener."

"Two days? And no effort was made to stop her?"

"We had no orders to that effect, Herr Eisener. In any event, we did not discover her whereabouts until yesterday morning, and she sailed a few hours later. It would have been difficult to attempt anything without alarming the Dutch authorities."

"Two days," Eisener muttered. "She could have been loading guns."

"Not in Terschelling, Herr Eisener. It is a small, intimate, fishing and tourist resort, and an island. The guns would first have had to be transported from the mainland, and the authorities would never have permitted it."

"And where has she gone now?"

"She cleared for Le Havre, Herr Eisener. She is on charter to an English group, and indeed two people joined her just before she sailed. But my agent in Terschelling is sure that one of those already on board was Frau Elligan."

"Le Havre. Who have we there?"

"I do not think that is her actual destination, Herr Eisener. It is necessary to have one to clear port, but yachts do not take this seriously. As you may know, she cleared Cuxhaven for Den Helder, and put into Terschelling instead."

"But it will be necessary for them to put in somewhere, is that not so?"

"I wouldn't guarantee it, sir. A ship like *Christina* is capable of keeping the sea for some considerable time."

"This operation has been botched from start to finish,"

Eisener complained. "You have let the Elligan woman slip through your fingers, and now she has disappeared."

"Well, sir," the Gestapo agent said, "it is not possible for a ship absolutely to disappear, certainly in the narrow waters she will be using, if your estimation of her ultimate destination is correct. We will have a watch kept in the Straits of Dover, and we will also have a watch kept off Gibraltar. That is a very narrow passage, and we have a sizeable presence in Tangiers. Our people will base themselves on Ceuta, and monitor all shipping entering the Mediterranean. I estimate she will be passing through there in about ten days."

"You have made no allowance for her having to stop, somewhere, to pick up her cargo," Eisener pointed out.

"No matter how long it takes, we shall be waiting for her. What are your orders, Herr Eisener? Are we to seize her?"

"Can you do that?"

"Oh, we *can*, sir. But it would be piracy on the high seas."

"Even if she is carrying guns?"

"Merely carrying guns is not in itself a crime, Herr Eisener. And the vessel is at present flying the Dutch flag. We have no right to stop and search any vessel outside our own territorial waters."

"But you say it could be done. Have we any naval units in the Mediterranean?"

"No, sir. And even if we did, I very much doubt Admiral Raeder would give us permission to use them where it might cause an international incident. However, our people in the Mediterranean have the use of fast motorboats. It would not be difficult to overhaul a sailing ship. In that event, of course, the ship would have to disappear without trace. Also its passengers and crew."

Eisener stroked his chin. He was getting into deeper water with every minute. Pemberton had merely asked that Sophie Elligan be prevented from obtaining a ship. It had been his decision to raise the matter to a higher plane. But when he had done that, he had assumed the Gestapo would merely pick up the wretched woman in Hamburg and deal with her there, or at least put her off gun-running for the rest of her life. It had simply never occurred to him that a woman would shoot her way out of trouble. On the other hand . . . he picked up and read again the newspaper that was lying on his desk. Sophie Elligan appeared to make a habit of shooting her way out of trouble, with deadly accuracy. If only he had had this report available a few days ago. "Very good, Eichmann," he told the agent. "I will make a decision on what to do about this Dutch yacht in a few days' time. But keep me informed as to her whereabouts, and have your people in the Mediterranean standing by."

He hung up, and then picked up the phone again. The *boier* might well be able to keep the sea for a considerable time, but she would have to put in somewhere, some time, even if it was not until after she had delivered the guns. The French certainly maintained a naval presence in the Mediterranean, and now they were looking for a mass murderess. "I would like to speak with the Chief of Police in Marseilles," he said.

Roberta Wilcox blinked at the two men who had just entered her ward. She did not like the look of either of them, and she liked the look of the little black bag one of them was carrying even less. Additionally, Dr Pizzoli had started to reduce the sedative doses, and she was in some discomfort. The nurse also apparently did not like the look of the men; she stood by the head of the bed, protectively. "You may go," said the first man, a little fellow with a moustache.

"I am required to stay with the patient," Angelica said.

"And I have said you will go, Signorina."

Angelica looked at Roberta. "They're afraid I may say something you shouldn't hear," Roberta said, attempting humour.

Angelica left the room, and the second man carefully closed the door. The little man pulled up the chair and sat beside the bed; the second man stood at the foot, staring at Roberta. "How are you feeling today?" asked the little man.

"I hurt."

"But your strength is coming back? You are eating normally?"

"Yes, thank you." She could feel her muscles tensing; he was being too polite, too interested in her welfare.

"That is good. Do you know who I am? I am a captain in the military police. My name is Rodrigo. You will call me Rodrigo, and I will call your Roberta, and we will be friends. Would you not like to be my friend?"

"If you are a soldier, why are you not in uniform?"

"Because I belong to a special branch of the military police. That dealing with the extraction of information from prisoners-of-war."

129

"I am not a prisoner-of-war," Roberta snapped. "I demand to see the British Consul."

"The British Consul does not know you exist. And I doubt he would be interested if he did. Because, you see, you are quite right; you are not a prisoner-of-war. Albania is now a part of the Italian Empire. There is no war. What we are engaged in doing is eliminating certain outlaw bands. Those people have no rights under the Geneva Convention. And you were fighting with them. Therefore *you* have no rights under the Geneva Convention."

Roberta was commencing to pant; she was beginning to be more afraid than angry. "I was not fighting with them. I have never fired a gun in my life. I have never even held a gun in my life."

"Those who give aid and comfort to outlaws are themselves outlaws," Rodrigo pointed out. "That is the law. Admit that you are the mistress of the man Andrews."

"Oh, for God's sake. That is so absurd it is childish. His mistress? He has only ever known me in a state of collapse. And he is old enough to be my father."

Rodrigo looked puzzled, as if he did not see what that had to do with it. "We know your friend, Signorina Ames, is working for him."

"You have news of Catherine?"

"Only that she is wanted for murder."

"Catherine? Murder? You have got to be joking. Catherine wouldn't hurt a fly."

"You may think so. She appears to have hurt a great many flies, over the past few days. Including some of our own people. This makes us very angry." He gestured at his assistant, and the man came forward, and very deliberately pulled the sheet out of Roberta's grasp and down to the bottom of the bed. Roberta stared at them both, while again tensing her muscles to resist pain. "Now let me see this wound of yours." Rodrigo pulled the skirt of her bedgown above her waist.

Roberta didn't see the point in attempting to resist him, closed her eyes as he gave her pubes a gentle stroke. "I shall report this to the Consul," she muttered.

"Of course. When you see the Consul. *If* you see the the Consul, ha ha. That is a nasty wound. Let me look at it." His assistant unbandaged the wound. It was properly stitched closed now, but the flesh around it was still inflamed. "Hm. I am not sure this has been properly treated. I am surprised gangrene has not set in. Do you know what I think needs to be done, Signorina? I think the wound should be opened, and a massive antiseptic used. I think iodine should be poured into it." Roberta screamed. She had not meant to, but the thought of that . . . "Hush girl," Rodrigo said. "That is only an opinion. But of course, if it was to be mistaken opinion, then I suppose the leg would have to come off." Roberta had run out of breath, and lay there, gasping, hating herself for having to inflate her belly before the two men. "That would be a very sad business," Rodrigo said. "A pretty girl like you, with all her life in front of her, hobbling around on one leg, I think it would be very difficult for such an unfortunate woman ever to find herself a husband, and have children, and live a happy life."

"You bastard," Roberta shouted. "You—"

Rodrigo laid his finger across her lips, and hastily took it away again as she snapped at him. "That is no way for a young lady to behave. And I'm sure we can save the leg. Our doctors are very good. All that is required is for you to answer one or two questions."

Roberta continued to pant, terribly aware of the men's gaze. "So," Rodrigo said. "We know that you know two things. One is the date of the arrival of the goods for which Signor Andrews is waiting. The second is where they will be landed."

"What I know will do you no good," Roberta gasped. "Mr Andrews has a map, which is divided into squares. I am sure the people bringing the goods have an exactly similar map, divided into matching squares. All he had to do was give them the number of a square, and they would know where to go to be met."

"I see. And he gave them such a number." Roberta stared at him. "You have just admitted this, Signorina." Roberta licked her lips. "And you have just admitted that telling us this number will not help us. I agree with you. But I would still to know this number."

Roberta clamped her lips shut. If they had somehow got hold of a matching map . . . "You are a very silly girl," Rodrigo said. "Do you really think it is being brave, being loyal, to condemn a lot of people to death? Because that is what you are doing, you know. Without guns, without the promise of support from the outside world, these bandits will soon surrender. Once they have surrendered, they can be pardoned, and resume their lives as

131

members of a civilised community. If they do not surrender, they will be hunted down and killed. All of them. Men, women and children. Dogs and goats and chickens. Do you really want that to happen? Oh, I agree, if they manage to obtain some guns and ammunition, some Italian soldiers will be killed as well. Those deaths will also be on your conscience, Signorina."

"And Signor Andrews?"

"Well, he is a foreign national, is he not? If he surrenders, he will be deported."

"And the people bringing the guns?"

Rodrigo shrugged. "They are breaking the law, and will have to be dealt with as criminals. But they will have the opportunity to defend themselves in a court of law. What can be more fair than that?"

"I do not believe you. You will kill them all."

Rodrigo gazed at her for several seconds, then rested his hand on her good thigh, and moved it up and down, gently, from the knee to where he could touch her pubic hair, and back again. Roberta fought to keep herself from trembling, unsuccessfully. "Such a pretty girl. But . . . we must do the best we can. Very well, Signorina. As I have said, I think it will be necessary to look again at your wound. To take stronger measures, eh? But before we do that, I think it will be necessary to make sure your bowels are in good shape, eh? Alexandro."

Alexandro opened the bag and took out a bottle. "You may find this unpleasant," Rodrigo said. "It is very strong. But it will be good for you. Of course, in your weakened condition you may find it debilitating—"

Alexandro uncorked the bottle, and Roberta inhaled the pungent odour of the castor oil. "No," she said.

"You may stop us any moment you wish," Rodrigo said.

Alexandro advanced up the other side of the bed, the bottle in one hand, a metal cup in the other. "No!" Roberta shouted, and tried to push herself up the bed. Rodrigo got up and grasped her arms, one in each hand, pinning her to the mattress. Alexandro carefully half-filled the cup, then put the bottle on the floor. With his free hand he grasped Roberta's face, driving his fingers into her cheeks to force her lips and teeth apart. He grinned at her, as he held the cup to pour.

"What are you doing?" Both men turned, to look at Dr Pizzoli, standing in the doorway like an avenging angel, Angelica beside him. Roberta wanted to scream again, with relief. Thank God for Angelica.

"We are going to give the young lady a laxative," Rodrigo explained, unconcerned at the interruption. "I am sure it will be good for her."

"In her condition? You will kill her."

"I am sure you are mistaken, Doctor. Be a good fellow and take yourself off."

"No," Pizzoli said. "You take yourselves off. Both of you." Rodrigo glared at him. "Do you think you can give me orders?"

"Yes," Pizzoli said. "This is my hospital. I give the orders here. Release that woman, and leave this hospital."

Slowly Rodrigo released Roberta and straightened. "I have the power to have you arrested."

"Then exercise that power, Captain, and then inform our superiors why our wounded are not being properly treated."

Again Rodrigo glared at him for several seconds. "I also have the power to remove this young woman, whether you like it or not."

"No, Captain," Pizzoli said. "You do not have that power. Only your superiors can give you that power. Show me an order from them, and I will release the prisoner into your care."

"Ah." Rodrigo smiled. "Well, then, there is no problem. My aide will remain here while I obtain the necessary order."

"Your aide will not remain here, Captain. He will accompany you out of my hospital."

Rodrigo pointed. "I will make a full report of this, Doctor. It will reach General Graziani himself."

"Then no doubt I shall hear from General Graziani, himself." Another glare from Rodrigo, then he beckoned Alexandro and left the room. "Thugs," Pizzoli remarked.

"Will you not get into deep trouble?" Roberta asked.

"Perhaps. I will have a defence." He grinned. "We will share a defence. Will you trust me?"

"Yes," Roberta said. Do I have a choice? she wondered.

"Then this is what we shall do."

Sophie enjoyed the sensation of being at sea for several days. But she hated being entirely cut off from what was happening in the rest of the world; Captain Pfuhl's steamer had always had a radio. Now she stood at the rail as *Christina* ploughed her way west through still lumpy seas, and gazed at the hills of Cornwall. The land was some ten miles away, as Dennis was determined to stay out of any territorial waters where he could legitimately be stopped and questioned, but it was an enormous temptation to put into port, if only for an hour, to pick up a newspaper.

She knew that Albania had officially surrendered, but she also knew that various guerilla groups were holding out in the mountains of the south-east; she had to assume those groups included Clay Andrews and his people. But that they were there would be confirmed when they reached Clew Bay and contacted this man Gannon. She would also have liked to know how far the French were getting in their investigation into the Le Pouget Massacre, as the report she had read in a newspaper in Terschelling was calling it. But at least she was beyond their reach out here.

Not that she lacked problems, even out here. Richard was indulging in an enormous sulk; she wouldn't put it past him to act the fool instead of Ned Carew when they reached the rendezvous. But that would be cutting off his nose to spite his face, and he had to know that she was not a forgiving woman. Catherine was a greater source of concern. The girl was behaving magnificently, in her acceptance of the situation, of the bizarre twist her life had taken just by going for a bicycle ride. But of course there was a downside. Catherine had lived a very sheltered life up to a fortnight ago. The shelter had come less from physical protection, although rural England had to be about the most civilised place in Europe, than from her own inhibitions, her upbringing, which had insisted that there were some things a well-brought-up young woman did not do.

Now for that fortnight she had been forced to break every rule in her book. Having never seen a death before 7 April, she had now witnessed at least one death for every day of her life. Having never broken a law in her life, she was now an accessory to murder. Having always moved in carefully regulated directions, she had spent the fortnight roaming Europe as a fugitive. Having been chaste all of her life, she had been forced to share her bed with a man. The only two things she had not done were the ultimates: she had never personally killed anybody, and she had not yielded her virginity. But she was intelligent enough to understand that the

134

operative word in both those considerations was "yet". Small wonder that, the lid of her Pandora's box having been so suddenly and so violently lifted, she had emerged as an eager volcano of smouldering passion. Which was currently directed at Dennis Overcamp. As he was well aware. Sophie wondered why he had not yet done anything about it? Because he was unsure how it would turn out? Because he was so much older than the girl? Because of the colour question? Or because of *her*, whether that reason was because he was afraid of her or wanted her rather than an immature virgin? Or simply because he was the complete gentleman? Sophie had not met enough of those to be sure.

But she was afraid for the girl if things got out of hand. She had nothing against interracial relationships. But a great many people did. And from what Catherine had told her, her parents would. So, should she care? Her business was to deliver the goods and thereby help to avenge Ned, and to make as much profit as possible, and then . . . become a mother. She gave her stomach a gentle rub. Whatever was in there was too small to be affected by all this, yet. At least she hoped so. But it was something to which she intended to devote the rest of her life.

Dennis stood at Sophie's shoulder, offering her his binoculars. "Look on the port quarter."

Sophie levelled the glasses, and made out a grey shape, coming and going through the light haze. "I would say that's a destroyer."

"I would say you're right. Royal Navy."

"Is that important?"

"Only that he's been there now for two days."

Sophie levelled the binoculars again. "Are you sure?"

"Either him or a sister."

"And you didn't tell me?"

"I didn't see any point in bothering you until I was dead sure he was tracking us. Now I am. So, what would you like to do about it?"

"You think he knows where we're going?"

"No, ma'am. If he knew where we were going, he'd be there waiting for us. He's trying to find *out* where we're going, and then he probably means to nab us the moment we've loaded the goods."

"Has he a legal right to do that?"

135

"I don't know what his rights are in Irish waters. It's independent, isn't it?"

"It has a sort of dominion status," Sophie said. "I don't know the legalities of that either. Usually the dominion governments go along with the UK on just about everything, but Ireland could be different. They hate the British, for a start."

"So you're for standing on."

"I don't see what else we can do. We'll have to take advice from Gannon."

He grinned. "And hope to sneak back out. Clew Bay is a big area. With a bit of poor visibility it could be done."

"But won't a destroyer be able to catch up with us again? It's a lot faster."

"Even the Royal Navy doesn't have the right to stop a Dutch yacht on the high seas, ma'am, at least in peacetime. Once we're outside the three-mile limit he can look but not touch."

Dennis went below to check his charts and enter his position in the Log. Catherine sat beside him. "How do you know where we are?"

Dennis was using his dividers and slide rule, with expert ease. "At the moment I'm using what's called Dead Reckoning. I lay off from our last positive position, using our speed through the water, and allowing for tide and drift, to give me the speed over the ground, and there we are."

"It doesn't sound very accurate to me. You said our last positive position. How did you obtain that?"

"There are two sources. One is when you're in sight of land, as we still are. It's called a running fix. You take a bearing on a prominent known object, like say a headland, and you draw a line out to sea on the chart on that bearing. Then an hour later you take another bearing on the same object, and draw another line, and where the two lines cross is where you are. The second way is at sea, when you use a sextant to take the height of the sun, which gives you your latitude, and enter that in conjunction with your nautical tables, which give you your longitude. Of course you have to have a very accurate clock, which they call a chronometer."

"Which you have, of course. But supposing it's misty, and you can't see the land or the sun?"

"Then you're dependent on Dead Reckoning. It really is very accurate if you have good tide tables. And that clock."

"How come you know all this?"

"I have a master's ticket."

"Wowee. So, when do we arrive at our rendezvous?"

"Midnight four days' time, all things being equal."

"Aren't they?"

"We're being shadowed by the Royal Navy."

"Heck! You mean we're going to be stopped? Arrested?"

"Not until after we've picked up the guns. Then it's up to us to give them the slip and get back to international waters. You mean you wouldn't like to be stopped?"

"No. We can't be stopped."

He put down his dividers and made a mark on the chart. "Because of this guy Andrews?"

"Why does everyone suppose I have something going for Clay Andrews? The man is old enough to be my father. And he was not the least bit interested in me."

"Yet you took on this hazardous mission for him. There has to be a reason."

"There are two reasons. No, three. One is that he saved my life. The second is that I wanted to hit back at the Italians for killing two of my friends. The third is that I have to get back, and deliver the guns, to get my friend Roberta out of there."

Dennis nodded. "Sounds reasonable. So you don't go for guys old enough to be your father."

She shot him a quick glance. "Meaning what?"

He shrugged. "I'm thirty-five."

"Then you'd have had to start very young."

He grinned. "Maybe I did."

"Ireland," the commander said.

"That sounds right," Pemberton agreed.

"We don't know where, as yet, but they have rounded Fastnet, so we imagine it's somewhere on the west coast. Are our orders unchanged?"

"Surveillance only."

"There are a great number of bays and inlets on the west coast

137

of Ireland," the commander said. "Into which our people have no right to go without permission. We could lose her."

"I think you can let her get on with it," Pemberton said. "We know that when she's got the goods she'll be making for the Med. You can pick her up again then, if we decide that is necessary. The last thing we want now is a problem with the Free State Government."

"Wilco," the commander said.

"I have some items for you, sir," said the secretary, and laid the sheaf of papers on the desk.

There was a covering note. *You asked to see anything coming out of Albania.* Pemberton turned over the first page. *Report from our Consul in Tirana. It has just been released by the Italians that two British subjects were killed in the fighting following the "police action" in Albania. They have been named as Peter Bentley and Alan Chambers, who died during a bombing raid upon Muslim rebels. Two others, women, named as Roberta Wilcox and Catherine Ames, may still be fighting with the rebels. The next of kin of the deceased have been informed. The Italian Government very much regrets these unfortunate occurrences, but points out that these people had no business to be with the rebels in the first place, nor do they hold themselves responsible for what may happen to the two women if they persist in these "mad" activities.*

Pemberton put down the paper, and gazed at the wall opposite, on which hung a large portrait of Neville Chamberlain. Catherine Ames, he thought. Of course if it had been the Italian Government involved in the shoot-out at Le Pouget, they knew very well that she was alive. But she was keeping one step ahead of them. That young woman was setting up to be a second Sophie Elligan. That he could do without. He got up. "I am going down to the country," he told his secretary. "I may be late back."

"Why, Mr Pemberton," Lady Martingell said, herself opening the door. "How nice of you to call. Have you got something to tell me?"

"Quite a lot," Pemberton said. "I also have one or two things to ask you."

She ushered him into the lounge. "Whisky?"

"A short one, thank you." He sat down. "What newspaper do you take?"

Anne poured. "*The Times.* Why?"

"I don't think *The Times* deals with overseas crime, unless it is something very big. Did you know that a day or two before Mrs Elligan and Miss Ames called on you they had killed four people?"

Anne handed him his glass and poured one for herself. "Are you serious?"

"Very. They of course would call it self-defence. Also killed in what must have been quite a gun battle were Mrs Elligan's lover, who has been identified as Mr Edward Carew, and a maid. Presumably these were killed by the four men Mrs Elligan then killed, if you follow me."

"Ned Carew," Anne said softly. "Killed. She said they had separated. But who did it? I mean, who were the four men killed?"

"They have not been identified, but the French authorities are pretty sure they were Italian agents, sent to nip this gun-running expedition in the bud. Well, they didn't succeed. What I would like to know is this: did you and Mr Elligan know that Mrs Elligan is a quite deadly killer?"

"We knew she was capable of taking care of herself. She spent four years surviving in the Sahara, and again some time surviving in Abyssinia."

"Yet your husband was quite happy to go off with her."

"You don't suppose . . . oh, my God! But Sophie wouldn't kill Richard!"

"I have an idea that Sophie would kill anyone who got in her way. The point is that she is wanted by the French police. She is also wanted by the Gestapo."

"What on earth for?"

"Shooting one of their agents."

Anna stared at him in consternation. "And of course," Pemberton went on, "obviously she is also wanted by the Italians. The list must be as long as my arm. About the only country in Europe that she is not wanted in, is Great Britain. At the moment. Now tell me this, Lady Martingell. You came to me, so you said, because your lover had abandoned you for this woman. I would like to know if there was any other reason."

Anne flushed. "What other reason could there be? I was angry, and I wanted him stopped. Before he got into real trouble."

"He is in real trouble now, Lady Martingell. If any of those three nationalities catch up with Mrs Elligan, and Miss Ames, who appears to be quite as dangerous, there is liable to be another shoot-out; I don't see either of those women just surrendering to be tried and executed. And Mr Elligan is going to be bang in the middle. In those circumstances my promise of an amnesty for him isn't going to mean very much."

"But . . . can't you arrest them first?"

"I have nothing to arrest them for, this far. They have committed no crime in England, nor has any request as yet been made, from Germany, France or Italy for their extradition. Such a request in any event would not be legal until they actually return to this country – if they do. As they are using a Dutch vessel, no one has any right to arrest them at all, on the high seas. I had assumed that, using your original information, certain colleagues of mine in Germany would be able to prevent Mrs Elligan obtaining a ship, and thus that the whole thing would fall through. That has gone dreadfully wrong, cost another life, and she slipped through our fingers and is now as free as air. As His Majesty's Government has no wish or intention to fall out with Italy at this time, I am now obliged to pass on to the Italian Government all the information I possess and leave it up to them to stop this expedition whenever it enters Italian-controlled waters. As I say, when they do that, as I am sure they shall, we can expect several more deaths. I thought you should know this."

"Oh, my God, my God, my God," Anne muttered. "I don't want him killed."

"Well, then, my lady, if you have any means of getting in touch with Mr Elligan, I would advise you to use it right away, and warn him to get out now, while he can."

"I have no means of getting in touch with him."

Pemberton finished his drink and got up. "Then I am very sorry, Lady Martingell. I wouldn't give too much for Mr Elligan's chances."

The entire crew was on deck as the *Christina* sailed towards the lighthouse on Clare Island. It was quite dark now; they had passed the mouth of Galway Bay just before dusk. Now they slipped along in calm seas and to a light breeze. Dennis swept the horizon astern and out to sea, but there was nothing to be seen. "I don't get it," he said. "That fellow shadowed us for so long, and then just pulled away."

140

"He's there." Even Richard had come on deck. "He knows we have to go back the way we came."

Dennis went below to check the sailing directions again. Sophie went with him; she was as nervous as at any time in her life. "We leave Clare Island to port," he said. "And then swing up towards the Corraun Peninsular."

"But not as far as Corraun itself," she reminded him.

"We're supposed to get a light before then," he agreed. They returned on deck. The lighthouse was now bearing dead ahead, and was lost in the bulk of the island itself.

"Starboard two points," Dennis told his helmsman. "Trim those sheets," he commanded the other crewman.

The wind was south-westerly, and the boom needed only the slightest adjustment to keep the sail full as the *boier* entered the bay. "Is there water?" Richard asked.

"Out here," Dennis said.

Richard put his arm round Catherine's shoulders, and she didn't attempt to free herself; he could feel her trembling.

Gradually the light again came into view as they passed east of the island. "Port three points," Dennis said, and the yacht came round again, still with her sails full.

"There!" Captain Pfuhl might be the oldest person on board, but his eyes retained the sharpness of so many years at sea. In front of them a light was winking.

"I'll take her," Dennis said. "Carl, hand the mainsail." Carl relinquished the helm and hurried forward to drop the mainsail; the other crew, Lewis, went with him. "Can you handle the light, ma'am?" Dennis asked Sophie.

The lantern had already been lit; Sophie raised it and stood at the rail to swing it to and fro. The light in front of them continued to blink, while *Christina* ghosted forward under jib alone. "I see more lights," Richard said. "To the right."

"Those'll be Mulrany," Dennis said. "It's a village on the isthmus joining Achill Island to the mainland. It's a good way away." He made a slight alteration on the helm, and the *boier* came round. in response.

"I see the second light," Sophie said.

"That means reduce speed. We have already done that," Dennis said. "It's the third light that matters."

141

It was now utterly dark, the night relieved only by the beam of the lighthouse, sweeping slowly to and fro. "Think they can see us?" Richard asked.

"If they're looking real hard," Dennis said. "That beam is only on us for about five seconds a time."

"I see the third light," Sophie said.

"Drop the jib," Dennis called. "And let go." The foresail came down, and the anchor chain went out with a rumble. The *boier* came to a stop, snubbing the chain and then falling back. "Sound," Dennis said.

Lewis went forward with the leadline. "Six fathoms."

"Close enough," Dennis said.

"How much do you draw?" Richard asked.

"Twelve feet. We've room. But I imagine it shoals pretty fast from here."

"Boats," Sophie said.

"Let's get with it." Dennis went amidships with his crew, followed by Pfuhl. Somewhat reluctantly Richard released Catherine to go with them.

The two women peered into the gloom as the large boats, almost lighters, came alongside. They were propelled by oarsmen, but moved slowly, as there were only four men to each boat, and each boat was very heavily laden. "Thank the lord there's no sea running," commented one of the Irishmen.

"Amen," Dennis said, sending down a hawser suspended from the crosstrees, and worked by a winch. The first crate was attached and slowly swung up, the two crewmen straining at the handle. Then it was swung inboard and slowly lowered to the deck.

"What happens if it slips?" Catherine asked.

"Depends what's in the crate," Sophie said. "Rifles or ammunition, it'd probably make a nasty hole in the deck. Explosives, and you can pick your favourite cloud."

"You can joke about it?"

"Not much point in crying. Here's our man,"

Sophie went forward, Catherine behind her, as the tall man wearing seaboots and a sailing cap came up the ladder and swung over the rail. He was carrying a briefcase. "Mrs Elligan?" He was unmistakably an American.

"Mr Gannon?"

He shook hands. "Spot on. I find that very reassuring."

"Thank you."

"And Mr Carew?"

"Ned," Sophie called. There was a moment's hesitation, then Richard came aft. "This is Mr Gannon," Sophie said. Again Gannon shook hands, then did the same with Catherine. "We have a transaction to complete," Sophie said. "Let's go below." The saloon was already being filled with crates of rifles and ammunition; the *boier* did have a hold but it was limited. "The end of our comforts for the rest of the voyage," Richard commented, pleasantly.

"There's room here." Sophie led them to the free end of the table. "Have a seat."

There was only one chair left – the others had been unbolted and stowed to make room and Gannon sat down, cautiously, Sophie, Richard and Catherine stood around him. He placed his briefcase on the table, opened it. "Here is a credit note from your Swiss bank. As agreed, the remaining payment is being made in two parts. Twenty-five thousand pounds has been credited to your account. The remaining fifty thousand has been placed in a holding account and will be transferred either upon presentation of the letter of accommodation, or on instructions from Mr Walters. This will be done whenever Andrews confirms that the delivery has been completed. I trust this is in order?"

"Sounds all right. There should be another transaction."

Gannon nodded. "Here I have another note indicating a transfer of six and a quarter thousand pounds from your account to that of a Mr Richard Elligan."

"Yippee," Richard said.

"Now I need some instructions," Sophie said.

From his briefcase, Gannon took a large-scale map which he spread on the table. "Here is the west coast of Greece and Albania, and the Ionian Sea, including of course the islands. I assume you are equipped with charts for the area?" Sophie nodded. "Well, you will use your charts in conjunction with this map. You will see that it is divided into squares. Mr Andrews has an exact equivalent. He wishes the goods delivered to square seventeen."

They bent over the stiff paper. "South of Corfu, north of Leukas . . . just about opposite Anti-Paxos," Sophie said.

"That looks a pretty desolate coast," Richard commented.

"It is, and thus is ideal for our purpose. Mr Andrews will expect to see your light at ten o'clock on the night of Sunday 23 May. Does that present any difficulties?"

"Three plus weeks. No, I do not think there will be a difficulty about that," Sophie said. "But the landing place is at least twenty-five miles from the Albanian border."

"Yes, it is. But Andrews says it is impossible to land the goods on Albanian soil; the coast is too well guarded by the Italians. It is also safest for you to stay out of Italian waters. He will provide the transport once the goods are landed. All you have to do is land them, and your part in the transaction is completed. You can then resume your voyage, return to France, and collect the rest of your money."

"I don't think we'll be returning to France," Sophie said. "Well, it looks straightforward enough, Mr Gannon. Providing Clay is there to meet us, I can't see any problems. But you say the landing is to be made at night. That requires signals."

"The same as we used tonight. The actual landing place will be at the mouth of a small creek. He assures me there is sufficient water. But if you follow the lights you will be perfectly safe."

Sophie recalled that on a previous occasion Clay had needed the goods to be landed at a fairly dicey place. But they had made it. "How's he getting on, by the way?"

"Things are fairly crucial. The Italians launched a drive into the mountains a week ago and caught the partisans on the hop. They suffered severe casualties, and had to retreat further into the mountains. They are dreadfully short of ammunition. But Andrews is confident that they can hold out for the three weeks until the munitions arrive."

"But . . . Roberta!" Catherine said. "She was with them, badly wounded. If they had to clear out in a hurry—"

"Would that be a Miss Roberta Wilcox?" Gannon asked.

"Yes, Roberta Wilcox. Do you know of her?"

"Yes. I'm terribly sorry to say, Miss Ames, that Miss Wilcox was captured by the Italians in that offensive. She was, as you say, badly wounded. And I'm afraid she died of those wounds, the day following her capture."

Lovers

"No," Catherine said. "No," she shouted. "No!" she screamed. Sophie grasped her hand. "She was going to be all right," Catherine shouted. "Clay said she was going to be all right!"

Gannon was looking extremely embarrassed, while Dennis came sliding down the ladder to find out what the noise was about.

"I'm afraid it is true, Miss Ames," Gannon said. "Apparently she had to be abandoned by the partisans, and by Andrews, when they began their retreat, and was taken by the Italian troops. The official communiqué merely said that she had been fighting with the partisans, and that she had died of her wounds."

"They killed her," Catherine muttered. "They murdered her."

"I'm afraid that may well be true. Our people in Tirana have received a secret report suggesting that her wound was attended to by the Italian doctors, but that she was questioned by an intelligence officer and in despair when left alone tore off her bandages and bled to death."

"Oh, my *God!*" Catherine pulled herself free of Sophie's hand and ran for the heads.

"I am most terribly sorry," Gannon said. "Were they close?"

"Very, I think," Sophie said. "Well . . . what's done is done. How's the loading going, Dennis?"

"Just about halfway. We're going to have to secure the remainder on deck. I have tarpaulins to cover them, but we're going to waddle."

"Just so long as we get there," Sophie said. "Well, thanks for everything, Mr Gannon. Are you still in touch with Clay?"

"Yes. We've managed to get him a radio."

"Just let him know we'll be there."

145

"I never doubted it." Gannon shook hands. "Will the young lady be all right?"

"I really can't say. But we'll do out best."

Sophie let the men escort Gannon on deck, then went into the heads. Catherine knelt on the deck, her arms still round the lavatory bowl. Sophie worked the flush, then lifted the girl up. "You need to lie down."

"God," Catherine said. "To do such a thing. To *have* to do such a thing. What did they do to her, first?"

"Better not to think about it." Sophie half carried her into their cabin and laid her on the lower bunk. "I'll get you a sedative." She opened her bag, found what she wanted. "You need to remember, always, that Roberta was a very brave girl. She knew they were going to get what they wanted out of her, one way or another, so she determined not to betray Clay, even inadvertently."

"I hadn't thought of that. Oh, Roberta—"

Sophie sat beside her, a cup of brandy in one hand and the pill in the other. "Drink this, and things will look better tomorrow."

She went on deck, where the last of the crates were being stowed, Dennis carefully checking to make sure the trim was balanced. "All I can say is, let's hope no one actually shoots at us. How's the girl?"

"Distraught. But sleeping, now. What do you think of her, Dennis?"

"She's a charmer."

"Not good enough."

He glanced at her. "You suggesting something? I thought she had it going with your husband?"

"He would like to get it going. She is not interested. But she's interested in you. And when she wakes up she is going to need all the help and the distraction she can get."

"Holy shit!" he commented. "I thought she was your protégée."

"I suppose she is, by accident. I certainly don't want her going round the bend with grief. Or hatred."

"And her virginity?"

"She couldn't give it to a nicer guy."

"You are something, Mrs Elligan. And suppose I said I'd far rather bed down with you? No offence intended to Miss Ames. But . . . like I said, you are *something*."

"You say the sweetest things."

"But you're not available. Will you tell me why? Something to do with my skin?"

"Nothing in the slightest to do with your skin, Dennis. I think you are one of the handsomest men I have ever met, as well as the nicest. But I'm still mourning my dead lover, and . . ." but she needed to tell someone. "I'm carrying his child."

"You—" instinctively he looked at her stomach.

"Oh, it's not two months yet. I hope to have completed the delivery and be back before I start to show. But . . . it's Ned's child, and it's going to stay Ned's child, if you follow me. I would also like what I have just told you to be a secret between you and me. Not even Catherine knows. And my husband certainly must not know."

"I follow you. A pregnant, gun-toting, gun-running beauty. Lady, you have got to be unique."

"She has the goods aboard, all right," the secretary said. "She has been sighted off the west coast of Ireland, making south, and low in the water. Our people estimate that she loaded in Clew Bay."

"That makes sense," Pemberton agreed.

"Do you wish her stopped?"

"Good lord, no. I assume she is still flying the Dutch flag, and she is now in international waters. We have no business interfering with her."

"Are we just going to let her go? What about informing the Italians?"

Pemberton surveyed the report on his desk, that yet a third Briton, the woman Roberta Wilcox, had died in the fighting. As before, the Italians were very apologetic, although they continued to point out that the British tourists had had no business being in the battle area at all, much less taking the sides of the partisans. It did not seem to occur to *Il Duce*'s people that they had even less business being in Albania. "I've changed my mind about that," he said. "Let them get on with it."

"And when the Elligans come back?"

"The word is probably 'if'. If they get back to England, well, I don't see there is a lot we can do about it." He wished there was some way of stopping the Germans.

"Yes, yes, I understand," said Francois Labarge into his phone. "But may I ask what is your interest in this, Herr Eisener?"

"The woman shot one of my people," Eisener said.

"Indeed? How remarkable. Why was she not arrested?"

"She got away. She appears to be as slippery as an eel, as I imagine you have found out. But we would like to have her back. Although of course, Monsieur Labarge, we realise that you have a prior claim."

"Thank you," said the Marseilles Chief of Police. "Well, I will keep in touch. You understand that we have no jurisdiction over a foreign vessel on the high seas."

"I think it is very possible that she will need to put in somewhere before she can deliver the goods," Eisener said. "She can hardly put into an Italian port, eh? And Spain is still in a mess. The only logical place would be a French or a French-controlled port, either on the mainland, in Corsica, or in North Africa. Once she is in port, you have her. And the wanted people will be on board."

"I understand. You may leave the matter in my care, Herr Eisener." He hung up, gazed at his deputy.

"News of the Elligan woman?"

"Oh, indeed. The Germans seem convinced that she is engaged in running guns to the Albanian patriots."

"That is her profession, is it not?"

"Apparently. And to think she has been living all these years outside Sete under a false name. Someone slipped up there."

"You know she and her lover are wanted in North Africa for the murder of an Arab sheikh?"

"And a few other crimes besides," Labarge said. "Oh, yes, we must get her back to stand trial. But to ask us to stop her delivering arms to the Albanians for use against the Italians, while Mussolini lays claim to Corsica and rattles his sabre in our direction, that is an absurdity, Henri."

"You mean to let her go?"

148

Labarge grinned. "I think she will, how do the English say? Again slip through our fingers on her outward voyage. When she has delivered the goods, if she can do that, and is on her way back, then we will pick her up."

"Suppose she cannot deliver the goods? Suppose the Italians catch up with her?"

"Then they will shoot her or hang her and we will be saved the use of the guillotine. And a sensational trial which I do not think would do anyone much good. But I wish an eye kept on her. Let the Navy know this."

"Dr Pizzoli wishes to see you, Signor General," said the secretary.

"Am I supposed to wish to see him?" Edio Rometti asked. He had no idea what had really happened with the death of the English girl, but he sincerely regretted it. And what the English press were going to make of it . . . "Oh, show him in."

Pizzoli entered, and carefully closed the door behind him, excluding the secretary. Edio gazed at him. "I wish this meeting to be private," the doctor said.

"Well make it quick," Edio said. "I have a great deal to do."

"I am being transferred," Pizzoli said.

"Is that of interest to me?"

"I think it may be, Signor General. I have a problem."

"Take it to your confessor."

"If you will allow me to explain. I have a patient, who I cannot take with me, and who I cannot leave behind. I have come to you because I believe you are a man of honour."

Edio frowned. He hated people who spoke in riddles. "It is kind of you to say so. One would not expect you to take any of your patients with you to your new post. But why cannot you leave this man behind? Has he got some rare disease?"

"He is a woman."

Edio sat straight. "She is dead. You reported her dead."

Pizzoli licked his lips. "I had to do something, Signor General. I had to save her from those intelligence thugs."

"So what *did* you do?"

"I opened her wound and let it bleed onto the bed, then I sewed it up again, gave her a transfusion, and took her to the

149

infectious disease ward. I put her in a private room with instructions that the patient was to be treated only by me and a nurse I can trust absolutely. When the intelligence captain returned with an order for her to be delivered into his care I told him that she had opened her wound and committed suicide, and that her body had been cremated immediately. This is as you know normal practice with prisoners as it is getting quite warm. They did not question this."

"Do you realise, Pizzoli, that I can have you shot for that confession? That is aiding and abetting an enemy."

"That was preventing a murder, Signor General. Signorina Wilcox is too weak to withstand the sort of questioning those bastards would have inflicted on her. They more or less told me they did not care whether she lived or died, so long as she answered their questions first."

Edio studied him; he was clearly a very brave, and very honourable, young man. "So tell me, what am I supposed to do?"

"Well . . . over this last week she has made good progress. She can now move about and I think she is strong enough to manage on her own. So—"

"You think she should be released back into the wild, like a captive animal."

"You see, sir, once I leave this establishment, my duties will be taken over by another doctor. Then the secret of what happened will become known, and—"

"You will be shot."

"I was thinking of the girl. The intelligence unit will have her."

"Just how many people know of this subterfuge?"

"Nurse Oriolo and I, sir. And now you."

"And if I do not arrest you, and Nurse Oriolo, now, I will be as guilty as you."

Pizzoli swallowed. "I came to you because—"

"You thought I was an honourable man. You do realise, Pizzoli, that the partisans are only holding out because they are anticipating receiving aid in the form of guns and ammunition. We know that aid is on its way. We even have a fairly good idea of who is making the delivery. What we do not know is where and when and how. This girl may well know these things."

"I think she was telling the truth when she said she did not, sir. Why should a man like Andrews confide in someone he had only just met?"

"He certainly confided in her friend," Edio pointed out. "However . . . there may be a way we can sort this out to our advantage. You say the girl can move about. Does that mean that if released she could regain her friends?"

"In the mountains? I do not know that she is *that* fit. She is still weak, and if she were to fall and open the wound again—"

"Then we will have to arrange an exchange. You may leave that with me."

"You mean you will let her go?"

"Suitably primed," Edio said.

Edio was taken to the isolation ward, shown into the private room by Pizzoli. "You have met General Rometti, I think," the doctor said.

"Yes." Roberta stared at the general, muscles tensed.

"You are a very foolish girl," Edio said severely. "And a very fortunate one. You know that Dr Pizzoli has saved your life, at very great risk to himself?"

"I am very grateful. Please tell me he won't be punished."

"He deserves to be punished. But as it has turned out, while his behaviour has been reprehensible, it has not caused any harm. I have decided to release you."

Roberta blinked. "Release me? You mean I can go home?"

"Not directly: you are officially supposed to be dead. It cannot simply be a matter of taking you to Tirana and handing you over to the British Consul. I am arranging a truce, at which you will be handed back to the partisans. To your friend Andrews. It is up to him to get you out, to Greece."

"You mean you are going to use me as the bait of a trap. I absolutely refuse."

"You are hardly in a position to refuse anything, young lady. And it is not a trap. I give you my word on that. You have simply become an embarrassment to us. And as you no longer have any information to give us—"

"No longer?" Roberta's voice went up an octave.

"You did not know? We have captured another of your

people, and he has given us all the information we need, as to where the arms are to be landed, and when. So you see, your suffering has all been in vain. Not all the partisans are as brave as you. So as I say, we no longer have any reason to hold you, and I believe you are, in fact, a non-combatant. So I am returning you to Andrews, and as I say, I presume he will get you out to Greece, as he got your friend Catherine Ames out. From Greece you will be able to go home." He stood up. "You will be taken into the mountains tomorrow morning."

Roberta could hardly believe her ears. "I would like to thank you, General."

"It has been a pleasure to meet you, Signorina. I only wish it could have been in happier circumstances." He kissed her hand.

"I hate to raise such a mundane matter as money." Richard leaned on the taffrail beside Sophie. "But how do I get my hands on this Swiss bank account?"

Sophie opened her shoulder bag, took out the bank access number. "You will need proper identification. Your passport will do."

"You mean I can draw money from this, now?"

Sophie gave him his cheque book. "Whenever you happen to be close to a bank."

"I was supposed to send this money back to Anne."

"She'll have to wait. It's only a few weeks now."

"And the second payment has gone ahead?"

"You know it has, Richard."

"But I can't touch any of it until the delivery is complete. You wouldn't be trying to double-cross me, by any chance, Sophie?"

She smiled. "I'm just making sure you don't get any ideas about double-crossing *me*, Richard."

Very cautiously, Dennis Overcamp opened the cabin door. It was mid-afternoon, and *Christina* was well clear of land now and making south-west to get a good offing before bearing south. She was heavily laden, and wallowed, close-hauled into the southerly wind. As he did not wish to burn any of his precious diesel – he was keeping that in case he needed to make any sudden escape later in the voyage – it was going to be a slow, hard beat all the way to Gibraltar, unless the wind changed. But they were making progress. With five thousand pounds on the end of it.

He wondered what had more influenced him to risk his all, and more importantly, his ship and sole means of support, on such a dangerous adventure? The money, or the woman? The money was important, of course. It would enable him to pay off his debts, and even have some to spare to tart up the ship and do a bit of advertising. But he was not sure he would have taken it on without the woman.

There was far more to it than sheer beauty. In fact, he did not think Sophie Elligan was actually beautiful at all. Her features were too strong, as was her character. Of course her figure was magnificent. But he had known several women with magnificent figures. Was it because she had shot her way out of more situations than he could imagine? That beneath that superb and invariably calm exterior there was utter ruthlessness? That concept was certainly exciting. But it was also, he was sure, compounded by the fact that while Sophie could act with the determined ferocity of a lioness at bay she was not a cold-blooded killer. She had a deal of protective warmth towards those she liked, or loved.

He had quickly determined that it would be very enjoyable to be loved, or even liked, by Sophie Elligan. He felt he had achieved the second phase, anyway. And the first? He had been enormously encouraged by what she had told him. The sort of loyalty that preserved her love for Ned Carew even after death was something he could both admire and hope to possess himself. Her decision not to have sex while pregnant was again understandable: she was determined that nothing should happen to her child.

Disregarding, of course, the fact that by undertaking this delivery at all she was risking the lives of herself and her child. But the dualism only made her more attractive. When it was all over . . . he felt all things might be possible.

But now . . . she had virtually commanded him to have sex with Catherine Ames. Well, that would be no hardship. Having spent the past ten days in the company of two extremely attractive women he certainly felt like it. And according to Sophie, the girl wanted it. And needed it. But what happened afterwards? He was a man who from necessity had learned to look ahead, wherever possible. There could be no future in a relationship with Catherine. Apart from the differences of race, nationality, age and very possibly religion as well, he was not in love with the girl.

Maybe Sophie hoped he *would* fall in love with her. Or maybe she was only using him for that short-term objective of taking Catherine's mind on to another plane than that of utter despair. But as he was here . . . Sophie was on deck, with Elligan and Pfuhl. She had intimated that she would stay there until he came up. He had at least an hour's clear run.

He stepped into the cabin, and the body in the lower bunk stirred. She was covered with a blanket, but he knew Sophie had undressed her. He sat on the bunk. "How do you feel?"

"Ugh," she commented, and blinked, suddenly realising who he was. She licked her lips. "My mouth tastes like a sewer."

He pumped some water, mixed in a little of the brandy, and gave it to her. She sat up, and the blanket slipped. She caught it to raise it to her throat, then, deliberately, released it again. Slowly it slid down to her waist. She drank, also slowly. "I didn't come here to talk about your friend," Dennis said. "But I want you to know how sorry I am."

Tears welled out of her eyes and dribbled down her cheeks; they made her quite beautiful. Dennis wiped them with his handkerchief, then took away the empty glass.

"Say we'll get back at them," Catherine begged.

"The delivery of this cargo will be getting back at them." Gently he lifted the blanket from her thighs. She watched him with huge eyes, but she wasn't afraid. "Do you want this?" he asked.

"You mean, if I said no, you'd stop?"

"Yes."

Another Clay Andrews, Catherine thought, who either considered her a child . . . or was really interested only in Sophie. But Clay had never gently stripped her naked. "I want it," she said. His expression did not change, but he slid his hand slowly up her leg, caressed her knee for a moment, then moved on up her thigh to touch the pale hair. As he did so, he leaned forward to kiss her on the lips. "Oh, I want it," she said.

*   *   *

154

Dennis Overcamp pointed to the east. "Fastnet Lighthouse," he said. "They run a race out here during Cowes Week every other year. But that's not until August."

"It looks bleak," Catherine said.

"It can be very bleak. And soon will be, I reckon." He was looking at the sky, which was a mass of streaky cloud.

"Does that mean something?"

"Wind."

"Are we in any danger?"

He grinned. "Not really. But it won't be comfortable with this heavy load."

She leaned against him. Was it only yesterday they had left Clew Bay before dawn, yesterday her life had taken on a new dimension? She could still feel his touch, the gentle insistence of his hands, the sudden violence of his thrusts . . . and she would be feeling it again, this afternoon.

She had made a brief attempt to thank Sophie for so arranging things, and Sophie had kissed her. "Just be happy while you can."

Sophie knew a great deal about being unhappy, but she remained always perfectly calm and poised. Not so Richard, who was on deck now, further aft, staring at the lovers with simmering eyes. "What are you?" he asked Sophie, who was sitting in a deckchair beside him. "Some kind of madam? And with a—"

"Just don't say it," Sophie recommended.

"I think I deserve a quid pro quo," he remarked, still watching Catherine and Dennis.

"Well, you are not going to get one. Not even a hand job."

"You're still my wife, you know."

"My misfortune."

He brooded, then looked up. "I don't much like the look of that."

Sophie also looked up, frowned, then got up and went to the helm to join Catherine and the captain. "How far to Gib?"

"From Fastnet? One thousand three hundred miles."

"Days?"

"With this load on board we're only making about a hundred and fifty miles a day. So we're talking about eight days. We behind schedule?"

155

"Not yet. I'm thinking about the weather."

"There's some on the way"

"Will that hold us up?"

"It won't be comfortable, but it's coming towards us, and we're going towards it, so at least it'll only be a matter of hours. We may lose those hours, though, given the wind direction."

The weather broke that evening, with a heavy rainsquall. "Rain before wind means trouble," Dennis said, and had all the lashings checked and doubled; were any of the heavy crates on deck to shift they'd risk a capsize. Then he took a couple of reefs in the mainsail, and changed down to a storm jib.

Satisfied, he took the helm himself to face the heavy black clouds which came scudding up from the south-west. The wind direction meant that he could not steer the course he had intended and, rather than stand in towards the French and Portuguese coasts he elected to go west, into the Atlantic, keeping as close to the wind as possible, hopefully to have a clear reach in to the Straits when the weather cleared. Soon the wind was howling, and seas were breaking over the bows and streaming aft along the deck, but the heavy *boier*, even if over-loaded, coped with them very well, driving into the waves with tremendous resolution.

Sophie retired to bed. She used Dennis's bunk in the aft cabin, as she had moved him in with Catherine; not that he was going to be there tonight. She lay on her back in the darkness, listening to the whine of the wind, the slaps of the waves against the hull, body sliding to and fro across the sheet to the gentle roll, but with her leeboards down *Christina* was, as always, a very stable platform.

Sophie was not the least afraid; she had every confidence in both the ship and the skipper. But she found it difficult to sleep as the vessel occasionally lurched, or was stopped by a larger than usual wave. And she had a lot to think about. Eventually, there was the future. She was wanted for murder in both France and Germany, not to mention Italy. England was her adopted home, but she did not think she would be entirely welcome there, now – and England had extradition treaties with all of those countries, Spain was just finishing a civil war that had devastated the

156

country and left very deep hatreds. Portugal was as Fascist as either Spain or Italy.

Cross the Atlantic, with her baby, and hope to set up a new home? But would they let her in? The Americans were very investigative of people's backgrounds. The best possible bet at the moment seemed Holland. She liked what she had seen of the people, and she liked Dennis. The drawback to Holland was that it was a very small country in which to disappear completely – and it was very close to both Germany and France.

But, closer to hand, there were some very bothering considerations. The French were looking for her, but they could not possibly know where she was. The Germans were looking for her, now . . . but they had been looking for her from the moment she entered Germany. Following her, tracking her, and at last attempting to arrest her.

Why? It was four years since she had last been in Germany, last seen her parents. Then she had been buying guns for the Abyssinians, and to obtain a licence she had had to perform a rather unpleasant act with a gauleiter. But she did not think she had broken any laws except moral ones, and the present German regime was not interested in morality. But this time . . . how had they known she was coming? She found that a very sinister consideration.

To top it all, once they had put to sea, they had been shadowed by a Royal Navy destroyer. It was possible that the Nazis, having worked out that she must after all have escaped on the Dutch yacht, might have contacted the British to look out for her, but she did not think the German and British admiralties were that close.

So who had informed the German police that Sophie Elligan was going to pay them a visit looking for a ship? Only four people in the world had known that: herself, Catherine, Richard . . . and Anne Martingell. Unless someone in the American Embassy in Paris had blown the whistle. But no one had known where she itended to find her ship. Although she supposed, given any knowledge of her past record, it might have been easy to surmise that it would be Germany.

If she had been betrayed by someone in the American Embassy, then they were all in deep shit. And yet . . . the guns had been loaded as promised, and the payments made as promised. If it was Richard or Anne . . . but Richard would have been endangering his own neck, and any possibility of being paid, by having them nabbed before the delivery.

Anne Martingell, she mused. She did not know Anne very well; they had actually only met on half a dozen occasions. But she knew a lot about her. She knew that she had killed her first husband to save Martingell's life. She knew that she had killed her own son by that husband to save her own life. She knew that she had shamelessly seduced Richard while still apparently happily married to Martingell, and while Richard had been officially courting her stepdaughter. She was a woman with a ruthlessly selfish streak, who was every bit as deadly as herself, Sophie realised. Yet *she* was the one everyone was hunting!

She rather felt she might go hunting herself, when this delivery was completed, she thought as she fell asleep.

"It is a trap," Dino grumbled, peering down through the tangled bushes and rocks at the road, and the Italian column of trucks that had just pulled up.

"Yes," Clay said. "It is a trap." But not the sort of trap Dino was thinking of. The Italians had made the offer to return Roberta Wilcox. They had asked nothing in return. That was not logical. But he did not think they would have gone to such elaborate lengths just to ensnare him. Besides, they did not even know where he was, at this moment. And he intended to control events.

Soldiers disembarked from the trucks, but they did not assume any very military formation, merely stood around and smoked cigarettes. As he had insisted, there were no machine-guns or artillery to be seen. From the last truck there now descended a man wearing the uniform of a general. Clay focused his glasses and gave a low whistle. "You know that man?" Dino asked.

"We have met."

Now the girl was brought out. She wore pants and a blouse, sandals; her hair was loose. And she was standing, even if she moved tentatively. His glasses told him she had lost weight, and her face was even tighter than he remembered, but she looked better than he had expected.

158

Edio looked up the hillside, which to his eyes would be empty. Then he signalled the medical orderly who had taken his place beside Roberta, and the three of them began to climb the slope, very slowly, because of the girl. The soldiers on the road watched with interest, but still no aggressive demeanor.

The party of three continued to climb, pausing every few minutes to rest and wipe sweat from their brows. Clay studied the land below them and to either side. There was still no artillery, no sign of any aircraft – although he knew these could be summoned in a matter of minutes. He waited, wiping sweat from his own brow, until the Italians and Roberta were within twenty feet of him. "Far enough, General Rometti," he said, quietly.

Edio's head turned, left and then right. "You are covered," Clay said. "Let the girl come on alone." Edio nodded to Roberta, who glanced at him as if she would have spoken, then resumed her climb. "Go straight up, Roberta," Clay said. "There are people waiting for you in the next gully."

Roberta hesitated, trying to see where he was, and then climbed some more, panting, and even more as she realised she was now surrounded by armed men, crouching amidst the rocks. If Clay were to break the truce . . .

"There," Edio said. "You have her, Signor Andrews. She is not yet fully restored to health, so treat her carefully. I will withdraw, and look forward to our next meeting."

"Not so fast," Clay said.

Edio, already turned, turned back. "Treachery?"

"Not on my part, General. But you'll forgive me if I say I need time to withdraw myself and my people, together with Signorina Wilcox. We will go now. One of my men will remain, concealed, but with his rifle trained on you. He is a very good shot. You will remain where you are for one hour, then you may return to your people."

"One hour," Edio said, and looked up at the sun. "Can it be that you do not trust me, Signor Andrews? Did I not keep my word the last time we met, and permit you to leave Abyssinia, unharmed?"

"I've a notion you may be regretting that act of generosity. Sorry, General, but this is the way we are going to play it."

159

Edio shrugged. "As you wish." He sat on the ground, and lit a cigarette. The medical orderly followed his example. Clay waved his arm, and his people began to withdraw.

A litter had been prepared for Roberta, and she was carried over the mountain trails to the cave which was now Clay's head-quarters. Here they were joined by the marksman, who reported no problems. After an hour the general had been allowed to rejoin his men, who had then got back into the trucks and driven away. "I wish I knew what was happening," Roberta said, as Clay sat beside her to eat their evening meal.

"So do I. I'm hoping you are going to enlighten me."

"I haven't a clue." Roberta told him about Pizzoli's ploy to keep her from being tortured. "Then his general came along and told me I was to be returned to you."

"Wouldn't it have been more correct to send you to the British Consul in Tirana?"

"He explained that he couldn't do that, because his command had already reported me dead."

"Hm." Clay was actually very glad to have the girl back, and looking so well, but he had to consider her a poisoned chalice. "And Rometti made no further attempt to question you about the arms delivery?"

"No. He said that was why they were letting me go. As they now know exactly where and when and how the arms are to be delivered, they were no longer interested in anything I might tell them. Or refuse to tell them."

"How did he claim to have learned that, if not from you?"

"He said they had captured another of your people, who had told him."

Clay looked at Dino, who was seated opposite. "There were those brothers, who disappeared," Dino said. "We thought they were dead."

"Whether they were dead or alive, they did not know anything about the shipment."

"They could have overheard something."

"I do not believe they could have overheard enough to make Rometti let Roberta go." Clay began to think. Edio could not know where and how the guns were to be delivered; he only knew they were *going* to be delivered. But he would also know that the delivery had to take place at a predetermined place. And if they were coming by ship, and were expected sometime soon, the ship would already be at sea, and certainly maintaining radio silence. Therefore he was trying a gigantic scam. By releasing Roberta with the story that she no longer had anything to offer the Italians, he was hoping to panic the partisans into attempting to change the delivery arrangements. When the whole thing could easily foul up.

"What are you going to do?" Roberta asked.

"I think we'll chance our arm, and proceed as planned," Clay said.

The gale blew for several hours, the skies cleared, the wind dropped and the seas started to go down. The heavily laden *boier* continued to plough along, the wind now on the starboard beam so that she made relatively good time. The decks dried, and the two women were able to sit aft and enjoy the sunshine. "How do you feel?" Sophie asked.

Catherine glanced at her. "You sent him to me, didn't you?"

"I had the impression you needed it. That you might even enjoy it."

"Oh . . . of course I did. He's just marvellous. But Sophie . . . Roberta—"

"I know."

"But life must go on, eh? As you carried on after Ned's death."

"What's the alternative?"

Catherine brooded at the sparkling water. "I want out. Forget my share. Just put me ashore somewhere with enough money to get home. Please, Sophie."

Sophie sighed. "You know that's not on, Cathy. We dare not put in anywhere, with this cargo. We have to see it through."

Again Catherine considered the heaving waves for some time before speaking.

"Are we going to make it, Sophie?"

"I intend to," Sophie said.

But it was increasingly nerve-wracking to be some completely cut off from the outside world. Sophie stood beside Dennis, using their binoculars as Cape St Vincent came in sight, and then the beaches of the Algarve. The sea had now calmed right down, although the normally big Atlantic swell was still running. There was quite a lot of shipping about, some freighters but mostly the inshore Portugese fishing fleet. There was also a small warship to be seen. "Fishery protection vessel," Dennis said. "She's not interested in us."

They stayed outside the three-mile limit, and next day the Rock came into view. "Crisis time." Richard joined Sophie by the helm.

"There's no reason for it," she said. Yet the British knew who they were and what they were doing. Slowly the harbour came abeam. There were several warships to be seen, including even an aircraft carrier. But *Christina* stayed on the south side of the channel, and with the tide they made good time.

"Hurrah!" Richard said, as the Rock began to slip astern. In front of them the seas were even calmer, as there was no swell.

"Gosh," Catherine said. "I was scared."

"Plain sailing now," Dennis assured her. "At least until we're past Italy."

Edio entertained Admiral Carzanti to lunch, and outlined the situation. "I do not understand why you do not simply launch a major offensive into the mountains," the Admiral said. "And finish the job once and for all."

"There are three reasons," Edio explained. "The first is that *Il Duce* has announced to the world that all fighting is finished, and all Albanians have accepted the situation and are now good and faithful servants of Italy – with the possible exception of a few bandits. Thus obviously if we resumed a real shooting war that perception would be shown to be untrue."

"But you *are* engaged in a war," the Admiral argued.

"They snipe at us, we capture and execute some of them," Edio agreed. "On that basis it is easy to maintain the fiction that they are no more than bandits."

"You mentioned three reasons."

"The second is that such an offensive would not work, simply because, if defeated, the partisans would retreat across the border into Greece."

162

"Where they would be interned, surely."

"I doubt it. The Greeks hate us. It is a matter which will have to be settled sooner or later. But for the time being I doubt they would do anything more than deny any Albanians are using their territory."

"And the third reason?"

"The third reason is this shipment of arms. We know a trickle of weapons, and more important, ammunition, is coming in from Greece. But this is insufficient to affect the issue. The partisans are holding on in the mountains because they are expecting a sizeable shipment of arms, and again, most importantly, ammunition, from the West. We know this. What we do not know is how and when this shipment is coming, although it must be on its way by now. The point is that if we prevent that shipment from reaching the partisans, with of course the promise of more shipments to come, I believe their morale will crumble and they may well surrender. They will certainly run out of ammunition in very short order. Now, I have tried to have the shipment nipped in the bud, as it were. I know who is behind it and conducting it. But unfortunately our agents have not been successful, and after a considerable loss of life. We have lost track of the principals, and as far as we know they are at sea with the goods."

"And you wish me to stop them? As you said just now, General, *Il Duce* is anxious to have this matter finished and done with. He will not give us permission to stop and search any neutral vessels on the high seas, and thereby perhaps cause an international incident, and proclaim to the world that the Albanians are far from meekly surrendering."

"There is no law against shadowing such a vessel?"

"You say you do not know what she is."

"Would it not be possible to patrol the bottom end of the Adriatic and note every foreign vessel using these waters?"

"Once she moves inside the Ionian Islands she would be in Greek territorial waters."

"That would still narrow down her destination considerably. I do not think she would dare come north of Corfu. The landing will be made on the Greek coast, somewhere inside the islands. I am prepared to deal with that. What I need, more than the place, is the date. Your shadowing vessel could supply me with this.

163

Twenty-four hours will be sufficient. Once I know the date, you may leave the rest to me."

Carzanti scratched his nose. "You would risk a raid into Greece?"

"If necessary. A very quick one. In any event, the goods would have to be transported. There are only one or two roads available for heavy traffic. But if I know the date, I believe we could seal the matter up before they ever reach the border."

The Admiral spread the chart of the Ionian Islands and considered them for several seconds. Then he said, "Leave it with me."

"They have passed through the Straits, Herr Eisener," Eichmann said.

"When?"

"Yesterday morning."

"And I am only now being informed? Have you lost them again?"

"No, no, Herr Eisener. We know their speed, and we know their probable course. We will easily find them."

"I hope so." Eisener knew very little about the sea. "Has there been any French activity?"

"They were approached by a French naval vessel. But as far as we know no actual contact was made."

"And you say your people can find them at any time?"

"Of course."

"Well, then, I think we should put a stop to this farce once and for all. Where would be best?"

"Presuming they are steering for Greece, and certainly meaning to pass well south of Italy or Sardinia, they will be in fairly empty waters on the approach south of Malta. I would estimate tomorrow."

"It must be done clandestinely. And we would like to have Frau Elligan alive if possible."

"Understood. The others?"

"Are of no importance. And the ship must disappear without trace."

"Understood," Eichmann said. "It will happen tomorrow night."

164

The Delivery

"It is the end that crowns us, not the fight."
Robert Herrick

Pirates

"A Dutch *boier* passed through the Straits of Gibraltar yesterday," the secretary said. "Her course once clear of the straits was east by north."

"She means to keep well clear of French-Algerian territorial waters," Pemberton commented. "What sort of speed is she making?"

"Rather slow, sir. About five knots under sail, which she increases to six whenever she uses her engine."

"Because she's so heavily laden. So what in your estimation is her first critical position?"

"When she turns into the Sicilian Channel to pass south of Sicily. The Channel itself is nearly a hundred miles wide, but it is the narrowest point between Italian and French territory, and it is possible that one or the other might try to pick her up there. It would be illegal, of course, as long as she doesn't stray into either territorial waters, but if they seriously intend to stop her—" he paused, as his superior peered at the map.

"It would be illegal," Pemberton said thoughtfully. "When do you estimate she will pass through the channel?"

"At her present speed, we're talking about four days."

"Well, it might be a good idea for one of our units in Malta to make a routine patrol as far west as say, Sardinia and back, starting in two days' time."

"With what instructions, sir? Does she arrest them?"

"Good heavens, no, Billy. She goes about her normal duties. If, of course, she were to come across an incidence of piracy . . . it would be piracy, would it not, to attempt to arrest a private vessel on the high seas in time of peace?"

"It would be illegal, sir," Billy repeated, carefully. "I am not sure that our ship would have the right to intervene, if it might actually come to a shooting job. The repercussions would be enormous. We appear to be committed to keeping the peace with Italy, no matter what, and France is our ally."

"Quite so. However, I am sure the mere presence of a British destroyer close to the scene of, shall we say, the action, would prove a deterrent to others taking extreme measures. Do you think you can get all that across to the Admiralty?"

"Without letting on that you would actually like this cargo to get through, sir?"

"My interest is justice," Pemberton said, enigmatically.

"I do think it would be better coming from you, sir. Shall I fix you up a meeting with the First Lord?"

"It'll have to be today. If we are going to get anything done in time."

"We have a report that a Dutch yacht passed through the Straits of Gibraltar, yesterday, Commissioner." Henri placed the sheet of paper on Labarge's desk.

"Do you think she is the one?"

"Oh, certainly."

"Course and speed?"

"Estimated course east by north, estimated speed five to six knots. She will be abeam of Algiers tomorrow."

"But if she holds that course she will be well offshore."

"The next possible stopping place for her will be Tunis. That will be another three days, after she has passed through the Sicilian Channel."

"We shall see," Labarge said. "And we will stick to our original plan, Henri. Let Madame Elligan get her munitions to Albania, if she can. We will be here when she tries to get back out."

"The Dutch yacht *Christina* passed through the Straits of Gibraltar yesterday," remarked the flag captain. "Making east, and travelling slowly, although she is under full sail. Our best estimate is that she will be in the Sicilian Channel in about five days. There would be a convenient place to have her stopped."

"We have no right to stop her on the high seas," the Admiral pointed out.

"Well, sir, who's to know? If she is carrying contraband, she is hardly likely to hurry into Valletta and complain to the British."

"It would still be an illegal act," Carzanti insisted.

"Even if she were to stray into our waters?"

"That would be a different matter. But she is hardly likely to do that. No, Captain, continue to have a watch kept for her, particularly after she passes Taranto. Our business is only to shadow her. General Rometti will do the rest."

"This has got to be the most peaceful sea in the world," Dennis remarked, taking a noonday sight with his sextant.

"Have you sailed here before?" Catherine asked.

"Only a couple of times." He made a note on his pad. "Oh, there is weather from time to time. When there is a mistral blowing up in the Gulf of Lions it can get quite choppy. But there's not enough fetch for really big seas to build, and mistral winds seldom get this far south in any event."

Catherine stretched. She lay in a deckchair, wearing bra and knickers. She felt relaxed. The dreadful trauma of Roberta's death was starting to fade, and she was in the hands, often very literally, of a most splendid man. Whoever would have thought it could have turned out this way?

Thanks to Sophie! What a remarkable woman she was. To think they had actually had sex together. Water off a duck's back, to Sophie. She had felt like it, so she had done it. Catherine wondered if she would ever have the mental freedom to think like that? She wanted to believe that, because it was a problem she was going to have to face, when this was over. Did she just kiss Dennis goodbye, it's been great knowing you . . . and attempt to pick up the threads of her life? As a schoolmistress? Dennis apart, would she be able to do that? Could she ever stand before a class of inattentive girls and teach them Greek history without constantly recalling every minute of the past month? Every traumatic moment?

But Dennis wasn't apart. Dennis was the here and now. Catherine knew that, at the moment certainly, there was nothing she would rather do than spend the rest of her life on board this ship, sailing with Dennis. He had told her that with the money he hoped to earn he could really fix up the yacht, make her much more luxurious, and really develop the charter business. She felt she would love that, would cheerfully cook for their guests, and clean for them as well. With Dennis always at her side.

169

And her parents? But she had already rejected her parents. Again, Sophie's doing. But Sophie, and by extension, Dennis, stood for all the exciting things in life, for living, instead of merely existing . . . and for dying young? But both Dennis and Sophie were still alive.

If only she could be sure he felt the same way. He treated her as if he loved her, at once gentle and perceptive and eager to please. But he had been commanded to do so by Sophie. Always back to Sophie. Would he want to spend the rest of his life looking after her? Apart from the fact that he was so much the older, their backgrounds were as different as their colours. Their upbringings, their ethos and their mores, had to be aeons apart. Right now they were living in his world, and she was happy to go along with that . . . but her world would have to impinge, at some stage.

Ah, well, she thought, as she watched him write up his logbook, if he doesn't want me I can always stay with Sophie. She thought that was going to be exciting.

Sophie sat at the saloon table, surrounded by boxes of ammunition, and studied the chart. Captain Pfuhl was beside her. "I think you're nervous," Richard remarked, leaning on the bulkhead behind them, swaying in time to the movement of the ship.

"Just considering options," Sophie said. "In two days' time we'll be coming up to the Sicilian Channel. If they're ever going to try to stop us it'll be there, I should think."

"They being the Italians?"

"There's nobody else interested."

"Aren't you wanted for murder in both France and Germany"

"That's France and Germany. This is the Meditenanean."

"And you think the Italians know we are coming."

"They know something is coming," Sophie said. "Or they wouldn't have attempted to stop us before we even began. They will have patrols out looking for any strange vessels."

"But without the right to stop us unless we enter their waters," Pfuhl pointed out.

"The legal right, Captain. We shall have to wait and see."

She went into the after cabin, heard the door open and close behind her. "How long is this farce going to continue?" Richard asked.

"What farce?" She sat on the bunk.

"You sleeping alone in here, while Catherine shacks up with the darkie and I am left sharing with Pfuhl. Did you know he snores?"

"So do you, if I remember correctly."

"Sophie." He sat beside her. "Okay, so we've had our ups and downs—"

"Remind me about the ups."

"You are a bitch. We loved, once. We shared, once. We fought shoulder to shoulder, once."

"I treasure those memories, Richard. Believe me. But I think they were with a different man."

"In what way?"

"The man I adventured with, with James Martingell, in Afghanistan and China, was totally committed, to me, and to our project. I just can't relate him to the man who, after I had disappeared into the Sahara back in 1930, did absolutely nothing about it. His own wife!"

"For God's sake," he snapped. "I had a broken leg, remember? Which is why you were there in the first place, remember? And you were breaking the law. What was I supposed to do, call out the police? And then I was reliably informed that you were dead."

"The man I married would have come looking, the moment his leg was mended," Sophie said coldly.

"So you're going to hold that against me for the rest of your life."

"Not really. It's a memory that prevents me wanting to get too close to you again, though. I'm grateful, really. Because of it I had the happiest nine years of my life. With Ned."

"Until he up and left you. There has to be a moral in that."

"He did not leave me," Sophie said. "He was shot down by Italian agents while trying to save my life. Which he did."

Richard stared at her. "You told me—"

"I told you what I felt you ought to know, at the time."

He continued to stare at her for several seconds Then he asked, "Just how many people know this?"

"You mean apart from the French and Italian police, and probably the British as well as the German?"

"I meant, on board this ship?"

"Everyone, now."

"They all know, while I supposed—"

"Does it matter?"

"Yes, it does," he said angrily. "Not only does it make me look a proper Charlie in all their eyes, but it also means you don't trust me."

Sophie shrugged. "I don't."

"And now?"

"Now it doesn't matter. I needed a replacement for Ned, to convince Walters there'd be no problem, and you were the ideal person. Once the munitions were loaded, you became superfluous. That I didn't have the captain throw you overboard out in the Atlantic was because I'd taken you into partnership, and I'll see the partnership through. All I ask is that you pull your weight if it comes to trouble. I presume you can still do that?"

"And you and me?"

"Forget it."

He glared at her. "I ought to—"

She looked at his bunched fists. "It's a long way to land, Richard. Everyone on board this ship is mine. You're welcome to join the club. If not—" she gave another shrug.

"Bitch!" he said. "Bitch! And I suppose you've been having it off with the darkie."

"I think you should stop using that word," Sophie recommended. "Or I'll have you say it to his face. I have not been having it off with anyone, Richard. If it's any satisfaction to you, I'm carrying Ned's child."

He gaped at her. "On a caper like this?"

"It's what Ned would have wanted."

"And when it's done?"

"I'll retire some place quiet and have my baby."

He got up, went to the door. "And you reckon the world will always rotate to your requirements."

"It always has done." He slammed the door. Until the day Ned was killed, she thought, and felt the tears dribbling down her cheeks.

"Look over there," Dennis said, handing Sophie the binoculars.

It was just on dusk, and *Christina* continued to sail well before the fresh north-westerly breeze. The indicated direction was south-west, and she could make out the shape of a ship, some-what low, and perhaps ten miles away. "A warship?"

"I don't think so. But she's not under sail. And she isn't giving smoke. That means she probably has a diesel engine, maybe two. She's fast."

"Is that bad?"

"Not in itself. What bothers me is that she is maintaining station. Whereas she should be overtaking us and drawing away."

Sophie continued to study the alien vessel for several minutes; she was showing no lights that were visible at this distance. "Should we alter course?"

"I don't think that would do too much good. We'd have to beat, unless we go towards her. If we beat she'll follow, and she can catch us up whenever she chooses. We'll hold our course, but we'll take a few precautions." He had his crew drop the sails, and started up his own engine; the white canvas would show up in the darkness. But even the engine did not greatly increase the *boier's* speed. "Now I think we need to arm ourselves."

"There are enough of them about," Sophie agreed.

They opened one of the crates and took out six rifles. As Catherine had no idea how to handle a rifle, from another crate they took three tommy-guns, and gave her one of these. "What do I do?"

"Point it at anyone you don't like and squeeze the trigger," Sophie told her. "You don't have to aim except in the general direction."

"Suppose I hit somebody?"

"That is the general idea. Hopefully you'll kill him. But no shooting until I tell you. Right?"

"Right," Catherine said, looking suitably determined.

They equipped themselves with ammunition, and closed up the crates again. "You realise that if that fellow means to sink us, and puts a shot into where those explosives are stored—"

"Bingo."

"That doesn't scare you?"

"I'm counting on the fact that he'll want to be sure it's us, first."

They had supper, and then prepared. Dennis doused all lights, even his navigation lights, so that they were hopefully invisible at more than a hundred yards. "Trouble is," he said, "there's a moon due about nine."

"And you still don't think it's worth making a run for it before then?"

"Not if you want to be on time for your delivery." That had to have priority.

Lewis went into the bows to act as lookout in case there was something coming towards them from the other direction. Carl was on the wheel. The four marksmen took up their positions just forward of the helm, Richard and Sophie to starboard, Dennis and Pfuhl to port. Catherine was right aft. "Just like old times," Richard said.

"We've never fought a battle at sea," she reminded him.

"Scared?"

"People are always asking me that. I'm apprehensive."

"But not enough to stop you killing someone."

"Not enough."

Christina chugged steadily ahead, and the night grew very dark. But soon they saw the glimmer on the eastern horizon, and then the moon surged into view, full, sending a swathe of light across the water. "There," Dennis said.

The mystery vessel had increased speed, and was now quite close, still utterly dark. "Stand by," Sophie called.

Lewis came aft and nestled behind the bulwark, rifle cradled in his arms. "Ahoy!" came the amplified voice across the water. "Yacht *Christina*! Heave to!"

"No reply," Sophie said softly.

The other ship was now no more than a hundred yards away, again matching their speed. "I am coming alongside," the voice called.

Sophie levelled her binoculars, could make out men putting out fenders along the port topsides of the approaching ship. "We could pick those fellows off," Richard said.

"The shooting has to start with them," Sophie said. "They could be legit."

The stranger came closer yet. Now they could see several men standing on the foredeck, and others on the bridge; they all had rifles in their hands. But *they* would be able to see nothing on the *boier* save the helmsman; even Catherine was crouching behind the after hatch. Now only feet separated the two ships, and grapples were hurled, crunching into the wooden gunwale of the yacht. "Just like good old Teach," Richard commented. "You letting those fellows come on board?"

"No," Dennis said. "Just hold it," he called.

"So there you are, Captain," the voice said. But he still couldn't see Dennis.

"No one comes on board," Dennis called.

"Stop us," the voice said. The stranger clattered alongside with a thud that made the *boier* reel, and several men leapt across the rail.

"Fire!" Sophie shouted, stood up, and levelled her own tommy-gun, squeezing the trigger. Beside her, Richard was also firing, as were Dennis and Pfuhl and Lewis; Carl prudently dropped to the deck beside the helm, but he too was firing. The pirates, as such they had to be considered, returned fire and for a few seconds there was a hail of bullets going in both directions. Then the boarders were too close. Sophie dropped her tommy-gun to draw her pistol and fire into one body looming above her, then was struck a blow on the side of the head that tumbled her into the scuppers.

"That's the one," someone shouted in German. "Get her, and we can blow the rest out of the sea."

Sophie sat up, head swinging, realised she had lost her pistol. She scrabbled for it, and a body fell right over her, crashing to the deck. She had no idea who it was, as her arms were gripped and she was jerked to her feet. She kicked at the nearest man, but did not connect, and a moment later she was picked up and slung over the shoulder of a very large man. She pounded his back with her fists, but she couldn't kick again as he was holding her very tightly round the thighs. "Stop shooting!" Richard was shouting. "They've got Sophie!"

She was carried to the rail and thrown across onto the deck of the German ship, landing with a thump that jarred all the breath from her body "Free those grapples," the German commander shouted.

"No you don't," Pfuhl shouted, swinging his empty rifle at the back of the man trying to obey the order.

Sophie sat up, panting, and had her shoulders seized to draw her back towards the saloon door, beneath the wheelhouse. On her way she tripped over a dead body. "Who the shit are you?" she shouted at her captor.

"Gestapo, Frau Elligan. You have a date with a German court."

"You—" the saloon door was open, and she was thrust inside, tripping down a brief ladder as the light was switched on. She gazed at a bearded man wearing a seaman's sweater and a peaked cap. With him was a younger man, clean-shaven. And the grapples had been freed; Sophie could feel the ship drifting away from the yacht; the grinding noise of hull against hull was gone. But there were still shots being exchanged.

The door opened and another man came in. "Your orders, Captain?"

"Get an offing, unship the gun, and blow her out of the water." He grinned. "She is carrying explosives, so there may be a big bang."

The lieutenant nodded, and stepped back outside. "What do we do with her?" the other man asked.

"Take her below and lock her in a cabin."

"Can I tickle her up a bit? She's a looker."

"Do what you wish. But she is not to be marked. I think Herr Eisener wishes to interview her, as he did her mother."

"Bastard!" Sophie had now recovered her breath, and she did not seem to be hurt beyond a few bruises. And she was fighting mad. The man came to her, reaching out to grasp her, and she clasped her hands together and swung them upwards into his crotch. He gasped, and swore, and fell forward, and she swung her still clasped hands left and right, crashing into his face and throwing him sideways and right over one of the chairs bolted to the deck. He landed heavily.

"Bitch!" shouted the captain, in turn reaching for her. But Sophie had jumped clear over the chair, to crouch beside the sailor and draw the pistol from his belt. Now she reared back, and as the captain groped for his own gun, she shot him through the chest. He fell back with a crash. The other man was just recovering, so Sophie shot him through the head, then got to her feet, watching the door. Sure enough it was dragged open, just far enough to let her shoot the sailor in turn. He staggered backwards, struck the rail, and went over the side.

176

Sophie dashed on deck. The two ships were now about thirty feet apart, and below her the engines were starting to surge as the mate opened the throttle to gain the necessary offing to open fire. Sophie tucked the pistol into her belt and swarmed up the ladder to the second steering position on the flying bridge. From here she looked down on the after deck, where a gun, a two-pounder she estimated, was being uncovered. It would fire a relatively small shell, but a single shot put into the *boier's* waterline would either blow *Christina* up or sink her. The small arms firing had stopped, and it was difficult to determine what was happening on the yacht, but clearly there had been casualties.

It still remained her future, with whoever was left. She grabbed the wheel and twisted it, and the diesel cruiser came round in a wide circle. The men on the after deck began shouting, and one came up the aft ladder. Sophie let him come, reckoning he would make the same mistake as the others and suppose he was dealing with only a woman. She waited until he had gained the bridge, then put the engines into neutral and shot him. He dropped at the top of the ladder, and she grasped his shoulders before he could slip back down, and dragged him onto the platform. She had seen what she wanted, a string of grenades hanging from his waist. She plucked this loose, freed one of them.

The remaining men on the afterdeck were now shooting at her, as were those forward. Sophie ran aft along the upper deck, reached the little funnel. She drew the pin on the grenade and dropped it down the hole, then hurled herself over the side.

Sophie struck the water at the same moment as the engine-room exploded. There was an enormous woomph, and she seemed to be hurled through the depths before coming up again, gasping for breath and instinctively swimming even as she turned back to look. The cruiser was disintegrating in every direction, as even the diesel fuel caught fire; guns and grenades exploded, men screamed as they were set alight or hurled into the sea. For a moment the night was as bright as day. The *boier* was illuminated, only a hundred yards away. Her engine was still running, and she appeared to be drawing away. But there was nobody on the helm, and she was coming round in a slow circle. "Dennis!" Sophie screamed. "Richard! Catherine!" Desperately she began to swim again.

Someone had heard her, and took the helm. *Christina* turned towards her. "Stop engines!" Sophie shrieked, not wishing to be run down.

Slowly the *boier* lost way as she approached. Behind her the cruiser was settling, her upper works ablaze, as water rushed into the engine room through the split seams. "Sophie!" Catherine was leaning over the rail, trying to see as the light faded.

"Here!" Sophie shouted. Now she was beneath the topsides. But by now she was exhausted. "A rope!" she gasped. One came down and she grasped it, made a bowline and dropped it over her head and under her arms. "Winch me up!"

It seemed to take a long time, but slowly she was lifted from the water and dragged upwards, using her feet to keep herself off the hull until she reached the gunwale and could get a leg over. Then she fell into the ship and lay on the deck, gasping. Catherine knelt beside her. "Oh, Sophie! We thought we'd lost you."

Richard standing above her. "Fortune favours the brave."

Sophie sat up, and Catherine helped her to her feet. "Sophie! Dennis was hit. He's bad, Sophie."

All Sophie wanted to do was lie down. She looked around herself at a scene of utter carnage, with four bodies lying on the deck, with various fittings cut to pieces by the flying shot, with discarded weapons in every direction. "How many of ours?" she asked. "Apart from the captain?"

"Pfuhl stopped one," Richard said. Sophie bent over the old captain, and felt her heart sag. They had adventured together over such a long time, and had risked so much together. When she remembered him taking his steamer up that creek in East Africa . . . now he lay on his back, his chest a mass of blood. "Sophie," Catherine said. "Dennis—"

Sophie heaved herself to her feet and went to the far gunwale, against which Dennis lay. He was on his side, making no sound. Sophie turned him over, afraid of what she was going to see. But he was alive, breathing stertorously, and losing blood. He had been hit in the side, she reckoned, and at least one rib was broken. But the bones had deflected the bullet away from heart or lungs. "Help me."

Catherine knelt beside her, and between them they got the captain's sailing smock and shirt off. Catherine gave an hysterical giggle. "I've done this before. I helped Mr Andrews do

178

Roberta. Sort of. Oh, Roberta!" She burst into tears. "He's not going to die too, is he, Sophie? Say he's not going to die." "He's not going to die," Sophie promised. "Let's have a light." Richard held a flashlight and she peered at the gash. There were two ribs broken, but the bullet had exited cleanly. "Fetch my bag." Catherine half fell down the companionway. "What happens now?" Richard asked.

"We patch Dennis up."

"And then?"

"Ask me when we've patched Dennis up." Catherine returned with the first aid kit, and Sophie cleaned the wound as best she could. Then she applied antiseptic, and this brought Dennis back to life, with a groan and then a moan of pain. "Bandages." Catherine held them out, and Sophie wrapped them tightly round the captain's body. "Now, let's get him to bed. Richard, you and Carl . . . where's Lewis?"

"I'm afraid he's dead, ma'am."

"Shit!" Sophie muttered. But it could have been worse. Richard and Carl carried the captain down the ladder into the saloon, and then into his cabin, laying him on the bunk. Catherine went with him. "Let's get these bodies over the side," Sophie said, when the men returned.

"Just what have you got in your veins?" Richard asked. "Ice water?"

"You'd better believe it. And be grateful." Between them they carried the two German sailors to the rail and threw them over. By now the cruiser had entirely disappeared, although there were still one or two patches of burning wood and oil.

"What about our own?" Richard asked. "Decent burial and all that?"

"I don't think we can spare the time. But we can at least weight them and say a prayer." Carl joined them, and they tied lead weights to the ankles of the two men, then stood together and said a private prayer as they consigned the bodies into the dark water. "Good men," Sophie said. "Oh, good men."

"Sophie!" Catherine stood in the hatchway. "He's so restless. I think he has a fever."

Sophie went down. The cabin lights were on, and she looked at her bloodied hands. Her wet clothes were also soaked in blood,

179

whose she didn't know. She washed her hands, went to Dennis. He was tossing and turning and muttering incoherently. She mixed up a sedative, and Catherine held his head up while she poured it down his throat. Then he slowly subsided. "Oh, Sophie," Catherine said.

"He's going to be all right." As long as infection doesn't set in, Sophie thought. But she had done all she could.

Sophie returned on deck, took deep breaths of fresh air. *Christina* lay quietly in the water, her engine growling in neutral, rolling gently. Now there was no trace of the German vessel, and the moonlight was streaming across an empty sea. She kept holding her stomach. She felt nothing down there. But if the baby had been harmed . . . then nothing else would be worth while.

"That chap had a wireless aerial," Richard said. "Think he got off a message to his friends?"

"What friends?"

"That's a fact. What do we do now?"

"Clean up." They fetched buckets and hoisted sea water over the side to wash down the deck. Carl got a brush and pushed the blood into the scuppers and thence over the side. "I'm sorry about your mate," Sophie said.

"He was a good friend," Carl said. "But the Captain—"

"He's going to be all right," Sophie assured him in turn.

"What do we do now?" Richard asked again. "Seems to me we're all fucked up. You're wanted in Italy and France, not to mention Germany. And after this . . . if the Germans know where to find us, now, you can bet the Italians do too. Now we don't even have a skipper. I reckon we'd better cut our losses, dump the cargo, and see if we can make it back to England."

"Forget it."

"You're not going on?"

"I have been paid to deliver this cargo to Clay Andrews on 23 May. And that is what I intend to do."

"You are out of your tiny mind. When next we make port—"

"We are not going to make port, until after the cargo has been delivered."

"Oh, yes? And who is going to navigate us?"

"I am. With help from the captain when he regains consciousness."

He snorted. "Lights, and signals," Carl said.

Sophie levelled her binoculars. She reckoned it was a destroyer, approaching at speed, its lamp flashing. "Who reads Morse?"

"I do," Richard said. "He's telling us to stop and identify ourselves. In English."

"That's a relief. Leave the talking to me."

The destroyer lost speed as it came up to them. Although the residue of its wake had them rolling. "What ship is that?" the voice came through the loud hailer.

"The yacht *Christina*, out of Terschelling," Sophie shouted back.

"We saw an explosion."

"So did we," Sophie said. "So we came to investigate. We think a ship blew up. There are bodies in the water. Can you help?"

A launch was already being put down, equipped with a powerful searchlight. "What caused the explosion?" the voice asked.

"We have no idea. We heard it, and saw it, from some distance away. By the time we got here the ship had disappeared."

"I would like to board you."

"Why? We are a Dutch vessel. You have no right to interfere with our progress on the high seas."

"There will have to be a statement as to what happened."

"I will make one, when we reach port," Sophie said.

"What is your destination?"

"Athens. Piraeus. I will make a statement when I get there. Good night to you, Captain." She went to the helm, engaged gear, and the *buier* started to move through the water, away from the floating bodies and the destroyer's launch. As they drew abeam of the warship a searchlight was played over their decks. "Give them a wave," Sophie said.

Carl and Richard obeyed, and the searchlight died. "You realise you have just tossed off the Royal Navy," Richard remarked.

"I am within my rights to do so."

"And what do you think is going to happen when he picks up those bodies and finds several of them with bullet wounds?"

"He cannot prove we put them there, Richard. Will you take

181

the helm, please. I must report to the Captain. Course is zero eight zero until dawn."

"Disappeared?" Pemberton asked.

"Actually, blew up," the commander said. "That is the report received from the captain of the destroyer we put on patrol in the Sicilian Channel. He saw the explosion from a distance, and steamed towards it. But it appears there were no survivors."

"Well, well," Pemberton commented. "I suppose it was always a risk, when your cargo is arms and ammunition. A careless match—" but what a shame, he thought, that Sophie Elligan should go in such a fashion.

"I don't think you quite understand, sir. It was not the *boier* that blew up."

"Eh?"

"It was an unidentified vessel, sir. Our destroyer, when it reached the scene, spoke with another vessel, entered in her log as the Dutch yacht *Christina*."

"Good God! And she was all right?"

"Our people were not allowed on board, and they had no legal right to insist on boarding. They were spoken to by a woman, who seemed in command. She said they too had seen the explosion, and gone to the scene."

Pemberton considered. He did not suppose there could be any doubt that if a ship blew up in the vicinity of Sophie Elligan she had had a hand in the blowing up. A one-woman army of destruction. "There is a curious development," the commander went on. The destroyer captain reports that they picked up several bodies. None of them had any identification. However, what is really interesting is that nearly all the bodies had gunshot wounds. It was as if there had been a gun battle shortly before the explosion. In fact, it is the opinion of the doctor on board the destroyer – he hasn't had the time yet to carry out a proper post-mortem – that they mostly died from gunshot wounds, rather than drowning or blast. And an additional point of interest is that although the destroyer picked up a considerable amount of flotsam, including three lifebelts, none of them carried any name. I find that highly suspicious."

"Suspicious of what, Commander?"

"Well, sir, piracy. We know that pirates still do operate out of the smaller North African ports. So it occurs to me that, if the *boier* was involved, and there was some kind of shoot-out before the other vessel exploded, there would be gunshot damage to the yacht. This surely gives us the right to seize her and search her."

"Only if we are are positive we would find such evidence, Commander. Otherwise we would be acting illegally, and there would be one hell of a row."

"So, what do we do, sir?"

Pemberton regarded the portrait of Neville Chamberlain on the wall opposite; he was becoming quite attached to that portrait. Sophie Elligan. Shooting her way to hell and back. He wondered who had tried to stop her this time? Probably the Italians. They should have known better than to attempt it with anything less than a battleship! And the best of luck to her. "Why, Commander, we do nothing. It is not our province. As you say, the *boier* may well have been set upon by pirates, and defended herself. No doubt she will report the incident in due course."

"Disappeared?" Eisener said. "Ships do not just disappear."

"I'm afraid they do, Herr Eisener," Eichmann said. "In this case, there was apparently an explosion. This was reported by a British warship in the area. Apparently it was not possible to identify the vessel."

"Then we do not know it was ours."

"I'm afraid we must presume that it was, sir. For three reasons. The first is that Captain Mueller radioed in at nine o'clock last night, that he had his target in sight and was closing. That was twenty-four hours ago, and he has not called again since. The second reason is that he has not returned to port. And the third is that the British destroyer picked up some bodies. No report has been made on their condition. But they would also have picked up various flotsam, including almost certainly a lifebelt. Yet they say they have no indication of the ship's name. We know that our vessel put to sea with all identification removed, including the name on the lifebelts."

"You are telling me that our vessel, which was both fast and heavily armed, and was manned by a picked crew, actually got up to this yacht, and was then destroyed?"

Eichmann gulped. "I'm afraid that looks the most likely

scenario, sir. Of course we do not know what caused the explosion. It might just have been bad luck—"

"Where Sophie Elligan is concerned, there is never any luck involved," Eisener snapped. What a shitting mess. Canaris had been unhappy about the whole thing from the beginning. What he was going to say now, he thought, that when they finally did catch up with Sophie Elligan, and had her tried and convicted, he would see to it that she was not merely beheaded by the blow of a sharp sword, but that her neck would be cut through, slowly, with an old and rusty saw.

"Have you any further orders, sir? Eichmann asked. "I'm afraid the yacht will be in the vicinity of Malta by now, which means she is within thirty-six hours of the Ionian Islands, even at her slow speed. And it will take is at least that long to arrange another interception."

"And have another ship blown up? Arrange another interception, Eichmann, but this is to take place when she is on her way back. It's the woman we want, not the guns." Presuming the Italians can't handle her, he thought as he replaced the phone. But if the Gestapo couldn't, what chance had the Italians?

"I thought you might be interested in this, sir," said the flag captain, placing the sheet of paper on the Admiral's desk.

Carzanti studied it. "Can this be the ship we are looking for?"

"Unfortunately, no, sir. You will see that the British destroyer which reported the incident says it spoke with a Dutch yacht when it reached the scene. It is highly unlikely that there would be two Dutch yachts in the vicinity at the same time. I would say the Elligan party had a hand in the destruction of the other ship."

"But what was this other ship?" Carzanti inquired, somewhat plaintively. "I hope she was not one of ours, Renaldo."

"It certainly was not authorised, sir. And none of our ships has been reported missing. Meanwhile, the *boier* is proceeding east. Do you wish her stopped?"

"We have been through this before, Renaldo. We have no right to stop her unless she enters Italian waters. But I wish her shadowed, from here on in. And you will keep General Rometti up to date with her position." Renaldo saluted.

Interception

"I should come up," Dennis protested. "You should lie absolutely still, you mean," Sophie told him. "It is not so much the bullet wound as the loss of blood. You need rest. All I need to know is what to do."

"Do you know our position?"

"We have Malta in sight, maybe ten miles, on the port beam."

"Then alter course to zero five zero, to enter the Ionians between Anti-Paxos and Leukas. That will take you to the landing area." He listened. "You are under sail."

"I thought it best to save fuel."

"Sensible. So what are you making?"

"There's quite a good breeze, southerly. We're doing about five knots."

"Then there are three days to go. Will that be on schedule?"

"With a day to spare. We can linger, once we're in Greek waters."

"The Greeks are very officious when it comes to visiting ships," Dennis said. "They will not board you if you behave properly, but if indeed we have a day to spare, I suggest you put into Leukas and make a formal entry. You can anchor off and not be overlooked, but they will require someone to go ashore with a crew list, reason for visit, etc. Can you handle that?"

"I reckon. What about a doctor for you?"

"Definitely not. Once they discover you have a man with a gunshot wound on board you'll have the Greek police swarming all over you."

Sophie nodded and went outside, where Catherine was waiting for her. "Is he going to be all right? My God, Sophie, if anything were to happen to him, after Roberta—"

185

"He's going to be all right. Now go hold his hand. But nothing else, mind. He needs his strength."

She went on deck. "We have company," Richard said. He was looking at the sky, and Sophie saw the airplane circling above them and gradually coming closer. "Italian," Richard said.

"That figures."

"So now they know we are coming."

"They always did. What they still don't know is where and when."

"Well, I would say that having spotted us, they are going to have a fairly good idea."

"Maybe. But they can't do anything about it while we're out here, and they can do even less once we're in Greek territorial waters."

"You reckon? What about that bloke a couple of days ago?"

"He was German, not Italian."

"You certainly seem to have stirred up a lot of enemies since the last time we worked together."

"One does, in this business. I thought you knew that."

She was leaning against the rail, and now he stood against her and put his arms round her. "Sophie, let's let bygones be bygones. I adore you. I always did. Okay, so you're carrying Ned's child. I'll be happy to raise it as my own. If we can pull this off—"

"We *are* going to pull it off," Sophie said, fiercely.

"Great. And then—"

"We go our separate ways, Richard. Again."

"You—" he changed his mind about calling her names. "Haven't I done everything I can for you, on this voyage?"

"You have done everything you have been told to do, yes. Thank you."

"You are a very hard woman, Sophie."

"I've been conditioned to it." She moved his arm and went to the helm. "My watch, Carl."

Edio read the report, flicking his moustache. "She is a difficult woman to stop. Who did this?"

"No one has any idea, General." Renaldo had crossed the Adriatic by flying-boat. "We presume it must be the French, as she is wanted for murder in France."

"The French do not go about committing piracy, as a rule," Edio pointed out. He had his own opinion. He did not like the Nazi regime, and considered that Mussolini had made a big mistake in tying Italy to it.

"However," Renaldo went on. "We have them in our sights now. One of our reconnaissance machines saw them, east of Malta, and steering a course which will take them into the Ionian Islands, as we surmised. Shall we alert the Greek authorities?"

"Certainly not. This is our business. And the Greeks would only obstruct us. You say you know where the *boier* is at this moment. Can you give me an ETA?"

"I could, if I knew where she was going. She will enter the Ionian Islands at about dawn on 22 May. If she proceeds straight to her landing place, she would be late that morning. Certainly by afternoon. That is presuming the landing place is on the mainland coast."

"They are hardly going to put the guns ashore on an island, which will mean another transportation problem." Edio studied the map.

"She could, of course, mean to turn up north of Corfu, and put the guns ashore in Albania," Renaldo suggested.

Edio shook his head. "That would be suicide, and our Sophie is too smart for that. No, the guns will come ashore here." He prodded the map opposite Paxos. "Within a mile or two."

"You are meaning to arrest them on landing?"

"Once they get into the mountains, they will be difficult to stop."

"But . . . you will be invading Greek territory."

"Yes," Edio said thoughtfully. "I have done this sort of thing before." For the same reason. When he had crossed the border from Libya into French Sahara in 1930, again to get hold of Sophie . . . even if he had not then known she existed. That expedition had been a disaster, but because of the weather more than anything Sophie had done. This time the weather would not be a factor, with summer just around the corner.

"It will be very risky," Renaldo argued. "There will be diplomatic repercussions."

"It is a matter of getting in, and out, before anyone knows what is happening," Edio said. "We are only talking of twenty-four hours. It is my responsibility, Renaldo. All I require from you is a constant updating of the *boier*'s position. And the ship. Is that arranged?"

"She will be here tomorrow," Renaldo said. "But we still need to be sure of the *boier*'s position. This ship is a steam yacht. She is not very fast. If you were to lose the Dutchman—"

"Have you no people in the islands?"

"Yes, we do. There is a man on Corfu, of course, one on Leukas, one on Zante, just in case she moves further south . . . but there are other islands."

"Send someone to Anti-Paxos," Edio recommended. "And I am sure you can risk an overfly, from time to time. The Greeks may complain, but they are hardly likely to shoot down one of our aircraft. Now tell me about this steam yacht. Will she carry a hundred men?"

"For a short time. Facilities will be primitive."

"One night, Renaldo. Is the commander a good man?"

"I believe so, General."

"What is his name?"

"I will command the yacht myself, General."

"You are sure?" Clay Andrews asked into his radio. It was brand new, and had been obtained from the American embassy in Greece and smuggled across the border. As always, when he was using the magic machine, people crowded round to listen. Roberta knelt beside him. Her strength was returning every day, and she was gaining some weight as well.

"That is our information," the man in Greece said.

"I hope you are right. But if it was not the *boier* blew up, what was it?"

"I would say it was someone trying to stop the delivery. Probably Italian."

"And Sophie blew it up? Great stuff. So, as far as you know, she is on schedule."

"As far as we know."

"Then we'll be there. Over and out." He looked around the expectant faces. "The guns are coming. And the ammunition, and the explosives. And the machine-guns. We will soon be a full fighting force." The Albanians clapped their hands. "However,

188

as you heard, there can be no doubt that the Italian know she is coming. They may try to stop her again."

"After the last time?" Dino scoffed.

"They are certainly going to try to stop us bringing the goods here," Clay said. "Now, I am going to move out with the mule train the day after tomorrow. I will cross the border by the mountain route. I will take twenty men with me. Dino, I wish you to mount a diversionary attack on Fier at dawn on 22 May. That will be the day the goods enter Greek waters. They will be landed the following night. There is no need to press home your attack. It is to be a diversion, nothing more. We do not want heavy casualties. Once the Italians have drawn in their forces to defend the town, you will withdraw to the mountains. Understood?"

Dino nodded. "Will they not try to block the roads?" someone asked.

"They will, But they cannot block the mountain trails," Clay pointed out. "It will be your business to keep those open, Dino. Once we are away from the coast we should not have a problem. Apart from aircraft. We will move by night, and shelter by day. Marco, is all organised with your people on the coast?"

Marco grinned. "They are Greek, therefore they hate the Italians. They await only your signal."

"Great stuff. Now, prepare yourselves. I will select my people later."

They wandered off, chattering enthusiastically to each other. "Is it really going to happen?" Roberta asked.

"I believe it is. And you're going to get out. You'll come with us to the coast, and I'll hand you over to Sophie to be taken out when she leaves."

"Gosh! Do you think she'll have Catherine with her?"

"I should think that's extremely likely," Clay said.

"These men are all volunteers?" Edio asked.

"One hundred, sir."

"They understand that we shall not be wearing uniform, that if we are by any chance forced to surrender we could well be tried as spies or bandits?" He grinned. "Or pirates?"

"They do, sir. But . . . you mean you intend to lead this expedition yourself?"

"I do. Finally to nail Clayton Andrews is a pleasure I have long promised myself. Especially if it carries with it the chance of nailing Sophie Elligan as well."

"Then I also wish to volunteer, sir."

Edio gazed at the young captain. "You, Umberto? You have a wife and children. I specifically insisted that only unmarried men could be included."

"The volunteers are mostly from my command, sir. Where they go, I also would like to be."

Edio nodded. "Very good. We board at zero eight hundred hours. Here is the list of equipment each man must carry."

Catherine helped Dennis up the ladder to sit in a chair on the afterdeck. It was not quite dawn, and the lightening sky was shot with vivid colours. But ahead of them were winking lights. Richard was on the helm; both Carl and Sophie were below, sleeping. "Well, Captain," Richard said. "Just about the end, eh?"

"The end is when we are back in Holland," Dennis said.

"If that's where we're going to wind up, to be sure. You been paid?"

"I have received half, according to my contract."

"She tells me I've received my half as well. Not that I've seen hide nor hair of the money yet."

"Why must you always try to stir trouble?" Catherine asked. "Without Sophie, where would we be?"

"I suspect, just where Sophie means us to be. You two got plans? For life after Sophie, I mean."

"Look," Dennis said. "Mind your own business, right? Concentrate."

"Pardon me for speaking, Captain, sir."

"Don't mind him," Catherine whispered. "It's just the way he is."

"How long have you known him?" Dennis asked.

"Just about the length of this adventure."

"He ever have you?"

"You know he didn't."

He reflected, leaning back in the deck chair. "So, what are *your* plans, Cathy?"

"Who can have plans, at a time like this? Survival, I suppose."

"And if you do?"

"The word is we."

"It's not going to be easy."

"Of course it is. Sophie's paying you five thousand, and me seven. And we'll have the ship. We'll have places to go, Dennis."

"I meant, well—"

"If people don't like it, they can lump it."

"Including your folks?"

She sighed. "I wonder if they ever were."

Sophie came on deck at dawn. "There's your land," Richard said.

"Good boy. Go get some sleep. We may need all our energy, later."

He gave her waist a squeeze, and went below. Catherine stood beside her at the helm, as the sun came up, rising above the low serrated peaks of the island in front of them. "I'm scared stiff."

"Aren't we all?"

"But you've made so many deliveries before."

"It hasn't always gone smoothly." Had it ever gone smoothly?

"You mean you think this has gone smoothly? My God, when I think of Le Pouget, all of those dead bodies, of that ship . . . all for a hundred thousand pounds."

"Just so a bunch of patriots can continue a war," Sophie said. "Don't go soft on me. Anyway, you're part of it now. How many of those pirates did you shoot?"

"Not one. I never squeezed the trigger on that gun, once. I just couldn't." Sophie glanced at her, and she flushed. "That makes me a total washout?"

"That makes you what you are, one of the very few good things about this trip."

Catherine was silent for some minutes, watching the islands rising out of the sea. Now they could see the mainland beyond. "Are we going to make it?"

"Wondering about that is a waste of time. We are going to do what we have contracted to do, to the best of our ability. Within that parameter, we treat each problem as it arises."

"And afterwards?"

191

"Then too. Save that the parameters will have been enlarged, to include regaining the Atlantic."

"That seems an awfully long way away."

"It is. But we'll no longer have contraband on board, so we'll be able to put into port if the going gets rough. Can you handle her for a while?"

Catherine nodded. Sophie gave her the helm, and went down to the engine room to check the fuel gauge. They had sufficient left for another thousand miles, which would take them almost back to Gibraltar. Where they were going to stop was a problem she hadn't solved yet. That too could wait until after the delivery. She went aft. "All well?" Dennis asked. He was making a remarkable recovery, seeing that he had been wounded only four days previously. He couldn't yet stand for more than a few seconds at a time, but he had an immensely strong constitution.

"As near as we can make it," Sophie said.

"Right. When you get up to Leukas, alter course to starboard. There's a canal there, leading back to the port itself. It's broad and deep, but you will have to motor."

Sophie took the helm back and called on Carl to shorten sail. Then the engine was started, and an hour later they turned into the canal. By now Richard was back on deck. Another hour, and they were in Leukas Harbour, finding an anchorage off the docks where their decks could not be overseen. The dinghy was put down, and Carl rowed Sophie ashore to report to the harbour office. "Twelve hours to go," Richard said.

The steam yacht nosed into Anti-Paxos harbour. This was less of a harbour than a creek, sheltered and romantic. "How are things below?" Edio asked.

"Some seasickness," Umberto reported. "And very warm. Can they not come up? Or they may not be very efficient."

"Four at a time," Edio said. "For ten minutes. We don't want to make the locals suspicious."

"I must go ashore," Renaldo said. "To report to the harbour office."

Edio nodded, and went to the wireless room. "Anything?"

"Two messages, sir, just come in. One says that the *boier* is presently moored up in Leukas Harbour—" the operator raised his head to see if Edio might have a comment – the enemy was so close.

But Edio merely nodded. "And the other?"

"From Fier, Signor General. It says they are under attack by guerilla forces."

"Can they defend themselves?"

"They are doing so, Signor General."

"Then let them continue. That can only be a diversion." He went on to the upper deck, sat in a deckchair, and lit a cigar. He was placing his entire career at risk. But he had no doubt he was going to pull it off. And for the time being . . . he had always dreamed of owning an ocean-going yacht. This was the next best thing. For one night.

The mule train was checked at the border. There was a good road running north and south on the Albanian side, but it was as yet scantily patrolled by the Italians as it lay in the shadow of the partisan-controlled mountains. On the Greek side there were only small outposts and most of the guards knew Clay in any event, from his numerous comings and goings: all they required was sufficient payment. "We are on our way to buy supplies," Clay said, truthfully enough. "We will be returning in two days' time." The sergeant nodded and signed the papers. Clay laid the agreed amount of money on the desk.

"Whew." Roberta was riding one of the mules to save her strength.

"It's nearly over, for you." Clay walked beside the mule, holding her bridle.

"And for you?"

Clay grinned. "Just beginning another chapter."

"Will these guns really make a difference?"

"By themselves, no. Although we can sure use the ammo and the explosives. They're important for two reasons. One is morale. The guns will convince the partisans that they are not alone, that there are people out there who are willing to help them. The second is a spin-off from that. Once this shipment gets through, my friends in the States will be willing to risk another, and then another. We'll make Mussolini regret the day he crossed the Adriatic."

"But can you possibly win? I mean, the war."

"Sure. As long as we hold out. It may take a while. Maybe even a year or two. But Musso can't sustain such a wasting campaign for too long. Italy is pretty near bankruptcy as it is. We'll win."

"And how many lives will be lost in this year or two?"

He squeezed her thigh; the wound was on the other leg. "The price of freedom."

She shivered. "You know, the Italians were pretty good to me. The ones who got me out. Men like General Rometti and Dr Pizzoli."

"Sure. They're decent people. But they're still doing what the Pontine Bullfrog tells them to. That's the curse of all people. However basically decent they are, they do what they're told to by their leaders. And when there's a bad leader . . . when you get home, Roberta, be sure you tell people, people who matter, what you've seen here. That could shorten the war."

"I'll do that," she promised.

Catherine thought that this last wait was the most difficult part of the entire delivery. They were anchored in a delightful harbour, bathed in perfect sunshine, with just a gentle breeze to keep the temperature from rising too high; Carl followed proper yachting procedure, and spread a tarpaulin over the after deck to allow them to sit in comfort. They were surrounded by busy activity, fishing boats coming and going, children bathing on the beach, a ferry chugging its way slowly up to the dock, much excitement and shouting on the shore, holidaymakers in small boats sailing close by the *boier* to admire her unusual lines, for these waters, and to wave and shout hello.

They breakfasted, and lounged about, wearing as little as was decent, then lunched, and lounged some more, attempted to siesta. While all the time thinking ahead to the night. Dennis having gone to sleep, Catherine joined Sophie in the after cabin. The ports were open and the breeze drifted through; it was actually cooler than on deck, but they both preferred to be naked, sprawled on the bunks. "What do you think about, at a moment like this?" Catherine asked.

"One tends to go over and over in one's mind, everything that should have been done, and try to reassure oneself that it has all been done."

"What about thinking through it?"

"There's a time for that. But it can be dangerous. Best to think up to it, and like I said, take what comes afterwards. If everything goes the way it should, we'll have unloaded the cargo by dawn tomorrow, and be on our way home, without anyone being able to prove we're not what we claim to be."

"And if something goes wrong?"

"Then we may have to fight for our lives. But I'm trusting Clay to have made sure nothing can go wrong. Come over here and give me a hug and a kiss then try to get some sleep."

From a hilltop Clay could survey the Ionian Sea beneath him, glistening blue in the late afternoon sunlight. The islands were blobs of green and brown. There was quite a lot of traffic down there, but only one that mattered; even at this distance, some ten miles, with his powerful binoculars he could make out the distinctive shape of the *boier* in Leukas Harbour. He swung the glasses up and down the sea, then focused on Anti-Paxos, which was directly in front of him across the channel. Boats came and went, surrounded the few yachts that were moored in the creek. That was obscured by trees, but he could see that one of the yachts was quite large, a real ocean-going steamer, flying . . . he frowned. The Italian flag. Well, he supposed there were quite a number of Italian millionaires able to own a vessel like that. But would they really come cruising in the Ionian Islands, next door to a war zone, with the risk of damage, however inadvertent?

He stroked his chin, heard Roberta coming through the bushes to kneel beside him. The mule train was hidden in the gully behind them. "Everything okay?"

"I'm not sure it is."

"What do you mean?"

He shook his head. "Nothing. There's nothing we can do about it now, anyway." Even if he had his radio with him, there was no way he could risk calling Sophie, without the chance of someone overhearing the conversation. "Let's get some rest. We'll move down to the coast at dusk."

* * *

195

The afternoon drifted by, the sun set. The crew of the *Christina* had dinner on the afterdeck. Catherine and Sophie washed the dishes, and they waited some more. Gradually the lights on shore started to go out. It was ten o'clock when Sophie said, "Let's go."

Dennis insisted on being on deck with them, even if he had to remain in his chair. Sophie gave him a tommy-gun. The tarpaulin was taken in, and she started the engine. Carl winched up the anchor. Richard had also armed himself, and took up a position amidships. Catherine stayed right aft with Dennis.

Sophie herself took the helm. The canal was lit, but it was a dark night and she didn't want any mistakes at this stage. With the engine running dead slow they gradually inched their way up the channel and into the open sea. "Course zero four five," Dennis said.

Sophie nodded, but she kept the speed slow as they closed the shore.

"A call from Leukas, Signor General," said the wireless operator. "The *boier* has put to sea."

"Then we have her," Edio said.

"Now, General?" Renaldo asked.

"Give them scope. I want Andrews as well. We do not strike until they are actually landing the guns."

Christina slipped quietly through the water, the only sounds being the low rumble of the engine and the swish of the water away from the hull. Carl was now right up in the bows as lookout. "I see the first light, madam. Dead ahead, And there is the other."

"There will be a third," Sophie said. "Stand by. Richard, would you use the lead."

Richard went forward and cast the line. "Six fathoms."

"The shore shelves steeply, according to the chart," Dennis said. "There is room yet."

Sophie held her course, heart pounding. To run aground at this stage would be utter catastrophe. But she trusted Dennis's judgement, and the lights beckoned her onwards. "Three," Carl said.

Sophie lined them up, one above the other. Now she could see trees looming out of the darkness to either side, and even a lot of people. They were in the creek. "Three fathoms," Richard called. Eighteen feet!

"Cut your engine," Dennis said. Sophie went into neutral, and the ship lost way. "Let go," Dennis called, and Carl released the anchor. *Christina* came to a halt as she snubbed the chain, and then fell astern as the stream took hold.

Already they were surrounded by boats, attaching their lines, and over the side came Clay Andrews. "Glory be," he said. "You are the sweetest sight any man could see." Sophie allowed herself to be embraced. "And . . ." he raised his eyebrows as he saw Richard, "You two back together?"

"For this voyage," Sophie said.

"I'd expected Carew."

"Ned couldn't make it."

"Right. Well, let's get this gear ashore. Can my people come aboard?"

"Help yourself. We only want to be out of here."

Clay signalled his people and their Greek allies to come aboard. They started unloading the deck cargo first, using the ship's winch to lower the heavy boxes over the side into the waiting boats, where more men were waiting to ferry them ashore and others to start loading the carts. "If you knew how happy I am to see the back of that lot," Dennis said.

"And you are?" Clay asked.

"He's the skipper," Sophie said.

"He doesn't look too good."

"We had a bit of trouble, and he stopped one."

"We heard about the trouble. Where's my girl?"

"I'm here, Mr Andrews." Catherine emerged from the gloom.

"You deserve a medal. Now, I've a surprise for you."

Roberta was climbing over the rail. "Roberta?" Catherine asked. "Roberta!" she screamed, running forward to embrace her friend. "We were told you were dead!"

"It's a long story."

"But to see you . . . how's the leg?"

"Mending."

"And how is your war going?" Sophie asked Clay. "We've been a little out of touch."

197

"It's going to go one hell of a lot better now we've got these goods." The deck had been cleared, and his men were starting to bring the boxes up from below. "You're not really back together with Elligan, are you?"

"I told you, for this voyage only."

"And if Carew has gone—" he waited.

"He's gone."

"Then when this is over, you're going to be footloose and fancy free. I don't suppose—" he grinned. "We never did get together. Not for want of trying."

"You were going to rape me, once, if Ned hadn't shown up."

"I'd like to make that up to you."

"You're fighting a war, Clay. Maybe we'll talk about it when you stop fighting other people's wars."

"I'll keep that in mind. What the—"

A huge shape was looming out of the darkness behind the yacht. She was carrying no lights. "You'll surrender, Sophie," a voice said through a loud hailer. "Or we shall fire into you."

"Jesus!" Sophie gasped. "That's Rometti!"

"He's in command of the forces opposing us," Clay said. "Or he was. What he's doing down here, in Greek waters—" His men continued to move the gear, now in desperate haste.

"You're breaking the law, General," Sophie shouted.

"So are you, Sophie. I have a hundred men here. Don't make me kill you."

Sophie stared into the darkness. She could make out the steam yacht quite clearly, now, and there were definitely a lot of people on board. She looked left and right. Richard and Carl waited amidships. The two girls were standing beside Dennis. They were all waiting for orders. "Your play," she told Clay.

"We can't surrender, Sophie. They'll hang us."

"Get the rest of the goods ashore. I'll stall."

"Move it," Clay told his men.

"You have five minutes," Edio called.

He could tell there was movement in the darkness, but he couldn't be sure what was happening. Nor, Sophie realised, did he know how many men were opposing him. The last of the boxes was brought up from the hold. "That crate," she said. "Break it open. It has the machine-guns."

198

"You're going to fight?"

"Like you said, it's that or a hanging. You with me, Dennis?"

"I reckon. You girls get ashore."

"I'm staying with you," Catherine declared. Roberta chewed her lip. To have come so far on a promise of safety . . .

The machine-gun was assembled, and Clay was feeding the ammunition belt. The last of the boxes was being lowered over the side. "Tell your people to start moving," Sophie said. "And you'd better go too."

"No way. Sophie's last stand? My people can help." He gave orders, and the Albanians broke out rifles for themselves. Two others carried the machine-gun aft.

Sophie surveyed the situation, which was by no means as desperate as it had first appeared. The *boier* was half-concealed behind the trees and bushes, and her hull was protected by the sides of the creek. And they would have the advantage of surprise. "One minute, Sophie," Edio called. "Then I shall open fire."

"And the best of luck," Sophie muttered, settling herself behind the machine-gun. "Take cover and shoot!" she shouted, and squeezed the trigger. Clay lay beside her to make sure the belt fed evenly. She aimed at the yacht's deck, sent a hail of bullets into it, and along it. Men screamed and fell left and right as they sought shelter. Only a few returned fire. While all the Albanians, as well as those on shore, were also firing.

"My God!" Renaldo shouted. "It is a massacre." He ran for the wheelhouse door, but as he did so bullets scythed into him and he struck the deck heavily. Edio stared at him, and at the several casualties he had already suffered. Once again he had underestimated the ability, and the willingness, of this woman to strike first and strike hard. He had automatically stepped into shelter when the firing had started. Now at least his men were returning fire, but he had nothing to equal the machine-gun.

Save the ship itself! He sent a few futile shots into the darkness, then ran round the other side of the wheelhouse, got inside, and threw the engine into gear.

* * *

199

"They're pulling out," Clay said.

Sophie ceased firing. Bullets were still whanging about her, but none seemed to have come close. "Okay," she said. "You get ashore with your people. We'll wait for him to get right off our back, then we'll disappear."

"Sophie . . ." he held her hand. "Ships that pass in the night, eh?"

"You could say, literally. Last time, Clay. It's been fun, but—"

"Look out!" Dennis bawled.

Sophie rose to her knees, staring into the darkness. The steam yacht had turned away from the shore, as if leaving. But she had kept on turning, performing a complete circle, and was now coming back towards them, a steel juggernaut, not travelling very fast, but fast enough. "Holy Jesus Christ!" Clay shouted.

"Abandon ship!" Dennis shouted. He knew they were helpless.

Sophie looked down at the machine-gun. That was useless now, too. The steam yacht was very close. "We have to help Dennis," she snapped, and ran forward. Again bullets whanged about her, but only a few of the Italians were still shooting. The rest were hanging on in expectation of the impact.

She reached Dennis, who was leaning against the rail. "For God's sake, Sophie," he said. "Get ashore. And take this stupid girl with you."

"I'm not leaving him," Catherine snapped.

"So we'll take him. Come on, Dennis. Now is no time for heroics."

They each grasped an arm, and urged him across the deck to the port rail. They had just got him there when the steam yacht's prow bit into the *boier*'s side.

Arrest

The impact was enormous. Even at no more than seven knots the steel stem pushed the *boier* over; that she did not go down on her beam ends was because the port leeboard dug into the bottom before snapping under the weight of the ship. At the same time the steam yacht's prow tore open the starboard side of the *boier*, allowing water to gush in. This brought her back onto an even keel for a moment, before she went straight down, very rapidly.

Roberta and Clay were already over the side and into the last of the boats. Dennis and the two other women were thrown to the deck, sliding first this way and then that as the ship heeled to and fro. "Over!" Sophie shouted. "Get over!"

Catherine pushed Dennis to the rail and helped him over. Clay was waiting to catch him as he fell, and Catherine jumped behind him. The steam yacht had pulled back now, and was turning. Her decks were lined with men, who were recommencing firing. Sophie gasped as she climbed up the sloping deck on her hands and knees. Above her head there was a tearing, snapping sound and the mast came down, crashing forward. At the same time there was a crunching sound from beneath her as the *boier*'s keel struck bottom.

Sophie reached the after hatch, and slid down the ladder into the saloon. Water was bubbling over the deck, although the actual fatal gash was forward in the hold. She lurched across the saloon and reached the door to the aft cabin, wrenching it open. Now the hull was starting to settle, sideways, and she had to hold on to stop herself from sliding across the deck. But her precious shoulderbag, with its even more precious contents, was still lying on her bunk. She seized it, threw the strap over her head, and listened to a burst of firing.

*   *   *

In the same instant as the steam yacht's bow crashed into the doomed *boier*, Edio heard the forward keel scraping on the bottom. Hastily he threw the engine astern, and the big ship floated back. He peered into the gloom, and was joined by Umberto. "You have done it, General. You have sunk her." He stared at Renaldo's body.

"He's dead," Edio told him. "And we have done nothing save sink their ship. Anchor, and swing out our boats, on the starboard side. We must get them before they can leave the shore."

"But . . . that will be an invasion of Greek territory, Signor General."

"Do you not suppose we are already invading Greek territory, by being in these waters at all? We are here. We must finish the job. Anchor!"

Umberto ran from the wheelhouse, and Edio followed. All seemed to be pandemonium ashore; he could not see clearly, but the partisans and their friends could not possibly have loaded all the guns and munitions as yet. He assembled his men. "Sergeant Greco, see to the wounded. Captain Umberto, I am leaving you in command. Maintain fire into the *boier*. Fifty men will come with me. Into the boats."

Bullets crashed and smashed into the wooden hull of the *boier*, but the three-quarter-inch planking absorbed most of them. The ship had now finally settled half on her port side, water gurgling in and out of the shattered hull. Sophie crawled across the saloon floor and up the ladder to reach the deck, immediately exposed to fire, even if it was random – no one on the yacht could actually see her. "Sophie!" Clay was calling from the boat, still sheltered by the hull. "Sophie!"

"I'm here," she shouted, crawling uphill now to each the rail, to be alerted by shouts from the shore. She looked over her shoulder, and saw the two boats appearing round the bow of the now anchored steam yacht. They were filled with men, who had to be Italian soldiers. If they got ashore . . . she rose to her feet, slipped and went down, and remained on her hands and knees, crawling aft to where the machine-gun remained wedged. No one saw her, as the Italians were busily firing at the shore. She reached the gun, checked the belt, and aimed at the lead boat.

This burst was even more effective than the first. Men fell about screaming, and the boat lost way, so suddenly that the second boat rammed it. Sophie continued to spray them both with bullets until the belt jammed. Panting, she listened to a loudhailer being used from the steam yacht. "General," Umberto was shouting. "There is a ship approaching."

Sophie chuckled with glee. Someone had heard the firing. If the new arrival was nothing more than a Greek coastguard cutter, the Italians had a problem. As they realised. They were turning the boats and making back for the steam yacht. Sophie waited until she was sure they were leaving, then slid down the deck. Clay was still alongside. "Come up and help me dismantle this machine-gun," she said. "We don't want to leave it behind."

He climbed up beside her, took her in his arms. "You are *something*," he said. "Don't ever leave me again, Sophie."

Ashore all was in a state of confusion, with the mules hysterical because of the shooting, and the people pretty excited too. "You really should try to get away from here," Clay told Sophie.

"Just now you were begging me not to leave you."

"I meant emotionally. Now we just have to get back to Albania before the Greeks begin to feel we are being too blatant about using their territory. I'm sorry I can't let you have a guide; I need all of my people. But it should be possible to negotiate with the locals."

"How far is it to Athens?"

"A couple of hundred miles."

"Across the mountains? On foot? With two wounded people? How are they, anyway?" she asked Catherine.

"Bobbie's all right. Just exhausted. But Dennis hurt himself getting off. His wound is bleeding."

"Do you have medical supplies at your base?" Sophie asked Clay.

"Some."

"Then we'll come with you. It's closer, and I have to have more antiseptic, otherwise gangrene could set in."

"You'll be entering a war zone."

"So what's new? And it'll only be for as long as it takes to

203

patch my people up. If Dennis doesn't get some attention he's going to die."

Marshal Badoglio indicated the chair in front of his desk. "Sit down, Edio. You look tired." Edio sat down. He was less tired than apprehensive of the coming interview. "Perhaps you would care to tell me what really happened? The Greeks appear to be entirely puzzled. But very concerned. Not to say angry."

"I understand that, Signor Marshal. I did what I thought best."

"You invaded Greece, entirely on your own initiative. You behaved like a second lieutenant instead of a general. Just how much co-operation did you obtain from the Navy?"

"Correctly, only in the form of surveillance, sir."

"And incorrectly?"

"Flag-Captain Renaldo Greve arranged the charter of the yacht, sir. And captained it for me."

"You are saying that Admiral Carzanti knew nothing of this?"

"Yes, sir. It was a private arrangement between Captain Greve and myself."

"And where is Captain Greve now?"

"He is dead, sir."

"Along with several of your men."

"Regrettably, sir. We had eight fatalities on board, and another six missing. There were also twenty-seven wounded."

"In exchange for what?"

"I can't say, sir. But the partisans must have suffered some casualties."

"The Greeks say they have picked up four bodies from the sea. All wearing civilian clothes. Were these yours?"

"Most probably, sir."

"They are talking about acts of piracy. They say you fired on their coastguard cutter."

"Correction, sir. They are saying the mystery ship, the pirates, fired on their coastguard cutter."

"Edio, that mystery ship is presently sitting in the harbour out there, riddled with bullets. The Greeks are certainly going to make representations. They are already doing so."

"I had to fire on the coastguard, sir, in order to make our escape."

"Oh, quite. So will you tell me, what did you achieve, for the loss of at least twelve men dead, twenty-seven wounded, one expensive yacht reduced to a wreck, and a diplomatic incident? When you cannot even be sure you killed a single partisan?"

"I'm afraid I achieved nothing, sir, save sinking the gun-runners' ship. My aim was to stop a considerable shipment of arms and ammunition from reaching the guerillas in the mountains. Now I must tell you that the munitions were landed and removed, despite my efforts. However, sir, I may add that when it comes to representations, those guns could not possibly have been landed and taken twenty-five miles to the Albanian border, without Greek connivance."

"I'm sure," Badoglio agreed. "However, for us to make representations about that, we would have to admit that our people, you, Edio, were involved in that gunfight. And that we are not prepared to do. We shall simply plead utter ignorance, as you have suggested."

"And the guns? And, incidentally, the gun-runners? They will also be in Albania by now, as they have lost their ship. Unless they have gone to Athens."

"As you say. Thank you, Edio."

Edio frowned, and remained seated. "You do not understand, Signor Marshal. The arrival of those guns gives the partisans a very considerable offensive capacity; it included machine-guns. What is more, the successful deliveries will encourage the principals behind this business to undertake more deliveries. We are allowing a potentially dangerous situation to arise in those mountains."

Badoglio picked up the report and scanned it again. "And you also have a personal vendetta with these people, Edio. Clayton Andrews. You were required to destroy him in the Sahara, and you failed. Then you were required to destroy him in Abyssinia, and you failed. Now he is humbugging you again. Is that not correct? And then this woman, Sophie Elligan, who actually made the delivery. Another old adversary, eh?"

"That is true, sir. And now I know where they both are,"

"What are you suggesting?"

"That we clean out those hills, sir. Once and for all."

"Have you not tried to do so, already?"

205

"We have undertaken sorties, sir. Seek and destroy missions. What is required is a large-scale offensive."

Badoglio was back to stroking his chin. "It will be expensive."

"It will be worth it, sir, to end this business."

"It will mean admitting that the country is not yet totally subdued. *Il Duce* will not like that."

"With respect, sir, it is a fact of life that needs to be faced."

"And suppose you do manage to bring these people to battle, and defeat them, will they not just flee across the border into Greece? Or are you seeking permission to follow them into a neutral country?"

"Neutral!" Edio snorted. "If they flee into Greece, sir, they will have to be interned. Now there is something we can make representations about."

"Hm." Badoglio considered for some moments, while Edio found he was holding his breath. "I assume you would command this offensive yourself, Edio?"

"With your permission, sir."

"Hm. I should cashier you, for that Ionian adventure. But I understand your motives. However, I also feel that your motives throughout this entire business have been affected by your determination to bring Andrews and Signora Elligan to book. That is a dangerous trend. I will give you one last chance—" he held up his finger. "To eliminate these partisans, or at least render them unable to mount an offensive. I will have to obtain permission from *Il Duce*. To do this I will, of course, have to tell him the fully story of what happened last week." He smiled. "Possible it may appeal to his own nature, which is essentially piratical. However . . . one last chance, Edio. Do not fail me in this."

"It's all a bit confused, Mr Pemberton," the commander said. "The Greeks are saying that some kind of gun battle took place on the coast inside the Ionian Islands, in which a Dutch yacht was sunk. That certainly sounds like our friends."

"What are the Italians saying?" Pemberton asked.

"That it is all a mystery to them."

"Does the Greek report mention any names? Any casualties?"

"Their coastguard, who were fired upon by an unidentified

206

vessel, picked up four bodies from the sea. All men, and wearing civilian clothing, but in the opinion of our man in Corfu, all definitely Italians."

"What about the crew of the *boier*?"

"No report of any of them being found, sir."

"So it's reasonable to suppose they got ashore," Pemberton said. "What about the guns? Are they mentioned?"

"No, sir, there is no mention of any guns."

"Hoorah for our Sophie. She's got away with it."

"She's lost her ship, sir. She still has to get back out."

"I'm sure she'll manage. When you think of what she got through to deliver."

"And our position, sir?"

"I think we'll just keep a low profile, for the time being. What happens when, or if, they return here, that's a different matter."

"You have read the report, Commissioner?" Henri asked.

"Several times," Labarge said.

"Do you think these are our people?"

"Undoubtedly. This Madame Elligan is a formidable creature."

"Have you any instructions?"

"I think we will leave her to the Italians, for the time being," Labarge said. "But I wish our people in Athens to monitor the situation very closely. If she survives the Italians, Madame Elligan may well return west."

Henri grinned. "Knowing what is waiting for her, she may well opt to remain in Greece."

"Then we will apply for her extradition, on a charge of murder."

"So," Eisener said. "This wretched woman has triumphed."

"Is that any concern of ours, sir?" Eichmann asked. "Her success in delivering the guns is an Italian problem. We are concerned with where she goes next."

"I would say she will seek to leave Greece at the earliest possible opportunity. And once she does that we may lose her again. You are sure she is presently with the partisans in Albania?"

"That is the opinion of our people."

"Hm. Who do we have in Greece?"

"Bartoli commands. He has a sizeable squad."

"Have him pick a good man, or perhaps two would be better, and send them across the border into Albanian. They will pose as partisan volunteers."

"Their mission?"

"I wish Sophie Elligan," Eisener said. "I want her sitting where you are, Eichmann, with her hands bound behind her back and her knickers around her ankles, waiting for me to deal with her. That is what I want more than anything else in the world, right this minute. However, if it is impossible to capture her and bring her here for trial, I wish her to be dead. I will require proof of this."

The partisans gathered round the mule train as it came into the shallow valley. Hands reached out for the packing cases, and these were placed on the ground and ripped open. They gazed at the modern rifles, and even more at the piles of ammunition, the grenades and the explosives, the machine-guns. "Now we blow the Italians out of our country, eh?" Dino said.

"I doubt there is quite enough here for that," Clay said. "But we'll sure make them know we're about." He was exhausted, but triumphant. He had driven his people, and their unexpected guests, as hard as he had driven the mules, to get them across the mountains and into Albania before the Italians could bring sufficient pressure on the Greek Government to have them stopped. Apart from the terrain they had had again to bribe a border guard, and they had had to ford the River Vijose, and they had had to cross the road that ran from Korce south along the border until it entered Greece itself. There were occasional Italian patrols along this road, but the invaders had been attacked on more than one occasion and they had not yet committed the strength properly to seal the route. In the event, the partisans had seen no enemy. And now they were home. He grinned at Sophie, and she grinned back. She was as exhausted as he, and she looked quite unlike her normal immaculate self. The still short red-brown hair was dishevelled, her clothes were torn, he knew she had several bruises as well . . . but she too looked triumphant.

Clay reckoned she had more cause for self-congratulation than he, even if she had lost her ship. She had fought her way out of France, through Germany, across the North Sea and then the Mediterranean, to make the delivery. "A bath," she said. "What I want more than anything else in the world is a bath. Catherine said something about a village."

"We had to abandon that long ago," Clay told her. "The Italians blasted it out of existence. These people . . ." he looked around the considerable number of partisans, men and women, and children and dogs and chickens and goats, who had assembled in the valley, "are quite homeless. Save . . ." he stamped on the ground with his boot. "For this. This is their home. But you will have your bath."

"Just let me know when." She went to where Dennis and Roberta were being lifted from their mules, slowly and carefully, while Catherine fussed like a mother hen. "How are they?"

"Dennis is bleeding again. Oh, Sophie—" Catherine looked near to tears; she was as exhausted as any of them.

"I'll re-do his bandages," Sophie said. Dennis was laid in the shade of a tree, and Sophie knelt beside him, took off his shirt. As she had supposed had happened, the bandages had slipped and his wound had opened. But it remained clean, thanks to her antiseptic. The problem was, she didn't have too much of that left. "How do you feel?" she asked.

"Fucking awful."

She took his temperature. "You have a slight fever. I'm sorry about the ship."

He forced a grin. "We're lucky we made it this far."

"Listen. I'll finance a new one."

"Why should you do that, Sophie?"

"You're my partner. Now rest. Catherine's here."

She went to where Clay was distributing the weapons, determining which should be hidden and which immediately used. "You promised me some medical supplies."

"You shall have them. How are the invalids?"

"I'm worried about Dennis. What is your plan?"

"As regards you? To get you out of here just as rapidly as I can."

"Into Greece?"

"It's your best option."

"Dennis should remain where he is, for at least a week. Or he could get into serious trouble."

"A week?"

She smiled at him. "Can't you stand my company, for a week? Now what about that bath?"

The women were taken to a mountain stream, and there left to themselves. "It was a place just like this that our war started," Catherine said. "Gosh, that seems a long time ago." She looked around herself. "You don't suppose this could be the same place?"

"No," Roberta said. "We left that a long way behind when we retreated."

"You must have quite a story to tell," Sophie said, rinsing her hair again and again.

"So must you," Roberta suggested.

"We'll collaborate on a book."

Roberta was looking past her. "Oh, heck." She sank lower into the water.

Sophie turned. "It's only Richard. He knows what we look like. Cathy and me, anyway." She stood up. "We were promised privacy."

He undressed and came into the water to join them. "I need a bath as much as anyone. And we need to talk. We don't want to hang about here, Sophie. Andrews has a radio, and a contact in Greece. He says he can only call once every twenty-four hours, but he should be able to arrange for us to be met and shipped out."

"As soon as we can move," Sophie said.

"What's keeping us?"

"Dennis. He took a beating on that march, not to mention getting off the ship. He simply has to rest for a few days, and regain some of his strength."

"While we get bombed out of existence by the Italians. You don't imagine they're going to take what happened lying down, do you?"

"We'll just have to sit it out." Sophie stood up, water streaming down her body. "That is my decision. If you want to get out on your own, do that."

"And miss the final payment, eh?"

"The final payment has already been made. It was to be on delivery, and we've delivered. Your money is in a Swiss bank account, as I showed you."

His eyes narrowed. "All twenty-five thousand?"

"My instructions were to make the last transfer as soon as the funds were paid into my account. So if you wish to get out and get at it, go right ahead."

Roberta was looking from one to the other in bewilderment. "It's always like this," Catherine explained.

Richard left the water, pulled on his clothes, and stamped up the slope to the encampment. "Will he go?" Roberta asked.

"No," Sophie said. "He knows he won't make it, without a guide."

"You won't believe this," Clay said. "But we've received two Greek volunteers."

Sophie gazed at the two men, who were bearded and nondescript, but they carried good rifles and bandoliers of ammunition. "Madame Sophie," one of them said. "We have heard so much about you. My name is Andreas. It is an honour to serve with you."

"Madame Sophie isn't doing any serving," Clay told him. "She is getting out of here just as soon as she can."

"Then it is an honour to have met you, Madame Sophie."

"Can you trust them?" Sophie asked.

"I doubt it. They'll run off at the first sign of any fighting. But it's nice to know the Greeks are more and more inclining to our side."

That evening Dennis's fever had increased, and he was restless. "I'm so worried," Catherine confessed.

"Give it tonight." Sophie wrapped the wounded man in blankets to make him sweat. "If the fever doesn't break by morning, we'll take him down to the stream. It's an old remedy, but it still works."

But she was herself worried, went off to find Clay as usual. He was seated by himself, away from the campfires, looking down the mountainside towards the sea, invisible in the darkness.

Although there were lights on the distant road. "The Italian army," he said. "Planning its next move."

"And you?"

"We're better prepared to meet them now. But I have in mind a raid. As soon as you've moved on."

"You wouldn't like me along?"

He glanced at her. "As you have reminded me, it's not your war, Sophie. If you were to be captured, they'd hang you. After roughing you up a bit."

"I know what they do. What about you?"

"The same, I guess."

"It's not your war either, you know. It never has been. What do your folks think about it?"

He sighed. "They're both dead."

"I'm sorry. I remember you speaking of them, when we first worked together. But if that's so, you must be worth a bit."

He grinned. "I've a share in Dad's stockbroking firm. And a seat on the board, if I ever decide to take it up. Yes, I'm a wealthy man. Which allows me to devote my time to doing what I like best."

"Getting killed."

"You're a fine one to talk."

She shivered. "I'm not here for the money, Clay. I'm here because I wanted to do something to avenge Ned. When I get out of here, I'm done. I'm carrying his child."

His head turned, sharply. "Avenge Ned?"

"Oh, he's dead. Shot to bits by Mussolini's hit men. Oh, I got the bastards. But that didn't bring him back."

"And you made this delivery, pregnant?"

"It's only two months. I won't show for a while."

"Then it's not guaranteed."

"It's guaranteed." She glanced at him. "Would you like it not to be?"

"Ned Carew was never my favourite person. Simply because he had you and I didn't. Sophie . . . when this is over—"

"Another man's child?"

"Yes," he said fiercely. "If I can have you as well."

"Well, like you said, when this is over. You care to put a date on that?"

"No. Because before it's over here, it's going to be going on

212

someplace else. You know Chamberlain has guaranteed Poland and Romania? It's pretty certain Hitler will move on Poland some time. Only his fear of Russia is holding him back."

"And when he does, what can Chamberlain do about it? He didn't do anything about Czechoslovakia."

"There's going to be a war, Sophie. A general settlement between the democracies and the Fascist states. I'm backing the democracies."

"Well, naturally. But it's not going to be over by Christmas, as they said the last time. By the time you come looking for me, I'll be a grandmother."

"It'll be sooner than that."

"Will America come in."

"I don't think so. Not officially. But she'll be there. And people like me will be *here*."

"And people like me are going to try to keep out of the firing line," Sophie said.

They kissed a bit, and she slept beside him. Neither undressed. She wouldn't have permitted sex anyway, with her old-fashioned ideas about pregnancy, but they were both acutely aware of the past. When they had first met, in 1930, they had sized each other up, and had both known they wanted to have an affair. Her marriage was in the process of breaking down, and he had been a lonely and attractive, and sex-starved man. But she had wanted to wait, even then. She had never been in the business of throwing herself into bed with a man, even a man as attractive as Clay Andrews. And while she had made them wait, they had been overtaken by events that had turned them into enemies, had her fleeing across the desert with Ned, with the Senussi, for whom Clay was working, in pursuit.

That episode could be called a draw, she supposed, and she had been happy to work with him again, in Abyssinia. But that had turned out even more disastrously. She would never be able to forget that he had stood by and done nothing when the Senussi sheikh whose uncle she had killed had come looking for vengeance. Had it not been for the interruption of Edio Rometti's brigade of cavalry she would have died the most ghastly of deaths, staked out on a hillside, her body mutilated.

She smiled into the darkness. Now Edio was also anxious for her blood. But where did that leave her relations with Clay? The odd thing was that she trusted him, as a human being, and believed he was genuine when he claimed to love her. But she also knew that he would sacrifice her, and all the others, and indeed, himself, if it would bring him victory over the Italians. Maybe that streak of single-minded ruthlessness made him potentially a great general. But as husband or lover there could be no certainty until all the fighting was finished. And he was talking of several years!

She slept towards dawn, and awoke with a start to find Dino standing above them. "There is a messenger."

Clay sat up. "From Greece?"

"No, no. He is from Korce. He says there is a large force assembling there, with tanks and artillery. He says they mean to move south along the road and close the border."

"Shit," Clay muttered.

"Where is Korce?" Sophie asked.

"It is a town to the north of here. We knew the Italians had garrisoned it."

"Can they get into the mountains from there?"

"No more easily than from the south. But if they attack from there they will be coming from both sides at once. And if they also seal the border—"

"Well," Sophie said. "We weren't going anywhere for a day or two, anyway."

Clay stood up. "Call in your people," he told Dino. "There is going to be an offensive."

"Bah," Dino said. "There have been offensives before."

"Not from both sides at the same time. They mean business. We shall have to fall back further into the mountains." He turned to Sophie as Dino hurried off. "Now I *have* to get you out."

"I told you, I'm not going anywhere until Dennis is strong enough to travel."

"He's going to have to be moved, anyway. I think our friend Rometti really means business this time. I suppose it had to follow. Shame you didn't get him down on that beach."

214

"I didn't really want to. He saved my life in Abyssinia, remember?"

"I think he reckons you're quits. Anyway, you'd better prepare your people for a move." He pointed at the aircraft that had just come into view, flying south from Tirana. "Here they are."

Sophie hurried back to where the rest of the crew had been sleeping. They were already awake, disturbed by the rustle of preparation going on around them. "The Italians are coming," she told them. "Planes first. So, shelter."

The Albanian women and children were already being herded into caves in the mountainside; it was a well-rehearsed drill. "They've been bombed before," Roberta explained.

With them went the explosives and some of the ammunition. The machine-guns were being carried to presumably good defensive positions. They were also accompanied by all of the goats that could be rounded up; the caves became an immense sound and stench, of muttering humanity, screaming children, barking dogs and braying goats. "If that entrance were to be sealed—" Richard said.

"For God's sake," Sophie said. "It hasn't happened yet. Has it, Roberta?"

"Not yet."

Soon they heard the crump-crump of the bombs falling, but they were widely dispersed. One or two fell into their valley, and they heard the roar of the plane engines as the aircraft swept low. But Clay had his people well in hand, unlike on the first attack back in April, and no one returned fire to give away their positions. After about an hour the noise stopped. Clay came to the cave. "I don't want any argument about this," he said. "You have to get out now. It seems pretty clear that the Italians are mounting a major offensive. It may last a long time, and it's going to be pretty grim. You have got to get the girls out, Sophie, and you have to take Overcamp with you as well." He glanced at Richard and Carl. "I assume you'll be going too."

Sophie chewed her lip in indecision, looking at Dennis. "I reckon he's right," the captain said. "The girls must go."

"But you're coming too," Catherine insisted.

"Now listen," Clay said. "I am going to come with you, as far

215

as the border. These people know what to do until I get back, and it should only take a day or two. We have to get across that road, but I reckon we can do that. Once you get to Greece, make for Athens. I'll call my contact there and tell him to arrange passages for you—?"

"Holland," Sophie said. "I think we're wanted for various crimes, just about everywhere else."

"Holland it will be. Prepare to move out in one hour. I'm going to round up some supplies and give Dino a few orders." He grinned at Sophie. "Like I said, our Greek volunteers have disappeared. First shots, eh?"

"Suppose they were spies?"

"Maybe they were, but there's not a lot they can tell Rometti he doesn't already know. As soon as we leave, Dino is going to move all his people further back and up."

He went off, and they looked at each other. "The man's right that we should get out," Richard said. "We really have no business getting mixed up in their war. We brought them their guns. It's up to them, now."

"Spoken like a hero," Sophie said. "But I suppose we have no choice. Come on girls, pack up. Carl—"

"I'll look after the skipper, Mrs Elligan."

As they all had only the clothes they had been wearing when they abandoned the *boier*, and their only luggage was Sophie's shoulderbag, they were ready in a few minutes. Clay had again organised mules for Dennis and Roberta. Clay and Richard and Sophie, as well as Carl, were armed with rifles, and Sophie still had her two pistols in her bag, while Clay had a revolver on his hip, as well.

It was mid-morning when they left the encampment. The planes had gone, although they had no idea if and when they would be back, but in the still air they could hear the grind of the tank engines from behind them as the Italians began their advance up the valleys. "Will you be able to hold them off?" Sophie asked.

"I don't know," Clay said. "The new weapons and more importantly the ammunition you have brought will help. What it eventually boils down to, however, is Edio's determination. He will suffer a great many casualties if he pushes too far into the mountains, yet when you come down to it, the Italians have more men, and more firepower, than we do. So, if they are determined enough, they can destroy us."

"And you."

He grinned. "If they are determined enough, probably."

They camped in late afternoon, to give everyone a few hours' sleep, as Clay was aiming to cross the road at night; they had seen a reconnaisance machine earlier, which had flown low enough to identify them. Now the road was only another two miles away. Catherine knelt beside the restless Dennis. "He keeps saying things I don't understand. I think he's delirious." Sophie took his temperature. It was a hundred and five. "That's terrible," Catherine said. "He's going to die."

"No, he's not," Sophie snapped. But she went to Clay. "We have just got to get that temperature down. Isn't that water I hear?"

"There's a stream close by."

"Then give me a hand."

Clay and Carl carried the groaning Dennis to the stream. Sophie and Catherine went into the ice-cold water with him, holding him between them, for half-an-hour. When they took him out, the temperature was down to just over a hundred. They dried him and wrapped him up. Clay checked his watch. "I'm afraid we only have another hour." It was dusk.

Sophie spread her blanket next to Catherine's, and had just lain down, with Clay on her other side, when he suddenly sat up and reached for his rifle. "Don't do that, Mr Andrews," Andreas said. "Or I will blow your head off."

Clay watched the two men emerging from the trees, rifles levelled. "Bastards!"

Andreas grinned. "We are only doing our duty."

"You came to me—"

"Our duty to the Reich," said the other man.

Clay looked at Sophie.

"The Gestapo has very long arms, Mr Andrews," the second man said. "My name is Heinrich Bergson, and I have come to arrest Frau Elligan," By now the whole camp was awake, but the rifles overlooked all of them. "We have no business with you, and your puerile little war," Bergson said. "Our business only concerns Frau Elligan. So, pack up your gear and leave. Oh, please, place all your weapons on the ground, first. You do not need them. If you get across the border, you will be safe. If you do not, the Italians will kill or capture you, no matter how well armed you are. Do it, now."

Clay was drawing deep breaths. Sophie rested her hand on his arm. "Don't be foolish."

"What do you intend to do with her?" Clay asked.

"I have said, we are to take her back to Germany for trial. She is guilty of the murder of one of my colleagues."

"Guilty, before the trial?"

Bergson grinned. "There will be a trial, Mr Andrews."

Clay again looked left and right. Everyone was waiting on his lead. The two girls were anxious to help, but they were unarmed, and unused to extreme violence. Carl was more concerned about Dennis, his skipper of many years. And Richard Elligan was a totally unknown quality, save that he was unlikely to risk his life to save his estranged wife, especially if his share of the delivery money was already banked. "Please, Clay," Sophie said. "There is no point in getting yourself killed. You have your war to fight. And these others are really innocents. If there is to be a trial, I have time."

"You'd trust these bastards?"

She smiled. "Not willingly. But we don't seem to have any choice."

"Time is passing, Mr Andrews," Bergson said. "If you wish to cross the road tonight."

Clay hesitated a last time. Then he said, "Dump your weapons."

The rifles were piled, and Clay added his own revolver. Sophie stroked her shoulderbag. No one knew what that contained, save possibly Dennis, and he was still half delirious. "Now be on your way," Bergson commanded.

They loaded Dennis on to his mule, Catherine and Carl to either side of him to stop him from falling off. Roberta also mounted. Clay looked at Sophie. "I'll see you in the funnies," she said.

He took his place at the head of the tiny group, Richard at the rear, and with a roar Richard suddenly swung round, as he did so drawing the revolver he had concealed beneath his shirt. "Bastards!"

But before he could level his gun Andreas had shot him through the chest. Richard's body seemed to explode in blood as he was thrown backwards to the ground. Catherine screamed and Roberta fell off her mule. Carl and Clay both turned as well . . . but they had no guns. Then Clay dived at the pile of discarded weapons. He got his hands on his revolver before Bergson shot him as well, his body arching backwards to the ground. Sophie opened her bag and grasped the Luger, pulling it out, only to be struck a savage blow on the back that tumbled her forward, the pistol flying from her grasp. For a moment she thought she had been shot as well, then she realised that Bergson had hit her with his rifle barrel. The pain was intense and for a moment she was incapable of action.

"That was very stupid," Bergson was saying. "Do you think we are children? Get on, or we will shoot you all." Gasping, Sophie slowly got to her knees. Bergson walked round her head and picked up the Luger. "You are full of surprises, eh, Frau Elligan? This is a Gestapo issue weapon. Taken from the man you killed in Hamburg, I would say. We keep records of the numbers of the guns issued to our people. It will be good evidence against you at your trial. Now let us see what else you have concealed about your person. Get up and turn round."

Sophie obeyed. She could only be patient until she could again get inside her bag; that had been thrown from her shoulder and lay some distance away, and Bergson obviously had not seen her take the gun from it – he assumed the Luger had been concealed in her clothes. But for the moment she could only think, Richard and Clay, both dead! Just as Ned was dead. All the men who had ever loved her.

Catherine and Carl were kneeling beside Clay. "He's breathing," Catherine said. "But that wound—"

"You may bind him up and take him with you," Bergson said. "If he is that important to you."

Catherine looked at Sophie. "Yes," Sophie said. "Do what you can. Get him into Greece. With Dennis."

Catherine tore her own shirt into strips to bind up Clay's

wound. Tears dribbled down her cheeks as she and Carl got the American into the saddle of Roberta's mule. Roberta was holding Dennis in place. My army, Sophie thought. Shot to pieces. But her grief was already turning to anger. She looked at the shoulderbag, which was several feet away. If she could just reach it . . .

But Bergson was taking no chances. He pulled her arms behind her back and she felt the touch of the steel at the same time as she heard the click of the handcuffs. "What are you waiting for?" Bergson asked Catherine. "Get out."

Catherine hesitated a last time, looking from the discarded weapons to Richard's dead body, to Sophie. "I guess he was a hero after all," she said.

"Or he loved you, after all," Roberta said.

"Sophie!" Catherine shouted. "Oh, Sophie—" Carl led the two women and the mules into the gathering darkness.

"Now," Bergson said. "There is just us. I was going to search you, wasn't I? Keep her covered, Andreas." He stepped up to Sophie, tore open her shirt, sent his hands scouring inside to fondle her breasts. "But you are more likely to have something concealed lower down, are you not?" He unbuckled her belt. Sophie spat at him, and he reared back as the spittle scattered across his face. "Bitch!" he shouted, and hit her with the flat of his hand.

Sophie lost her balance and fell, tasting blood. Bergson knelt beside her, tearing at her clothes, and Andreas tapped him on the shoulder. "Traffic."

Bergson's head jerked, but now Sophie could hear the grind of engines too, and she could see the glow of dimmed headlights, moving up and down as the vehicles bumped across the uneven surface. "Shit," Bergson said. "Take cover."

But it was too late. "Halt there," came a shout in Italian. Bergson hesitated, then stood up, his hands at his side. Andreas lowered his rifle. While Sophie sat up, watched the soldiers coming towards them. And leading them . . . "It's been a long time, General Rometti," she said.

Vengeance

E dio shone his torch on Sophie's face. "Ill met by moon-light," he remarked, and let the beam move lower, to reveal her disordered clothing. "Has this man raped you?"

"He was working up to it. You always arrive in the nick of time, General."

"This may be unfortunate for you. Release her."

"I am Gestapo Agent seven-five-three-six, Heinrich Bergson," Bergson said, importantly. "Carrying out a mission for the Reich."

Edio played his torch over him in turn. "You do not look like a Gestapo agent to me," he remarked. "You look like an Albanian partisan. I will hang you."

"I have identification," Bergson said. "Do you not know who this woman is? She is wanted in Germany for killing one of our agents. I was sent to arrest her."

"Were you also sent to rape her?"

"I was searching her."

"That's what they all say. Now release her." Bergson hesi-tated, then unlocked the handcuffs and Sophie could rub her wrists. She could also refasten her shirt, as best she was able with half the buttons gone. Edio was inspecting Richard's body. "I have seen this man before."

"He was with me in Abyssinia," Sophie said. "He was my husband."

Edio looked up with arched eyebrows. "Carew? Carew is dead."

"This is Richard Elligan."

"Ah. Being married to you is a dangerous business, Sophie. What about Clay Andrews? Our reconnaissance machine spotted you this afternoon, you know. That is why I decided to come down that road myself."

"I imagine Clay is in Greece by now."

"If he is still alive," Bergson said. "I shot him."

"We heard the shots," Edio said. "Well, you are all under arrest."

"I am an accredited Gestapo officer," Bergson protested.

"We shall investigate that. Have you anything to say, Sophie?"

Sophie shrugged. "It would be very nice if your men could bury Richard."

Full circle, she thought, and the end of her career, as she watched the earth being piled on the unmarked grave. Why had she bothered? No one would ever find it, and soon enough it would be torn open by the foxes. As Edio had said, being too close to her was a dangerous business, because all of her husbands and lovers insisted on attempting to defend her.

She sat in the back of the command car, beside Edio. She had been allowed to retrieve her shoulderbag, and no one had looked inside; Edio was too much of a gentleman to pry into a woman's private possessions. She could feel her second pistol, the Browning, through the material. But if she was going to make a break for it, the timing had to be perfect. She did not think now was the time, with several cars behind, and several motorbike outriders in front. Besides, she did not know if she had the mental energy to start killing again, and risk being killed herself.

They had made several sweeps up and down the road, and found nothing; it was now quite late, and it seemed obvious that the fugitives had managed to cross the border. That should have made her happy, but instead she felt unutterably depressed. Ned was dead. Richard was dead. She did not know if Clay would die or not, even if he had got across into Greece. The same went for Dennis. While as for those two lovely girls . . . she had not had the opportunity to get to know Roberta, but for Catherine she had feelings almost as if she had been her own daughter. Because above all, she wanted to survive, and give birth to Ned's child.

But was that practical? Edio Rometti might be the most perfect gentleman, but he also lived by the book. She was wanted for the deaths of quite a few Italians, in the Sahara as well as in France, and she was wanted for gun-running, which in time of war was a hanging offence as well. So, go out in a ablaze of gunfire? Or wait, and hope? It was easier to wait and hope.

"I really must congratulate you," Edio said. "That delivery was a work of enormous courage and determination. Such an achievement, for a woman,"

"Thank you."

"But at the end of the day it had to come to this. Do you not agree?"

"I had hoped not. Are you going to hang me?"

"*I* am not. Heaven forbid. Hanging women is not part of my duties, thank God. But I must hand you over to the military police, and there will be a trial, and . . . you are guilty of murder."

"I have never killed anyone save in self-defence."

"Well, you seem to have spent a lot of your life defending yourself."

"Suppose I were to tell you this is my last delivery?"

"It is."

"I meant, whether or not I was caught. I am pregnant. Ned Carew's child. I wish to bear it."

He turned his head, sharply. "I think you are crazy, to have come on an adventure like this, carrying a child. Oh, you will bear it, Sophie. We do not execute pregnant women."

"And afterwards?"

"Who can say."

"But you will not let me go."

"Sophie, I let you go once before, out of gratitude for what you and Carew did for Lalia. I warned you then that you must cease these activities, and you have chosen to ignore me. No, this time I will not let you go." He pointed. "My headquarters. Korce."

The little town was a bustle of men and machines, and arms, There were aides-de-camp waiting with reports, other officers waiting for orders. Sophie was marched behind Edio into the house he had appropriated; Bergson and Andreas were taken to a cell, protesting.

"Sit down." Edio gestured to a chair. "I must attend to these matters."

223

Cheese and bread and wine were produced by an orderly, who saluted and withdrew. "How is your offensive going?" Sophie asked, seating herself, the shoulderbag on her lap, and eating hungrily.

"Slowly, at this time; we always knew it would. But this time we are going to finish the job, before any more arms deliveries can be made." He finished reading the reports, issued a stream of orders into the telephone, then hung up. "Now, there are things I must ask you. About the partisans."

"I know nothing about the partisans."

"You were with them for several days."

"They sheltered us after you destroyed our ship, yes."

"So you must have some idea of their numbers, their organisation. You can certainly give me a detailed list of everything you brought to them."

"Why should I do that?"

"Because I have asked you, Sophie."

"And I will ask you again, Edio: will you let me go?"

He sighed. "In exchange for information? No, I am afraid I cannot do that. And if you force me to, I will have to hand you over to certain people who will obtain the information from you whether you wish to give it or not. Believe me. They are professionals."

"I'm sure. Tell me, Edio, do you regard me as a dangerous woman?"

He smiled. "Oh, indeed."

"How dangerous?"

"Well, you seem to have this knack of shooting your way out of trouble. I'm still not sure how you survived that storm in the desert, but then there was the sheikh in Tamenrasset, God knows how many Senussi during your escape – actually, we do not hold this against you as they were our enemies too. Had you merely surrendered to us you might have been treated as a heroine."

"I did not come to you because you said I would be gaoled for gun-running."

"That is true. But that is better than being dead."

"You were compiling a list."

"Well, there were several people in Abyssinia, then there were

224

our four men in France, then there was the German policeman in Hamburg, then there was that ship . . . I am assuming it was you blew up that ship?"

"It was me, personally."

"You'll be claiming next that it was you manning the machine-gun on the *boier*."

"It was."

"You are a one-woman army, Sophie. Are you going to admit all of this in court?"

"If I have to, certainly. One may as well die with one's name on everyone's lips. The point I am making, Edio, is that you understand that, as you have just said, I believe in shooting my way out of trouble."

"Absolutely." He smiled. "When you can." Then the smile faded as he found himself looking into the muzzle of the Browning Sophie had just taken from her shoulderbag. "Are you mad?"

"The whole world is mad, Edio. At least this part of it, though I have a feeling the contagion will spread. This gun is fully loaded with nine bullets."

"And you propose to shoot me, nine times, so that your name can be on everyone's lips?"

"I don't propose to shoot you at all, if you behave yourself. You and I are going to walk out of here, our arms round each other. I am sure you realise that your men are quite convinced you have something going for me, so it will arouse no suspicions. We will go downstairs, get into a car, and drive to the border. Once we are there, I will leave you. I do stand by what I said earlier, that this is my last gun-running mission. I am going to retire. So you see, I hope we will part friends. But Edio, I want you to be sure of one thing. My gun will be in your ribs every moment of the journey, and if you try to recapture me, or do anything I don't like, I am going to blow you into two pieces."

"That is the border," Edio said. "There is a Greek post a hundred yards away." They hadn't spoken much on the drive from Korce. Edio, always conscious of the gun-muzzle in his ribs, and whose finger was on the trigger, had made all the correct responses to the various patrols and checkpoints, while, as Sophie had predicted, his aides in Korce had exchanged glances and winks at the sight of their general taking his beautiful captive for a drive in the night. But he was also very conscious of the humiliation of his position.

"Then stop the car," Sophie said. He braked at the side of the road. "Walk with me."

He got out. "Do I need to put my hands up?"

"That won't be necessary." He walked in front of her until they were within sight of the Greek post. Sophie had already taken his gun. Now she removed the magazine and put it into her bag. "I'd hate you to get any ideas. Not that I suppose you would ever shoot a woman in the back."

"Or a man," he said.

"Touché. What will happen to you?"

"I imagine I will be cashiered for allowing this to happen."

"I'm sorry. Do you hate me very much?"

"I would consider it a kindness were you to shoot me."

"I'm not going to do that, Edio. We've been enemies too long. I owe you my life. Now I'm giving you yours. Try to forgive me." She stood against him, the Browning again in his ribs, and kissed him on the cheek. "It's been fun. Now go back to your car and drive away." She gave him back his pistol.

"Let me get this straight," Eisener said into the phone. "You had her, and you let her go?"

"That is not entirely accurate, Herr Eisener," Eichmann said. "Baltori's people had her, and were bringing her in, when they were superseded by the Italian Army who, it seems, also have her on their wanted list. Our people protested, but were overruled. They were all taken to Korce, whereupon Frau Elligan made her escape, taking an Italian general with her."

"My God!" Eisener said. "We are being made to look fools. I hope this general will be cashiered?"

"Oh, he will be, Herr Eisener."

"And where is the wretched woman now?"

"Well, sir, the last certain thing we know of her is that she crossed the border into Greece. According to our people, her accomplices had also made Greece, earlier. I imagine they will have linked up by now, and indeed will be on their way—"

226

"Where?"

"That is the question. But . . ." he hurried on before Eisener could explode. "Her options are limited. She is wanted for murder in both Germany and France, as well as Italy. She is wanted for at least gun-running in England, I imagine. As she is an international figure, it is safe to assume she keeps her main bank accounts in Switzerland, but that does not mean she has a base there—"

"Holland," Eisener said. "She is not wanted in Holland, and at least one of her partners is Dutch. Find out where this man Overcamp has his home, Eichmann. That is where she will go to ground."

"And then? You wish us to keep the place under surveillance, and move in when they return?"

"I wish you to keep the place under surveillance," Eisener said. "And inform me when they return. This business has been bungled too often. I intend to wrap it up, personally."

"Barthes is quite sure that it was the Elligan party that boarded the SS *Gloaming* in Athens yesterday morning," Henri said. "It consisted of three women and three men; two of the men were apparently ill, most probably wounded. The passage was arranged by Clarkson, who is an under-secretary at the United States Embassy in Athens. That is the proof, in Barthes' opinion. Why should an American under-secretary go to this trouble were the man Andrews not involved?"

"And this *Gloaming*?" Labarge inquired.

"She is a British ship, sailing direct for Gibraltar, thence Lisbon and Southampton. She does not touch French territory. I'm afraid she has got away, monsieur. Unless you intend to institute extradition proceedings in England, which will be very lengthy. Or you authorise executive action."

Labarge considered. "I doubt she will go to England," he said. "She knows she can be extradited, and held while proceedings are conducted. When does the ship dock in Lisbon?"

"Three days, monsieur."

"Leave it with me," Labarge said. "I will see what can be arranged."

*   *   *

"Our agent in Athens reports that the Elligan party embarked on the SS *Gloaming*, yesterday morning," the secretary said.

"He's quite sure it was Mrs Elligan?" Pemberton asked.

"Yes, sir, tall, very good-looking, short auburn hair—"

"Short?"

"That's what he said, sir. She was accompanied by five people, two women and three men. Two of the men were invalided on board. There is supporting information. Apparently temporary British passports were issued to the two young women at the British Embassy, Catherine Ames and Roberta Wilcox—"

"Roberta Wilcox is dead."

"She was able to prove that she is actually alive, sir. She and Miss Ames claimed their passports had been lost in a shipwreck on the west coast of Greece. That actually ties in with what we know. Our man checked about and learned that temporary passports were also issued by the Dutch Embassy to two of their nationals, and by the US Embassy to one of theirs. There is a discrepancy, however. Only two British passports were applied for. There is no mention of Mrs Elligan there. Or of Richard Elligan."

"Knowing Sophie, I'd say she sleeps with her passport tucked up against her tummy," Pemberton said. "And she probably has more than one, anyway. As for Elligan . . . maybe he opted out before the crunch. Anything else?"

"Yes, again odd. He reports that Mrs Elligan cashed a certified cheque, that is to say, she opened an account with it and immediately withdrew most of the money, in the amount of five thousand pounds. The cheque was drawn by her on a Swiss bank."

"Good old Sophie," Permberton said. "She takes care of every angle. So she got out, and will now hope to enjoy her ill-gotten gains. Where do you suppose, Billy?"

"Well, sir, Italy is obviously not on. North Africa is out. France is out. Germany is out. Spain is no place to be right now. Portugal . . . perhaps. Britain is out." He glanced at his superior. "Is it?"

"I would say so. Sophie is not specifically wanted for anything here at the moment, but if she comes here and any of those countries put in an application for extradition we would have to take it seriously. We'd have to lock her up while the case was decided, and that wouldn't suit Sophie at all. No, I think she'll go to Holland."

"Holland, sir?"

"Well, she was using a Dutch ship, remember? That supposes a Dutch skipper is her partner. And two of those temporary passports were issued to Dutch nationals. Get on to our people in The Hague and have them find out what they can about this yacht *Christina*, who owned her and where he is based. Have that done as soon as possible."

"And then, sir? Do you mean to extradite her?"

"I have nothing to extradite her for, Billy. But I do think it would be a very good idea for all of us if I were to have a serious chat with the lady and with Elligan. We simply cannot have British subjects rushing around the place shooting people and blowing things up, however worthy the cause. And Elligan at least will surely be coming back to England; he doesn't know it was his lady friend put us on to the whole thing. We'll await developments, Billy. But I would like round-the-clock surveillance placed on the Elligan house, and I am going to apply for a phone tap."

"As I said before, this is one peaceful sea." Dennis glanced at Sophie. "So long as we're not blowing things up." In the three days since they had left Athens he had largely regained his strength, having nothing to do except, as now, sit in a deckchair and be waited on hand and foot by Catherine and Roberta.

"Hopefully, that's done," she said, and went to where Clay lay, also in a deckchair, well wrapped up. The captain had been very doubtful about taking the two wounded men on board, and Sophie had had to offer him a substantial bribe. But as she was principally a freighter, the SS *Gloaming* only carried two other passengers, and they were more curious than upset by the odd band that had joined them for the voyage home. She couldn't believe it was over, and in more ways than one. "How is it?" she asked, sitting beside him.

"I'm there. Sophie . . . there's so much—"

"We have a lot of time."

229

"How long before I'm fit again?"

"The doctor said it'll be a couple of months. That bullet missed a lung by inches."

"But you . . . coming out alone."

She grinned. "I have my little ways. I'd like to talk about the future. There's no way you can go back to Albania."

He sighed. "I suppose not."

"And there's no way I am going to undertake any more deliveries."

"My people may still be interested."

"Good luck to them. But not for me."

"So what are you planning to do?"

"I was thinking of emigrating. Do you think your people would let me in?"

"Not if they found out too much about your background. On the other hand, this last venture was undertaken on behalf of the US Government, even if unofficially. I think we need to have a chat with Walters. On the *other* hand . . . if you were married to an American, they could hardly keep you out."

"That sounds a very sensible idea."

"Do you think we could make a go of it, Sophie?"

"I think we might. We'll be starting with a ready made family. You haven't changed your mind about that?"

"Not if the packet includes you. So—"

"I have some things to settle up first."

"Don't you think the sooner you get out of Europe the better? You must be at the top of the wanted list in just about every country there is."

"Not Holland. I have to see Dennis and Catherine, and Roberta, safely home, Clay. I have a duty to them. I also have to see, or at least contact, Anne Martingell."

"What on earth for?"

"I have to tell her that Richard is dead, and how he died. I think she'd want to know that. I also have to tell her how to access that bank account in Switzerland. We did a deal, and she's entitled to that money. I also need to find out what happened to my parents as a result of that fracas I had in Hamburg. I need to make sure they're all right."

"I think you're taking one hell of a risk."

"These things have to be done, Clay. I want you to wait for me in Lisbon."

"I thought we were booked through to Southampton?"

"That wouldn't be a good idea, right now. We're going to change ships in Lisbon. I've had the captain arrange it. But you'll stay there, and I'll come back to you." She smiled. "You can arrange our passage across the Atlantic."

He held her hands. "You will come back, Sophie?"

"Don't I always?"

Sophie also had Captain Bartlett radio ahead to book them hotel accommodation, and as they had virtually no luggage – only the couple of changes of clothing Sophie had bought them in Athens – they were ashore within minutes of the ship docking. "You going to be all right?" the captain asked. He had become quite paternal towards his odd passengers during the short voyage.

"Quite all right, Captain, and thank you for everything," Sophie said.

"Well, you're on the *Orangeboom*, sailing at dawn tomorrow for Amsterdam. Five berths. The tickets will be waiting for you at the hotel." He grinned. "It'll mean getting up quite early."

Sophie kissed him. "You've been just magnificent."

They took a taxi to their hotel. Clay still needed to use a wheelchair, but the staff were most solicitous, even if they were clearly bemused both by the appearance of the party and their nomenclature and various temporary passports; only Sophie's was normal. But she was paying. And the envelope containing the tickets was waiting for her, as promised.

The staff were also somewhat concerned about the room arrangement. Sophie had booked three; the two girls shared one, Dennis and Carl the second, and Sophie and Clay the third. "Is the gentleman your husband?" asked the assistant manager, looking at the passports again.

"I'm his nurse," Sophie explained. "You're not supposing someone so ill is capable of doing anything, are you?" The assistant manager flushed with embarrassment.

Catherine stretched naked on her bed; she had just had a hot bath. "Boy, does this feel good."

231

Roberta had bathed first. Now she was wearing a dressing gown and inspecting the dresses Sophie had bought for them; their own clothes had been in rags. "I can't believe it's over. There are so many things . . . Peter and Alan, that Italian general, and the doctor, they were so nice, those women and children in the mountains . . ." she glanced at her friend. "But you experienced so much more."

"Only Sophie. Experiencing Sophie makes everything else irrelevant."

Roberta hung up the dress and sat on the bed. "Were you ever . . . well—"

"Once or twice. Does that shock you?"

"I feel it should. But being shocked, or anything, also seems a little irrelevant, don't you think? Are you going to marry Dennis?"

"I want to. But he hasn't actaually asked me yet. Does *that* shock *you*?"

"Heck, no. I think he's super. But what about your parents?"

Catherine nodded. "I think there may have to be a parting of the ways. But Dennis is going back into the charter business; Sophie has promised to finance a new ship. So . . . we'll work things out. What about you?"

Roberta gave a little shiver. "All I want to do is get home and never hear a gun going off again in my life."

"Snap. You going to take up your job?"

"I suppose so. But you—"

"No way."

Roberta nodded. "I hope and pray it all works out for you." She turned her head as there was a knock on the door. "Cover yourself."

Catherine rolled beneath the sheet, and Roberta opened the door. To stagger backwards as she received a push in the chest. Catherine sat up, stared at the two men who entered the room and closed the door behind them. They were very hard-looking men, in raincoats and slouch hats. My God! she thought. The Gestapo! But the first man was speaking English with a French accent. "Madame Elligan?"

"No," Roberta said. "I—"

Catherine's brain was racing. "I am Madame Elligan." If they were after Sophie, she had to buy her some time.

232

The man gazed at her, obviously thinking that she looked a little young for the woman he had been told to arrest. "You will get up and get dressed, please, madame."

"In front of you?" As on that first day at the stream, Roberta was speechless.

"In front of me, madame. Make haste. You, mademoiselle, lie on the bed."

Roberta gulped, but lay down. The other man pulled her dressing gown cord free, rolled her on her face, and bound her wrists and ankles together in the small of her back. Then he tore the pillow slip into strips and gagged her. He was very efficient. Slowly Catherine got out of bed and dressed herself. The two French agents watched her with interest. "May I ask what this is all about?"

"You are under arrest for murder."

"I have murdered no one in Portugal," Catherine said, dropping her dress over her head and feeling a little more secure.

"The crime was committed in France."

"Then you have no right to arrest me."

"That is so, legally. But we are arresting you. Now, madame, we are going to leave this hotel and get into a car. I must ask you not to attempt anything stupid. Our orders are to deliver you to Marseilles, dead or alive."

Catherine swallowed, and looked at Roberta, whose eyes were rolling wildly. "Am I allowed to pack my things?"

"No. We must hurry. We—"

There was another knock on the door, which immediately opened. Sophie stood there, her shoulderbag in place, as always. The first French agent made a startled exclamation, and reached for his shoulder holster. But Sophie was far too quick for him, and before he could draw he was staring down the barrel of her Browning. "Just put your hands on your head," Sophie said, and closed the door behind herself. He obeyed. The second man backed against the wall, hands raised. "Take their guns, Cathy." Sophie said. The temptation to shoot them both was enormous. But she was determined to turn her back on killing.

"They came to the wrong room," Catherine gasped, as she extracted the two guns from their shoulder holsters. "They thought I was you."

"Untie Roberta," Sophie said. "You two, into the bathroom."
The Frenchmen backed into the bathroom, while Catherine
untied Roberta, who sat up, rubbing her hands together to
restore her circulation. "Bring those cords over here," Sophie
said. "We'll need some more. Roberta, tear up that sheet. You
two, lie on the floor."

They obeyed without hesitation, overawed not only by the pistol,
but also by her air of total command, total confidence. Now she
handed the gun to Catherine. "Keep them covered, and if you have
to, shoot." The men could not know that Catherine had never fired
a gun in her life. "No one will hear the noise in here, and if they do
they will think it was a backfire." The traffic noise on the street was
quite loud. Sophie bound and gagged the two men, then tied them
to each other, then tied them again to the washbasin upright; when
she was finished they could not move more than an inch or so.
"Someone will be in, probably tomorrow morning," she said, and
closed and locked the door. "Now tell me."

Catherine told her what the man had said. "So," Sophie said,
"we scratch Portugal. This means a change of plan. We are now
going for a walk, all of us. The hotel won't expect us back before
dinner, and we'll be on board the *Oranjeboom* by then."

"What about our things?"

"Easy come, easy go," Sophie said. "I'll buy you some more in
Holland." She hung the Do Not Disturb sign on the door.

She alerted the men, and explained the situation. "So we'll have
to abandon Plan One. You'll have to come with us to Holland,
Clay, and we can make our arrangements there."

"You've only five berths booked on this ship."

"So we'll take on a sixth. Happily, no one at the hotel knows
which ship we're taking." The staff smiled benignly as the
English party went down the steps, the porter and Carl assisting
Clay with his wheelchair, "We're going to sample the Lisbon
air," Sophie told the assistant manager.

"Of course, senhora. Dinner is at eight."

"We're looking forward to it. Now, gang, casual like. We
don't make for the docks until we're out of sight."

"I thought we weren't supposed to board until just before
dawn?" Roberta asked.

"So we're early. Getting up in the middle of the night isn't one of my favourite pastimes."

"When those guys get free—" Dennis said.

"That's not going to be for a good while. And then they do, what are the going to do? They're foreign policemen operating illegally. I imagine they'll keep their mouths shut and report to base just as rapidly as they can."

"Do you reckon we've finally made it?" Dennis asked, standing beside Sophie at the rail of the *Oranjeboom* as the ship negotiated the sandbanks off the Dutch coast preparatory to entering the ship canal. "The way those French agents were waiting for us—"

"It would have been easy for anyone in Athens to find out what ship we were taking, and where it would be stopping," Sophie said. "But there is no one in the world can know where we are right this minute. Don't go soft on me now, Dennis."

"I won't do that, Sophie. I'm thinking of the girls. They've really had enough."

"We've all had enough. They'll be all right. Are you going to marry Catherine?"

"I'd like to. Were you serious about a new ship?"

"Yes, I was. It'll be my wedding present. And then I'm going to disappear, utterly and completely."

"With Clay? I had the idea you and he were enemies."

"We've been on opposite sides, from time to time. But we've always had a yen for each other. And now that we're both retiring . . . besides, I have an idea I'll stay alive longer out of Europe."

"He's a lucky guy."

"I really don't want you lying in bed with Catherine and wishing she were me," Sophie said severely. "Look at it this way. When I was Catherine's age I was a sweet young innocent who'd never heard a shot fired in anger, much less fired one herself."

"Neither has she, fired one, I mean."

"You make sure she never does, or by the time she gets to my age, you may find you have another Sophie on your hands."

"I'll look forward to that," he said.

*   *   *

235

Holland was bathed in sunshine as the steamer moved slowly up the canal to Amsterdam. "It's so beautiful," Catherine said, holding Dennis's hand. "Where exactly is your home?"

"In Holland proper. That is, north of the Ijsselmeer. Close to a town called Sneak. Pronounce it Shnake. We'll go up there this afternoon, open the place up. You coming to visit, Sophie?"

"I'd like to, if you'll give me the address. I have a few things to sort out first, like our wedding, our passages across the Atlantic . . . and our various finances. I assume you trust me to do it all right?"

"I trust you, Sophie," he assured her.

"Marriage first," Sophie decided. "We'll need a special licence." It was such a treat to be able to relax, to feel it was all behind her. Her life had been one long adventure ever since she could remember. The three years of utter peace she had spent with Ned following their return from Abyssinia had been idyllic, but there had always been the knowledge that they were fugitives, wanted by the law in several countries, including the one they were living in, France, and that however anonymous they were as Mr and Mrs Smith, inevitably they would one day have to move on.

How ironic it was that when that day had come, the events had been instigated by two of the people she now valued most in the world, Clay and Catherine. And now she was wanted in even more countries. But not in the United States, and if Clay was right, she could even be welcomed. That would put the whole wide Atlantic between her past and her future. And her baby's future.

One of the first things she did on landing in Amsterdam was go to a gynaecologist to make sure everything was all right. And it was. That left Clay. But she had to believe it was going to work out. They had wanted each other for nine years. Only their odd professions had got in the way of a consummation. But if those professions were behind them . . .

"Happy?" she asked.

"Very, Mrs Andrews."

"Sophie Andrews. I like the sound of that."

There had only been two witnesses, as Roberta had opted to go up to Sneak with Catherine and Dennis. Now there was a single bottle of champagne, in their hotel bedroom. "When do we get to honeymoon?" Clay asked.

She kissed him. "I thought we'd already done that, briefly. We have all of our lives to honeymoon."

"After you've had the baby."

"I'll be showing in a few weeks. Then you won't want me."

"Try me."

She kissed him again. "By the time you are fully recovered I'll be as big as a house. Tell me about Connecticut. On second thoughts, I'll wait to see it. Now, our ship doesn't sail for three days, but we have a lot to do. So have you."

"What things?"

"First, I want you to get hold of Walters and confirm that the delivery was made as arranged. He should already have released the remainder of the money; if he hasn't, it should be done now. Then he has to arrange a visa for me, again, right away. Then, once I know all the funds have been deposited, I have to sort out my finances with Dennis and Catherine. I also have to get in touch with Anne Martingell."

"I wish you'd just stay here until we're ready to leave."

"Darling, no one save our friends know we are in Holland."

"They will once you start transferring money about."

"Swiss banks believe in secrecy," she reminded him.

Clay telephoned Walters, who seemed delighted with the success of his venture and eager to co-operate. It was with a growing sense of elation that Sophie spent the afternoon on the telephone herself, making the necessary arrangements. She had had the captain of the *Orangeboom* wireless ahead to book their passages on the first available ship to America, but these had to be confirmed. Then she telephoned Anne. "Sophie?" Anne's voice was incredulous.

"Alive and well. I have a lot to tell you. Can you come to the continent?"

"Where on the continent?"

"Belgium. I'll meet you in Ostend."

"Is that where you are?"

"It's where I will be, if you will come there. The Hotel Splendide."

"Ah . . . how is Richard?"

"Richard is dead."

There was a brief silence. "Just like that?" Anne asked at last.

"No, not just like that. He died very gallantly, in a shoot-out with some Gestapo agents who were trying to arrest me."

"God," Anne commented. "Is he . . . well, his body—"

"He was buried. I'm afraid the grave isn't marked, and there's no way we can go back and find it, right now. But you have some money coming. There is twenty-five thousand pounds on deposit in a Swiss numbered account. I will give you the number and the access code when we meet."

"Twenty-five thousand pounds," Anne said thoughtfully.

"That was the arrangement."

"Yes," Anne said, even more thoughtfully. "The Hotel Splendide, in Ostend—"

"The day after tomorrow," Sophie said.

"How did she take it?" Clay asked.

"I shouldn't think she did more than bat an eyelid. They may have been lovers once, but that was a long time ago. Recently they have been bedfellows because they couldn't think of anything else to do."

"I'm still not sure why you have to pay her a cent. You tell me she was against the delivery from the start."

"I owe it to Richard," Sophie pointed it. That was true, but she also wanted to see Anne again, and try to discover if her suspicions as to their betrayal were true. And then?

Next morning she opened an account in an Amsterdam bank with a cheque drawn on her Swiss account. "You understand we must wait for this to clear before we can allow any transactions, Frau Elligan," said the assistant manager, somewhat anxiously. It was not every day an attractive woman walked into his office with a cheque for twenty thousand pounds.

"Of course. But I must write some cheques. I will post-date them for a week, if that is what you wish."

"I'm sure that will be convenient," he agreed, and gave her a cheque-book.

She hired a car, using the cash she still possessed from her drawing in Greece – there was a considerable amount left, even after paying for the various sea passages and hotels – and drove up to Sneak, taking the easterly route round the Ijsselmeer. Clay remained in the hotel, waiting for a return call from Walters confirming all the transactions, and the issue of Sophie's visa.

It was another beautiful spring day. Sophie bought an English language paper before leaving the city, but there was nothing about Albania. That was a forgotten war, or she supposed it would now be called a civil uprising. She drove through rich countryside; the Dutch were engaged in a mammoth land re-clamation scheme, which in time, she knew, was intended to take in the whole bottom half of the Ijsselmeer, a huge area which would be turned into farmland. There was something utterly tranquil about the ambience of the place. How far away seemed the Albanian mountains!

Sneak was a delightful little town, dedicated to aquatic sports; there were boats and yachts of all shapes and sizes, moored in the small marina or along the canal banks. She even saw a *boier*. How she hoped Catherine and Dennis made a go of it. The address Dennis had given her was outside the town itself, and the road took her beside the canal until it turned in to access the back yard of the little thatched cottage, which had a frontage actually on the canal. Beside it there was a little wood. It was a perfectly idyllic spot.

Catherine was waiting to embrace her. "Isn't it just marvel-lous?"

"Cute."

Roberta and Dennis and Carl were also waiting to greet her and escort her inside; through plate-glass windows she looked out at the water, and a sailing school drifting by in the light air. "How's Clay?" Roberta asked.

Sophie showed them her new wedding ring. "And you?"

"I reckon we should contact Cathy's parents first," Dennis said.

"And I think we should get married first," Catherine said. "*Fait accompli.*"

239

"Dennis is ethically correct," Sophie said.

"Oh, boo."

"They may say yes," Sophia pointed out.

"It doesn't matter what they say," Catherine asserted. "I'm free, white—" she bit her lip. Dennis ruffled her hair.

"Slips like that are things you have to allow for," Sophie said.

"We'll work it out," Dennis said. "My plan is that we should go to England and have a chat. We're not wanted for anything in England, are we?"

"I don't think so, technically. You, anyway. It's not a good place for me, just in case someone has already filed an extradition request. I'm seeing Anne Martingell tomorrow, so she should be able to bring me up to date."

"Does she know about Richard?"

Sophie nodded. "Now, accounts." She gave Catherine a cheque for seven and a half thousand pounds, and Dennis another for two and a half. "You'll see they're dated next week. That's to give time for my cheque to clear. But they'll be honoured. I will also authorise you to spend up to ten thousand pounds, over and above this money, for a new ship. You'll have to contact me when you find one, as that draw will have to be made in Switzerland. This will be my address in the States." She gave them one of Clay's cards.

"Wowee." Catherine gazed at her cheque. "I've never seen that much money in my life."

"Me neither," Dennis said. "Sophie, working for you has been the greatest experience of my life."

"With me. You were working with me. Now, you, Roberta, I hope you are going home."

"I'll go when Dennis and Cathy go. I really don't know how to break the fact that I'm still alive. Dad has a heart problem."

"Which won't be helped by supposing you're dead," Sophie pointed out. "I think you should go home just as rapidly as possible." She wrote another cheque, for five hundred pounds. "That should take care of your passage."

"Now," Catherine said. "Lunch."

She turned her head as they heard gravel scraping on the drive. Sophie looked at Dennis. "I didn't think anyone knew we were home yet," he said.

There was a knock on the door. Catherine had moved to the window. "Four men. Just like those men in Lisbon."

"Only these aren't French," Sophie guessed. Shit! She thought. How careless can you get? Suddenly she felt unutterably tired, all the well-being flowing from her system like water from a ruptured pipe. She had supposed it was all behind her. She picked up her shoulderbag.

"You in there," said a voice through the door, in German. "We know Frau Elligan is with you. We mean you no harm. Just send Frau Elligan out."

"I have a gun," Dennis said. "In the bedroom."

"No," Sophie said. They had all been through too much, especially the girls. If there was a shoot-out the likelihood was that they would be killed, or at least badly wounded all over again, in the cases of Roberta and Dennis.

"Come out, Frau Elligan," the voice said. "Or it will go hard with your friends."

"Get into the bedroom," Sophie said. "All of you. Close the door and stay there."

"But Sophie—"

"I'll handle it," she promised them. "Just don't interfere." Dennis hesitated, but he was still too conscious of his own physical weakness. Carl was already helping him into the bedroom, and Roberta and Catherine followed. Sophie watched them go, keeping her face still with an effort. Her last friends, forced to abandon her. And she, having survived so much, had supposed she was home and dry. Now . . . she could only go out in a blaze of glory. Once she surrendered to the Gestapo, there was nothing in front of her but continued humiliation, continued pain, until they put a rope round her neck or cut off her head. She took a deep breath, took out her pistol, and moved to the door.

"All right," the voice said. "Break it down."

Sophie yanked the door open and stepped through, gun levelled. But before she could fire a man she had not seen, standing against the wall, struck downwards, his hand crashing into her wrist with paralysing force, to send the gun tumbling from her fingers. "Oh!" she gasped, following the gun and dropping to her knees with the force of the impact.

"A dangerous woman," Eisener said, and stepped against her,

241

grasping her chin to turn up her face. "Well, Fräulein Sophie, I have long wondered just what you looked like, how you managed to turn all those heads and wriggle out of such desperate situations." He nodded, and Sophie's arms were pulled behind her back and her wrists handcuffed.

I'm done, Sophie thought. My God, I'm done! But she was Sophie Elligan. She was a legend. She had to go out a legend, uncaring even of looming death. "At least tell me what you have done with my parents," she said.

Eisener grinned. "Oh, we executed *them*. As we are going to execute you. But before we get to that, I am going to have a great deal of pleasure interrogating you. It is a pleasure I have long promised myself. I am going to take you apart, inch by inch, and you are going to scream so loud you will break your windpipe."

Sophie pulled her head back, searched her mouth. And spat at him. "Bitch!" He slashed his hand across her face, drawing blood from her cut lip. "Get her up," he said. "Put her into the car."

Two of his men grasped Sophie's shoulders and pulled her to her feet. "Stop right there," Catherine said.

They all turned to look at her, standing in the doorway, her hands behind her back. "Who is this child?" Eisener inquired. "Your partner in crime, Frau Elligan? Disappear, little girl, and you will not be hurt."

"You disappear." Catherine brought her hand round to reveal an automatic pistol. She fired, and the bullet struck Eisener in the face and slammed him backwards. The men holding Sophie hastily released her and reached for their guns. The fourth man, who still held his gun, raised it and was cut down by Catherine's second shot. Her next two hit the remaining Gestapo agents, firing from close range.

"My God!" Sophie said, licking blood from her lips. "You have never fired at anyone in your life."

"One has to start somewhere," Catherine said, "and besides, I have had the advantage of watching an expert at work." The others had also come outside. Dennis knelt beside Eisener, felt in his pockets, and found the key to the handcuffs. Released, Sophie rubbed her hands together. "What happens now?" Catherine asked. She was trembling as she realised what she had done.

"Do you think anyone heard the sound of the shots?" Sophie asked.

"If they did it wouldn't matter," Dennis said. "People are always shooting in that wood."

"Right. Well, we need to think very clearly and move very quickly," Sophie said. "The Gestapo has very long arms. Get the bodies into their car." The two girls and Carl did this, as they could change their clothing to get rid of the bloodstains. "I'll drive their car," Sophie said. "You follow with mine, Cathy."

The bodies were in the back seat, lying on top of each other. Sophie drove out of the yard, checked the empty road, then took a side lane into the heart of the wood. Catherine drove behind her. Sophie went some distance into the trees, pulled off the lane, leaving the car half-hidden in the bushes. Catherine had stopped on the lane and she got in beside her. Catherine's hands were shaking. "What happens now?"

"Listen very carefully," Sophie said. "First, the Gestapo. If Eisener found out where Dennis lived, then all his people know it, and eventually they will come looking for him. You must leave within the next twenty-four hours. Pack up your things, go to Amsterdam, and buy that new *boier*. Then put to sea and find yourself a new home port. I'm afraid Dennis will have to write off that house."

Catherine gave an almost hysterical giggle. "It's mortgaged, anyway."

"That'll make it easier. If you really trust each other, your best bet is to buy the ship in your name. Then you can enter England without any problem. Dennis will just be your crew. When you marry, you can straighten that out. But there must be no panic. You must behave absolutely normally. There is no reason for the Dutch police to connect you with those bodies in the wood, whenever they find them. Dennis is known as a charter skipper, and he has merely left his home to buy a new boat. No one will be interested until his mortgage payments lapse, and by then you'll be in England. And from this moment on, you have never seen, heard of, or have any knowledge of someone called Sophie Elligan. Right?"

Catherine had been nodding at each point. "Does this mean we won't be seeing each other again?"

Sophie grinned. "Who knows? If I ever decide to charter a yacht again, I'll know where to come." She kissed her on the lips.

"You look all shook up," Clay said.

"I am all shook up." Sophie told him what had happened.

"Jesus," he said. "The sooner we're out of here the better."

"We sail tomorrow night. The Gestapo won't start looking for at least twenty-four hours, even supposing the bodies are found by then. And they'll be looking for Sophie Elligan, not Mrs Clayton Andrews."

"They'll connect, eventually."

"By then we'll be in Connecticut. If they come there, have I your permission to blow them away?"

"Only if I don't do it first. Are we really done with it, Sophie?"

"We're done, tomorrow night. I have one last duty. You know that."

Sophie drove across the border early the next day, and reached Ostend in time for lunch. She had telephoned ahead and reserved a room, even if she was not spending the night, and had given instructions that Anne was to be made welcome; she had stayed at the Splendide several times in the past. "Your sister is already here, Mrs Elligan," the clerk said. "She wished to be private, so I showed her up to your room. I hope that is all right?"

"That is most satisfactory," Sophie said, and took the elevator. As always, her bag hung from her shoulder, reassuringly light today. How long was it since she had travelled without a weapon? And now she need never carry one again. She opened the door, stepped inside, closed it behind herself. Anne Martingell sat in a chair by the window, as neatly dressed as always. She was not wearing mourning. "I'm sorry about Richard," Sophie said.

Anne shrugged. "He was a bit of a rat. I imagine you knew that."

"As I said on the phone, he died well."

"Trying to save you, you said. Everyone dies, trying to save Sophie."

"I would hate us to quarrel, at this late stage." Sophie placed her bag on the table, opened it, took out the various documents.

244

"These will give you access to your account, upon proper identification. Your passport will do. They are expecting you."

Anne got up, her own handbag dangling from her arm. She picked up the various pieces of paper, scanned them. "Twenty-five thousand pounds."

"As promised."

"I think you owe me more than that," Anne said. "I mean, Richard may have been a rat, but until you came back into our lives, he was my rat."

"He was also my rat, for a while. I reckon that makes us even."

Anne had already opened her handbag. Now she took out a small automatic pistol, levelling it in the same movement. "Just keep still," she said. "I know how dangerous you are."

Sophie gazed at her in astonishment. It had just never crossed her mind that Anne would try a fast one. Now she had to remember that this woman had killed both her husband and her own son when they had got in her way. "Move away from that bag," Anne commanded.

Sophie obeyed while she tried to decide what to do. Anne moved to the table, and emptied Sophie's bag on to the table. "No weapon? That's not like you, Sophie."

"I came here to keep my side of the bargain," Sophie said. "Not shoot anybody."

"You always keep bargains, don't you." Still keeping her pistol pointing at Sophie, Anne selected the chequebook she was looking for. "Sophie Elligan and Edward Carew. I like that." She flicked the stubs. "As I thought, you have been paying off your various partners. Well, I am one of your partners, am I not? Take this " she tossed the chequebook, and Sophie caught it. "Now, sit at that table and write a cheque for twenty-five thousand pounds, payable to me."

"Do you really think you can get away with this?"

"Of course I do."

"Because, once I have written the cheque, you will kill me."

Anne gave another shrug. "It seems a good idea. Or you would stop payment on the cheque, would you not? Whereas, if I kill you, I can have negotiated the cheque long before anyone in your Swiss bank discovers you're dead. It's how I shoot you, Sophie, that matters. Write the cheque, and it will be a bullet in the brain.

No fuss, no pain. Refuse to write the cheque, and it will be a bullet in the womb. Then I will leave you here to die, very slowly, and very painfully. No one knows who I am or where I came from or am going, and by the time they find you, you will have died in agony." She frowned, because Sophie had caught her breath and instinctively touched her stomach. "Well, well, can it be that you have a bun in the oven? I wonder who put it there? Richard? Or Carew? What a mess it'll be." Sophie licked her lips. "Sit down and write." Anne's voice was suddenly like a whip-lash.

Sophie moved to the table. Just to sit down and die . . . but the thought of a bullet smashing into her baby. For the first time in her life she was unable to make a decision for instant action . . . there was a knock on the door. Anne half turned in surprise, and Sophie leapt from the chair and hurled herself across the room. Anne turned back, firing as she did so, but the bullet went wide and smashed into the wall, and Sophie was already on her. The two women were much the same height, but Sophie was the stronger and fitter as well as the younger by some fifteen years. She swung her clasped hands to and fro, smashing them into Anne's face, causing her to shriek in agony and drop the pistol. Sophie stepped away from her, picked up the gun. Anne turned back, her face crinkling with a mixture of fear and anger, and the door opened.

"Mind if I come in?" Walter Pemberton asked.

Both women stared at him in consternation.

"Settling up, are we?" Pemberton glanced at the papers on the table.

"How the hell—?" Anne said.

"I followed you," Pemberton said. "We've had a tap on your phone for the last week or so. It really is time to wind things up. Do you remember me, Mrs Elligan?"

"I do, Mr Pemberton. It's been a long time."

"Too long. Now I must congratulate you on your remarkable success, although I understand it was fairly costly. Would you like to give me that gun?"

"I'm not sure that would be a good idea."

"Mrs Elligan, while I have no powers of arrest, here on the continent, I think I should remind you that as far as I am aware

246

you are wanted by the governments of Germany, France and Italy. I think you would find the odds far too heavy were you also to have the government of Great Britain out for your blood. You really should give it up. Providing you can find somewhere to take you in."

"I have already done that," Sophie said. "I am retiring, and am emigrating to the States. With my husband. I hope you are not going to try to stop me doing that."

"My dear lady, I wouldn't dream of it. I think your decision to take up residence on the other side of the Atlantic is admirable. And a great relief to us all. I suggest you leave this hotel, and Belgium, with all possible speed, and begin your journey. I will sort out that bullet hole in the wall."

"Well, then—" Sophie gave him the gun.

"You are just going to let her walk away?" Anne demanded.

"I have said I would, yes."

"And me?"

"You will accompany me back to England. I think you have done quite well out of this. Not as well as you intended, but at least you do not have another murder to your name."

Anne opened her mouth, and then shut it again.

Sophie had repacked her shoulderbag. Now she went to the door, and then checked. "Will you tell me one thing?" she asked. "How did you get on to us?"

Pemberton looked at Anne.

"As I thought," Sophie said. She looked at the gun he was still holding.

Pemberton shook his finger. "No, no Sophie. That's all behind you now. Even vengeance."

Sophie looked at him, then looked at Anne. Then smiled. "Maybe you're right," she said, and left the room.

Edio Rometti sat on the Tuscan hillside and looked down at the goats beneath him. It was a bright summer's day, and all seemed well with the world. If his career seemed to be at an end, he at least had this haven in which to spend his time.

He watched Lalia coming towards him, hips swinging as always. Perhaps, he thought, had she accompanied him to Albania, things might have been different.

"I found an American paper in town," Lalia said.

"So?"

"I was browsing, and I came across something that I thought might interest you. So I bought it." She held it out. "Page eight."

Frowning, Edio opened the paper. "Recent arrivals in New York? Does this interest me?"

"Read it," she recommended.

Edio read aloud. "Passengers on the *SS Nassau*, out of Amsterdam, who disembarked yesterday, included Clayton Andrews, the Connecticut stockbroker famous for his part in aiding the Albanian patriots against the Italian invaders. Mr Andrews was wounded in the fighting, but is making a good recovery. Accompanying him was his wife Sophie."

"Sophie," Lalia said. "Do you think—?"

"Oh, indeed," Edio said. "That's our Sophie. She always gets what she wants, in the end."